ST. PATRICK'S DAY MURDER

"Excuse me, Sergeant. Can you elaborate on this murdered leprechaun?" Rory asked. "For instance, why do you believe this person is a leprechaun, and what makes you believe he was murdered?"

"Good question, Campbell. The body of a man, a small man of middle age, dressed as a leprechaun, was found this morning on the open dunes near the lakeshore. The cause of death appears to be a blow to the head. Doc Riggles was called in to confirm this."

My hand flew over my mouth. "Oh, my goodness!" I breathed as my heart began racing. Sergeant Murdock's description of the victim was nearly identical to the man I had seen the day of the Leprechaun Parade. I hadn't gotten a good look at his face, but he did run headlong into my Jeep right after bludgeoning poor Fred Landry with a shillelagh, according to Mrs. Hinkle. This same man dressed as a leprechaun was undoubtedly the person Uncle Finn had seen as well. My heart sank at the thought.

"Do . . . you really think that this man is a leprechaun?" I asked the sergeant. Murdock closed her eyes and took a deep breath before answering me.

"Bakewell, I appreciate the question, but you and I both know that leprechauns do not exist. However, I will concede that the crime scene is a puzzling one. This unfortunate person, convincingly dressed as a leprechaun, had no identification on his body. The ME, Doc Riggles, is looking into it, and forensics have been called in to take control of the crime scene."

"Do you have any idea of the murder weapon?" Rory asked.

"As a matter of fact, fancy, hand-carved wal with what we believe to walking stick, I'm told,

Books by Darci Hannah

MURDER AT THE BEACON BAKESHOP

MURDER AT THE CHRISTMAS COOKIE
BAKE-OFF

MURDER AT THE BLUEBERRY FESTIVAL

MURDER AT THE PUMPKIN PAGEANT

MURDER AT THE BLARNEY BASH

Published by Kensington Publishing Corp.

MURDER AT THE BLARNEY BASH

Darci Hannah

Kensington Publishing Corp.
www.kensingtonbooks.com

For my wonderful mother,
Janet Rasmussen Hilgers,
For teaching me to read, to write, to bake,
to laugh, to love, and to live.
I am who I am because of you and Dad.

ACKNOWLEDGMENTS

I can honestly say that I had never given a thought to writing a St. Patrick's Day mystery until my wonderful editor, John Scognamiglio, suggested it. Thanks, John! I think it was the image of delectable cupcakes with swirls of green frosting and shamrock inspired treats that sealed the deal for me. Although I don't have one drop of Irish blood in me, I adore Ireland—the people, the food, the folklore! The thought of putting my own Beacon Bakeshop spin on St. Patrick's Day was too much for the writer/baker/lighthouse lover in me to ignore. As you might have already guessed, I jumped in with both feet.

Jumping was the easy part. Next came trying to wrap my head around what a St. Patrick's Day might look like in Beacon Harbor. One day I found myself standing in my kitchen staring at my coffee maker as another pot was dripping its way to completion, thinking on all things Irish. That's when my son Matt walked in, also looking to fill his coffee mug. Four of us were working from home at the time, and the coffee maker is the most adored appliance in our kitchen. While Matt and I were staring at the coffee pot, anxiously awaiting the moment we could pour a cup, I looked at him and asked, "Hey, I'm going to write a St. Patrick's Day mystery. Any ideas?" While all my sons are creative, Matt's devious nature was really on display that day. While we waited for coffee, he proceeded to plot my novel for me. Being a 25-year-old finance major, and never having read a mystery, cozy or otherwise, Matt's version of the plot wasn't exactly "cozy mystery" friendly, but his core idea was great, and it was just the inspiration I was looking for.

Along with John Scognamiglio for suggesting the idea, and my son, Matt Hannah, for the plot inspiration, I would also like to thank my tireless agent, Sandy Harding, for always being in my corner and for always having excellent suggestions. I would also like to thank the wonderful Larissa Ackerman, Rebecca Cremonese, and everyone else at Kensington Publishing who does such an amazing job with these books.

I would also like to thank my wonderful husband, John, for all the love and support, and our sons, Jim, Dan, Matt, and our daughter-in-law Allison for filling my life with love, laughter, and adventure. And a special thanks to my dear mother, Jan Hilgers, who once explained to me when I was young that on St. Patrick's Day everyone has a little bit of Irish in them. That made me feel special, and it still does. I also cherish our daily phone calls, the laughs, and all the great recipe ideas. I truly have the best team a writer could have right at my fingertips.

And a very special thank you to you, dear readers, for holding this book in your hands. I sincerely hope you enjoy your St. Patrick's Day visit to the Beacon Bakeshop!

CHAPTER 1

"Wellington!" My adorable, fluffy Newfoundland dog was still on the groomer's table as I entered Peggy's Pet Shop and Pooch Salon. "You look gorgeous!" I told him because it was true. Welly's silky black coat glistened like a polished onyx. He gave a wag of his bushy tail, indicating he was happy to see me. But he obviously wasn't loving his emergency morning trip to Peggy's salon. Welly was a dog with pendulous, silky black ears and expressive brown eyes, and he was using them to their fullest effect on me now. The look he shot me, lowering his fluffy ears to match his droopy eyes, was filled with such mournful gloom that I almost felt sorry for him. Almost. Welly's long stint on the groomer's table was his own doing. "I hope he smells as good as he looks," I told Peggy.

"He ought to," Peggy informed me as she set down her grooming brush. Peggy wasn't only the owner of Peggy's Pet Shop and Pooch Salon, but she was also a good friend. The moment I had left my finance career in New York City to open a bak-

ery in a lighthouse in the small village of Beacon
Harbor, Michigan, I knew that I was going to need
a good groomer for Wellington. My lighthouse was
right on the shores of Lake Michigan, and Welly
was a breed of dog that couldn't resist the pull of
water; be it giant lake or muddy pond, it made little difference. In the relatively short time I'd been
in Beacon Harbor, Peggy and I had become fast
friends. This morning, however, she had literally
saved me after Wellington had cornered a skunk
by the boathouse on his predawn sniff-and-dash
around the lighthouse grounds. Needless to say,
the skunk had gotten the last word in that brief encounter.

Peggy continued. "This one's spent half the
morning in the washtub. You'd imagine that a dog
like Wellington, who thinks nothing of swimming
in that frozen lake out there, wouldn't mind a
nice, sudsy, warm bath every now and again. But
you'd be wrong. This big guy sure puts up a fuss. It
took three of us and a half box of treats just to get
him into the tub."

"Sorry about that." My apology was genuine.
Peggy offered a smile and waved me through the
little half gate that separated the reception area
from the grooming tables. Welly, I noticed, was the
only client currently in the building. I stood beside
him and gave him a good sniff. "Wow! I can't believe you got that nasty smell out of his fur."

"After two baths with the recommended wash,
this boy was smelling a whole lot better. Should it
ever happen again, Lindsey, you can make the
mixture yourself. Just combine one quart of hydro-
gen peroxide with a quarter cup of baking soda,
and one teaspoon of Dawn dish soap. As you can

see, it works like a charm." Peggy was a dear, but I honestly couldn't see myself whipping up that concoction at four in the morning.

"I never expected the skunk to be out on such a frigid morning. I thought they hibernated." I offered a shrug. After all, it was March in Michigan, which wasn't a whole lot different from February in Michigan. Both months were snowy, dreary, and bitter cold. Although, to be fair, it was gradually warming up, or so the weatherman claimed, but one hardly noticed with the wind chill. Maybe skunks were just a tad more sensitive to the slightest change in temperature, I thought. Peggy, however, knew far more about skunks than I did. It was likely due to her clients having so many encounters with them.

"Skunks don't hibernate, Lindsey, they go into a torpor. It's nearly the same thing, but a torpor doesn't last as long as true hibernation. However, what you and Welly might not have been aware of is that March is prime mating season for skunks." She tied a cute bandana around Welly's neck, adjusted it, then gave his fur a gentle ruffle. "That little critter was looking for love . . . until Welly scared the stink out of him."

"Literally," I agreed with a grim smile. "My boathouse still reeks from the encounter. I hope it goes away soon. The grade-school Leprechaun Parade is about to begin any minute now and, as you know, the Beacon Bakeshop is the end of the parade route. I don't want that lingering nastiness from Mr. Skunk to throw any shade on our festive shamrock sugar cookies and green leprechaun punch. The kids are really looking forward to them, or so I've been told. We had a bit of a rough morning at the bakeshop due to that smell. For instance, Betty came in as usual, but she was holding a handkerchief over her nose. She then ordered her usual latte and cinnamon roll and took it to go. Can you imagine that?" Betty Vanhoosen was the owner of Harbor Realty, the president of the Chamber of Commerce, town busybody, and my good friend. She came to the bakeshop every morning that we were open and had never taken her latte to go!

"I can only imagine," Peggy commiserated with a shake of her head. "Well, I'm sure that brisk March wind coming off the lake will whisk it away in no time."

"I hope so. By the way, I love that white, shamrock-covered bandana you put on Welly. The kids are going to love it too."

"It's our March special," she said with a smile. "As you know, St. Patrick's Day is tomorrow. After that we'll pack these beauties away until next year. I also heard through the grapevine that this handsome big guy has an Irish girlfriend." Peggy gave Welly a loving pat, then clicked on his leash, allowing him to escape the grooming table. Welly was overjoyed by this tantalizing glimmer of freedom.

"He does," I agreed, giving my dog a big hug. The grade school kids were going to love the silkiness of his fur. Wellington was a big draw for the children of the town. It would never do to have him stinking to high heaven. I cast Peggy a grin. "He's smitten with Bailey," I told her as I proceeded to the register with her.

The Bailey in question was a beautiful, pristine white, Great Pyrenees dog that belonged to Finnigan O'Connor, my boyfriend, Rory's, Irish uncle. Uncle Finn, as he was called, surprised Rory last November when he told his nephew that he and his daughter, Colleen, were moving to Beacon Harbor to open an Irish gift shop and micro-pub called the Blarney Stone. Rory was ecstatic. Both his parents had passed before I met him, and he didn't have any close relatives in the area. Uncle Finn was Rory's mother's younger brother and, according to Rory, Uncle Finn was his favorite. My parents lived in Beacon Harbor during the summer months, and I loved having them around. Although they adored Rory and embraced him like family, I always felt a bit sad for my boyfriend for not having that love and support that only parents can give. Therefore, when Finn and Colleen decided to move from their home in Ireland to come to America, we were both thrilled.

On a personal note, Finn and Colleen's good news had kept me from focusing on the fact that my best friend, Kennedy Kapoor, had left Beacon Harbor to spend some time with her family in London. It had been a rough October. There'd been a murder on Halloween night in the village, and Kennedy and I had both gotten involved. I didn't blame my friend for leaving or, to paraphrase her own words, *wanting to find herself again.* However, by leaving Beacon Harbor, Ken had broken the heart of Tuck McAllister, a young police officer and a dear friend to both Rory and me. Of course, Kennedy and I had kept in touch because that's what besties do. However, the passing of time and the distance between us were beginning to wear on our friendship, not to mention her giddy text messages, short phone calls, and unsettling Instagram posts she'd felt inclined to share with the world.

I had just paid for Welly's grooming when Peggy hit me with another grin.

"I also heard another rumor," she ventured. "I heard that Kennedy is back in town."

I waited a heartbeat too long before I blurted, "She is. Got in last night. I better get going. I need to be at the Beacon before the little leprechauns arrive."

"Well, the parade has already started," she said, tapping her watch. "Great news about Kennedy. I realize that it's probably too early for her to open Ellie and Company for the summer season—"

"It is," I was quick to tell her. My bestie Kennedy Kapoor, who she was referring to, was not only a famous Instagrammer and fashionista, she was also a co-owner of my mother's seasonal clothing boutique, Ellie & Company.

"I thought so," Peggy acknowledged with a little nod. "Well, she must be visiting then. Good for her. I was simply remarking that Kennedy has quite an eye for pet grooming. When she suggested that teddy-bear cut for that darling poodle, Trixie, last October, I thought she was nuts. But boy was she on to something there. Thanks to Kennedy, Trixie and her owner, Cali, have started a new trend in town." A smile crossed Peggy's lips at the thought. "When you see her, tell her I said hello, will you?"

"Of course. But I'm sure you'll be able to tell her yourself. She's going to be at the St. Patrick's Day party at the Blarney Stone tomorrow."

"Ooo, that's right! It's opening day for that darling Irish shop. I hear there's even a little pub there that will only serve Irish beer and whisky. I've been hankering for a good Guinness! I also know that the Beacon Bakeshop is doing the catering."

"We are. FYI, we've been going through a lot of green food coloring as well as quite a bit of Guinness and Baileys. We're pulling out all the stops for this grand opening," I told her with a grin. "Guinness chocolate cupcakes with Baileys buttercream frosting, shamrock cupcakes, shamrock sugar cookies, crème de menthe brownies, and a Baileys cheesecake that will knock your socks off, not to mention samples of Uncle Finn's sticky toffee pudding, and Colleen's prize-winning Irish soda bread."

"I will definitely be there. And an FYI to you, Lindsey Bakewell. That Finnigan O'Connor is quite the charmer. With those dark Celtic looks and that Irish accent, you're going to have every single middle-aged woman in the county there vying for his attention. Hope you're planning on a big crowd."

"I am," I said, then headed for the door. At the very least I had to make it back to the Beacon before the parade got there. The annual grade-school Leprechaun Parade was truly going to be a spectacle this year. That was because Finn and Colleen O'Connor, with their gorgeous dog, Bailey, were leading the parade. Having just moved to the village from Ireland, and both possessing charming Irish accents, it was a no-brainer. Plus, their Irish shop was opening on St. Patrick's Day, and to celebrate they were giving vouchers to every student marching in the parade for a free shamrock good-luck charm at the Blarney Stone. Welly and I were just about to slip through the door when Peggy stopped me.

"Before you go, I have to ask you a question. Is it just the kids who are dressing up this year?"

"I think so. Why?"

"That's odd," she remarked with a troubled expression. "We had a strange occurrence about ten minutes before you arrived. Welly started barking at the window," she remarked, pointing at the large front window that overlooked the parking lot. Peggy's salon sat at the corner of Sixth Street and Waterfront Drive, which was a couple of blocks from the heart of downtown, and one street over from Main Street. "I thought he saw you coming in," she continued, "but when I turned to look, I swear I saw a leprechaun staring back at me."

"It was undoubtedly one of the children," I told her, and turned to the door again. Welly was in a hurry to leave.

"No." The way she said this stopped me in my tracks. "No, it couldn't have been. The person was the size of a child, but his costume was too good—too authentic. He looked like he stepped right out of the history books, wearing an old-fashioned green suit, knee breeches, with a matching green top hat. He had bright orange hair and a long beard of the same color, but I don't think they were fake. If it had been a child, his features would have looked smooth and youthful. He would have been a cute leprechaun, not the ugly, unsightly one staring right at me with those beady little eyes." There was a touch of concern in her voice as she spoke, but I had the feeling she was pulling my leg.

"Peggy, the leprechaun you saw was a child wearing a mask. I'm sure of it. They make pretty convincing masks these days, and kids love wearing them."

"Oh!" She breathed a sigh of relief, as if the thought had never crossed her mind. "That must be it! It was obviously just a mask. Either that or I saw a real leprechaun!" Her unsettling laughter followed Welly and me out the door.

CHAPTER 2

As I drove out of Peggy's parking lot, I realized that she was correct. Main Street was already blocked off for the parade. It wouldn't be a long parade, I thought, as I avoided the roadblocks by turning down another street that ran parallel to our main downtown shopping district. As I crossed Main Street from two blocks away, I could see the children already marching with their classmates and teachers toward my lighthouse while their parents, grandparents, and happy villagers lined both sides of the street, clapping and cheering them on. Dressed in their warmest winter gear, every child appeared to be wearing a green top hat and a red beard made from construction paper. For a town that didn't have a true St. Patrick's Day Parade, I found the grade-school Leprechaun Parade to be utterly charming. However, I was running late. I knew that Teddy, my fabulous assistant baker, and the rest of the Beacon's excellent staff had everything under control, but I wanted to be there when all those little leprechauns marched into the bakeshop to get their St. Patrick's Day treats!

"Hang on, Welly," I called to the back seat, getting ready to step on the gas the moment we passed the police station. I looked in the rearview mirror as I spoke and saw my dog already lounging across the seat as if he didn't have a care in the world. His fur glistened; he smelled like a rose. Obviously, the whole skunk incident of the morning had faded from his memory. "If we're late today, it's because of you," I reminded him. As usual, he thought I was talking about a treat and wagged his tail. Then, however, with a suddenness that belied his great size, Welly sprang to his feet and gave a loud series of barks out the window. My entire body flinched from the noise. At that very same moment something hard careened into the side of the Jeep, causing the entire vehicle to wobble.

"What the . . . ?" I blurted, hitting the brakes. Welly was still barking as my head swiveled to the passenger side window. It couldn't have been a car that hit us because we were in the middle of the block. I also couldn't see anything that made sense. Then something small and green popped into view.

"Heavens!" I cried, throwing the Jeep into park. I turned off the engine. The thought that I had just hit a child turned my knees to jelly. Technically, the child had run into the passenger side of the Jeep, but that didn't make me feel any better. It had been quite a loud thud. Feeling a bit sick, I sprang out the door and ran to the other side to see if the child was injured. Poor thing was probably late for the parade, like me, I thought as

I leapt onto the curb. Yet to my astonishment, no one was there. Welly, however, was still barking, only this time he was barking out the driver's side window. I ran around the Jeep again and was just in time to see a swiftly moving person, dressed as a leprechaun, turn down a narrow alleyway between two buildings, where he vanished. The thought that my eyes were deceiving me did cross my mind. The person, about the size of a fourth- or fifth-grader, was wearing a very convincing leprechaun costume, not at all like the construction-paper top hat and beard of the school children. He didn't run like a child either. He was swift, yet there'd been a slight limp to his gait, as if he had a knee problem . . . or was older than he appeared. Of course, hitting my Jeep could have been responsible for that as well. Another thing that struck me was that this small person was carrying a beautifully carved walking stick, the kind Rory's uncle Finn would call an Irish *shillelagh*. I closed my eyes and thought of Peggy. I had been so quick to dismiss her leprechaun sighting, and now I felt a bit guilty about it. I wasn't going to be able to explain my sighting either, for fear of sounding like a loon. I now understood how it felt to be that person in the woods who sees a Sasquatch, forgets to take a picture, yet still thinks it's a good idea to tell everyone about the sighting. *Ahem*, crazy!

Out of some deep-seated maternal reflex, I called across the empty street, "Are you okay?" My heart was still beating like a war drum! "Did I hurt you?" But whoever or whatever had hit my Jeep didn't answer. The leprechaun was gone.

I didn't have long to think about the strange encounter, because another startled cry hit my ears, this one coming from the opposite side of the Jeep. Welly, the knucklehead, had spun back around again and continued barking, all the while spitting tendrils of drool all over the insides of the windows. It looked as if a spider with a severe medical condition had tried to make a web in there. Highly disturbing. And I had just cleaned them too!

"Help! Quickly! Quickly!" The frantic voice not only pulled me from my messy window issue, but it had also struck a nerve. I ran back around the Jeep to the passenger side once again. That's when I saw Mrs. Hinkle running down the steps of the village hall building. The moment she saw me she began flailing her arms.

"Lindsey! Lindsey, oh, it's just terrible! We've been attacked!"

"Mrs. Hinkle, are you alright?" I ran to meet the older woman.

Clare Hinkle had to be in her seventies if she was a day. That's why seeing her move so quickly shocked me. Mrs. Hinkle came to the bakeshop every now and again. I knew her to be a sweet older woman who dedicated much of her life to serving the village of Beacon Harbor. Betty Vanhoosen had told me that Clare Hinkle had worked at Village Hall since she was in her early twenties. Now she was the village clerk, a duty she took very seriously.

"I'm okay, but did you happen to see a leprechaun run through here?"

"Umm . . ." *Wow. What was I supposed to say to that?* I cleared my throat and offered an unconvincing, "Possibly?" Oddly enough, Mrs. Hinkle seemed satisfied with my answer.

"I figured as much when I saw you there." She

took a deep breath and blurted with renewed anger, "That creature attacked Fred Landry—in broad daylight!"

Hearing that, I ran back to the Jeep and popped open the door, releasing Welly. If, by chance, Mrs. Hinkle was mistaken and the attacker was still inside the building, Welly's sheer size and protective instincts would make them think twice about pulling any more shenanigans. Mrs. Hinkle agreed, and together Welly and I followed her into the building.

The moment we entered the modest, red brick, two-story building, Welly seemed to pick up on a scent. He sniffed around the floor a moment, then made a beeline for the stairs that led to the second floor, and Fred Landry's office.

"The others have gone to watch the parade," Mrs. Hinkle explained as we followed my dog. "I was just on my way there as well when I walked out of my office and looked across the hall. That's when I saw a streak of green behind the desk in Fred's office. Then the leprechaun burst through the door and came towards me, forcing me back into my office. I shut my door, peeked out the window, and watched him disappear down the stairs. I immediately ran to Fred's office to see what the ruckus was all about, thinking it was a disgruntled taxpayer embracing the holiday. We get that all the time. Disgruntled taxpayers," she clarified. "Not leprechauns. However, when I found Fred lying on the floor, I realized what had happened. He'd been physically attacked. But that's not the strangest part . . ."

Mrs. Hinkle was undoubtedly going to tell me just what the strangest part of her story was when I believed I discovered it myself. Welly had pushed through the office door the moment I had opened it and went directly to Fred Landry. My heart stilled for a beat or two when I saw the poor man lying facedown in a pool of his own blood. More disturbingly, he was covered in green and gold glitter.

"All the glitter!" Mrs. Hinkle cried. "Why is he covered in glitter?"

"Good Lord! Mr. Landry's been murdered! Quick, call 911!"

"The police are just a few doors down, dear," she reasoned. "I was going to fetch the sergeant myself, until I saw you."

I stood beside the body, careful to avoid stepping in blood, when Welly started to whine. I was still staring at all the glitter. *GLITTER?* The word rang out in my head like a bullet from a shotgun. Blood and glitter were definitely not a good mix. It was highly disturbing and looked utterly surreal.

"What do you suppose the point of all this glitter is?" Mrs. Hinkle asked me.

"I haven't a clue, but his head's been bashed in."

"By that nasty leprechaun," she added, crossing her arms on her chest. I honestly couldn't tell what she thought was more disturbing, the thought of a vicious leprechaun with a penchant for glitter, or her dead coworker.

Mrs. Hinkle cleared her throat, adding in a much lighter tone, "I heard they were a bit ornery, but I've never heard that they were murderers. They're part of the fairy folk, you know."

Dear heavens, had everybody gone mad? Leprechauns? Fairy folk? A man was murdered by some person in a costume who then sprinkled the victim with glitter. This had the mark of a psycho serial killer to me. However, to dear Mrs. Hinkle I said, "Um, I rather think that this is not the work of a leprechaun."

"I saw him with my own eyes!"

"I did too. I don't really know what I saw. Did you make the call yet?" I prodded, changing the subject. Just then, however, Welly gave a hefty nudge to the dead man's arm. To my amazement, the dead man let out a soft groan.

"He's not dead, Mrs. Hinkle!" I cried, dropping to my knees beside Mr. Landry. "Hold the police. Call an ambulance first!" I would have done it myself if I hadn't left my cell phone in my purse, which was still in my Jeep. Mrs. Hinkle then surprised me by picking up the receiver on Fred's office phone.

"You just have to dial nine to get a line out," she informed me as she made the call. She then called the police as well. "They're closer," she reasoned. "The ambulance is coming from the other side of town and that parade will clog up the works, if you know what I mean. Best try to stop the bleeding."

"Right," I said, taking off my coat and rolling up my sleeves. I looked around the room, hoping to see a towel or something I could use to pack the wound on the back of his head. Mr. Landry's office was impressively tidy. I then noted that Mrs. Hinkle was wearing a smart dress that not only looked comfy, but expensive. I was wearing a pair of dark blue jeans and a lovely moss-green cable knit sweater from Mom's collection. The sweater could be replaced, but then another idea struck me. I asked Mrs. Hinkle, "Got a quarter?"

"Whatever for?" The wrinkles on her face were even more exaggerated as she asked this.

"The dispenser in the women's bathroom. A sanitary pad will stop the bleeding. I saw it on television."

"Right." She nodded, sending the ends of her neat, shoulder-length white hair fluttering. She then opened Fred's desk drawer and handed me a fistful of quarters. "Hurry!"

CHAPTER 3

"**Y**ou're finally here! I was getting worried. Is . . . that blood on your sweater? . . . *And glitter?*" Teddy Pratt, my excellent assistant baker, was holding a tray of green frosted sugar cookies cut in the shape of shamrocks as he looked at Welly and me. His eyes drifted to Welly, where he spied the green and gold glitter on my dog's nose and the top of his head. "I thought he was at the groomers?" Teddy looked both intrigued and a tad disturbed as well.

"Um, there was a little hiccough between the groomers and getting here." As I spoke I pulled Welly to the industrial kitchen sink with me. My big fluffy dog wasn't *officially* allowed in the bakeshop kitchen for sanitary reasons, but I felt the current circumstances allowed for an exception. Teddy set the tray of cookies on the counter and followed me.

"So, what you're telling me is that you haven't been blessed with the luck of the Irish yet? If you go out there with all those cute little leprechauns your luck is bound to change." He looked so certain that I almost smiled.

"I'm about to head out there, but I hope my run of bad luck doesn't follow me. First a skunk attack at dawn, then an emergency at Village Hall."

"Was it your water bill?" he questioned with a knowing look. "With all the baking and washing we do, it has to be shocking."

"Not my water bill," I assured him. "Welly and I were on our way back from the groomers when Mrs. Hinkle, from Village Hall, flagged us down and told us that Fred Landry had been attacked. Of course, Welly and I stopped to help her." I conveniently left out any mention of the angry leprechaun who had hit my Jeep.

"That's where that came from?" Teddy, staring at the stain on my lovely sweater, opened a drawer near the sink and handed me a clean washrag. "I don't know who Fred Landry is, but that's just awful, Lindsey. Is he okay?" There was genuine concern in his bright blue eyes as he spoke. Teddy's endearing look caused tears to well in my own eyes. The trauma of seeing Mr. Landry on the floor of his office suddenly hit me. I doubted I'd ever make sense of it, I thought, as I dabbed at my eyes with the clean rag before turning on the faucet. I then ran the rag under the warm water.

"The problem is, I don't think so, Teddy. He was alive when the EMTs came, but the man lost a lot of blood. Whoever attacked him meant to kill him."

"Lindsey, I'm so sorry."

"Thank you. But please don't say anything about this. I don't want to ruin the party."

"You got it, boss. Are you okay?"

"I'm fine. Just a bit of a mess." I flashed him a watery smile and began washing the blood and glitter off Welly's head and nose. The stain on my sweater was another matter.

"Well, you take your time, Linds. Everything has been taken care of. Tom and Elizabeth are serving up the leprechaun punch, and Wendy and Alaina have been handling the cookies. We were running low, so I thought I'd bring out the rest of them. FYI, those little leprechauns are adorable. Just pop out when you can."

"Thanks, Teddy. Will do." I watched as he picked up his tray of cookies again and headed for the door. Yet just before he pushed through to the café, he stopped.

"I'm confused. If a man was attacked, why is there glitter on your jeans and on Welly's nose?"

Sure enough, my jeans were glittering with sparkles of green and gold. And even my best efforts couldn't remove all the sparkle from Wellington's newly washed and brushed fur. I looked at Teddy and shrugged. "Would you believe a leprechaun?"

"Funny, but I would. The village is full of them today." Teddy flashed me a grin before walking out the door.

As anticipated, the moment Welly pranced into the bakeshop, the little leprechauns squealed with delight and began lining up to pet him. Although my staff welcomed me with worried glances from their stations, I was quick to ease their minds with a smile and a wave. Noting a little bubble of space near the punch station where Tom and Elizabeth were working, I pulled Welly with me, promising the children that everyone would get a chance to pet him.

"We were getting worried about you, boss," Tom said as he handed a cup of frothy green punch to an adorable little girl. She had big green eyes, strawberry-blond hair, and an impish smile. But what I loved most was that her green leprechaun hat was covered with white flowers and a heavy dose of pink glitter. Had Kennedy been at the bakeshop she would have loved this youngster's stylish flair. As it was, Kennedy had booked a room at the Harbor Hotel. I had offered my guest room, of course, but Kennedy had declined, stating that her new boyfriend, Niall Fitzhugh, was used to a certain level of luxury that the lighthouse just couldn't provide. Knowing a little something about this new man of Ken's, I highly doubted the Harbor Hotel would live up to his expectations either. I hadn't met Niall yet, but I was already beginning to dislike him. I was jaded, of course. Tuck was our good friend, and I hated to see him so glum. Kennedy had broken his heart last November when she had broken up with him and had announced that she was heading back to the UK for a while. The worst part was that I hadn't had the nerve to tell Tuck that Kennedy was back in town . . . with a new boyfriend. I was a spineless chicken. With effort, I banished all thoughts of Kennedy, Niall, and Tuck McAllister from my mind and turned instead to Tom and Elizabeth.

"We got delayed," I told them truthfully. "I'll tell you about it later."

"Fair enough," Elizabeth said with a nod. "Your green punch is a big hit with the kids. Nice work,

Lindsey. We should make some for the grand opening of the Blarney Stone."

"Elizabeth, that's a fabulous idea. Remind me to add it to the menu." The creamy green punch was a cinch to make. It was a mixture of frozen lime-ade, lime sherbet, and ginger ale. When we were asked by the school to provide treats for the parade, I hit the internet in search of inspiration and found the recipe for the green punch. I mixed some up, served it to my crew, and we all agreed it was delicious. I had planned to serve coffee and tea at the grand opening but adding this simple punch to the menu wouldn't be any trouble at all.

Welly loved the attention showered on him and waited patiently as we greeted the cheerful little leprechauns and their parents. However, I could tell that there was another lure in the bakeshop vying for his attention. Although the bakeshop was filled to the brim with grade-schoolers, teachers, and parents, I knew that somewhere behind the wall of green paper hats and smiling faces was Bailey, Uncle Finn's beautiful white dog. Welly, no doubt, knew this too.

"Be a good boy, Welly," I told him, slipping him a bacon and cheese–flavored Beacon Bite right before a little leprechaun boy gave him a big hug. Welly, thank heavens, knew the drill. Just to make sure, I had a boggling supply of Beacon Bites in the pocket of my sweatshirt. Realizing the stain on my sweater would require some real effort, I opted for the nearest clothing item at hand, an oversized sweat-shirt. I looked in the mirror, quickly brushed my long, ash-blonde hair back into place, and brushed on a little mascara as well, to accentuate my light-green eyes. Thank goodness my mother was a snowbird, basking in warmer climates, I thought. As the daughter of a former '80s supermodel, even I had to admit that I looked a tad shabby in the baggy gray garment with the words LAKE LIFE printed across it. Mom would take one look at me and shake her pretty head, muttering something like, *And I tried so hard to give you a sense of style! This is the best you can do?* Yep, I thought, children rebelled in odd ways. However, my jeans still sparkled, so that was something.

"Lindsey, lass! There ye are!" The moment I heard Finn O'Connor's voice, I turned to the bakeshop door. Over the sea of green leprechaun hats poked a familiar knotty walking stick. At the sight of Finn's shillelagh my heart gave a sudden, painful lurch. I had seen one just like it . . . in the hand of a leprechaun fleeing the scene of a crime. *Leprechaun,* I thought, realizing how stupid that sounded. I didn't know what I had seen, but I did know that whoever hit my Jeep and kept running was carrying a shillelagh. Nonetheless, I excused myself from the children and their parents, and headed for the door.

Finn was clearly no leprechaun. He was a man in his late fifties who stood just shy of six feet and had the same dark-haired, blue-eyed good looks of his nephew. Unlike Rory, however, Finn had a touch of gray at his temples, giving him an air of distinction. Finn and his daughter, Colleen, having led the Leprechaun Parade, had certainly dressed the part. Finn looked dapper in his driving cap of mossy green, a light brown tweed jacket over a cream-colored cable-knit sweater, and dark brown pants. Having glossed over my share of fashion catalogues in the past, Finn looked as if he'd just come from a long hike on the Irish moors rather than a short march down Main Street. Colleen, standing across from her father, was a black-haired, gray-eyed beauty who looked lovely in her long, white, cable-knit cardigan with bright green shamrocks on the lower hem and collar. Bailey, the Great Pyrenees, sat beside Colleen as she handed out slips of paper to everyone who walked through the door. Welly, of course, made a beeline for his new best friend.

"We heard about the skunk," Colleen said, offering a look of condolence. "We don't have them in Ireland, but I hear they're a nuisance. Maybe that's a myth too?" She raised an eyebrow as she looked at Wellington. "He smells just grand."

"It's definitely not a myth," I was quick to tell her. "Skunks spray a brand of nastiness that would knock the socks off a pig farmer. The smell is hard to get out as well, but Peggy managed to do it. Welly is good as new."

"He is indeed," she said, giving Welly a pat on the head. Welly was too busy licking Bailey's nose to notice. My pooch was such a shameful flirt, it was embarrassing.

"Sure, if this isn't the quaint town ye told us it was," Finn remarked with a grin. His grin faded as he added, "But 'tis full of leprechauns." The way he said this made the hair on the back of my neck stand on end. I got the feeling that Finn wasn't referring to the children of the parade. In fact, the way he was eyeing them with suspicion as he handed out coupons was a little unsettling.

"Uncle Finn, you were leading the Leprechaun Parade," I offered in a teasing manner, hoping to knock the air of suspicion from his eyes. I called him *Uncle* Finn because he had asked me to.

"Aye, but I've the unsettling feeling. Ye see, m' dear, there are children who dress as leprechauns, and then there are leprechauns who try to pass themselves off as children. Wee tricksters, they are. I thought maybe I had seen something strange in the ranks, ye see."

The hair on the back of my neck was not only standing on end, but it was also tingling.

"Away with ye, Da, telling your tall tales!" Colleen shot her father a chiding look. "Pay him no mind, Lindsey."

"A tale," I repeated, breathing a sigh of relief. "Right."

But the relief I felt was short-lived. Because at that moment Rory Campbell, all six-foot-four gorgeous inches of him, came moving at speed to the bakeshop door. The door flung back on its hinges, causing the little bell above to jingle a tad too frantically.

"Lindsey!" he cried with concern. "Are you okay? Tuck's just called. He told me all about the attack on Fred Landry."

"I'm . . . fine," I assured him, urging him with my eyes to *zip it.* It was hardly the time or place to discuss such a thing. However, Finnigan O'Connor's curiosity had been piqued, and the Irishman wasn't about to let the matter drop.

"Attack?" he asked his nephew. "'Tis a violent word, Rory, man. Who is this Fred Landry ye speak of, and what's he done?"

"He works at Village Hall. We really don't know more than that." I gave a nonchalant wave of my hand, hoping that Rory would get the message.

"Yes, we do," Rory contradicted, looking at me with concern. "You and Clare Hinkle were the first on the scene, according to Tuck. Officer Tuck McAllister," he clarified for his uncle. "According to him, Fred suffered a mighty blow to his head, causing a lot of—"

"Glitter!" I cut in. "So much glitter." Just then it dawned on Rory that he was surrounded by a sea of little leprechauns, most of whom were staring up at him with lime-green mustaches and partially eaten shamrock cookies in their hands. Welly, wanting to be noticed as well by his second favorite human, curtailed his face-licking barrage on Bailey to sit instead on Rory's feet. Wellington looked up at him and began to whine for attention. "Happy St. Patrick's Day, Rory, dear," I said. "Have a cookie."

CHAPTER 4

"I'm sorry I didn't call, but there was no time," I explained to Rory as we stood in the lighthouse kitchen. After the Leprechaun Parade we had closed the Beacon, cleaned up the mess, and I had held a quick staff meeting regarding the preparations for St. Patrick's Day and the grand opening of the Blarney Stone. It was going to be a busy day indeed, but with Teddy Pratt and the rest of my staff onboard, I knew we could handle it. What I was having trouble handling at the moment was Rory's look of disappointment. *Why hadn't I called him from Village Hall, right after I'd called Tuck?* he had asked, looking hurt.

Honestly, all I had wanted to do was get back to the bakeshop before the parade arrived. That hadn't happened, and quite frankly I had been a bit frazzled about the rogue leprechaun who had slammed into my Jeep right after assaulting Mr. Landry. Add to that a predawn skunk attack, and it had all the makings of an unsettling day! However, our day was far from over. Rory and I were hosting a pre–

St. Patrick's Day dinner party in my newly renovated boathouse, and I still hadn't told Tuck that Kennedy was in town. Unfortunately, he was about to figure that out for himself.

"Tuck said that you and Mrs. Hinkle kept mentioning a leprechaun." Rory cast me a sideways glance as he placed the dinner dishes on a large tray. "What was that all about?"

I gave the rich Irish beef and Guinness stew one last stir before returning it to the oven. The savory dish had been simmering in a large Dutch oven at three hundred degrees ever since I had gone to fetch Wellington from the pet salon, and it smelled wonderful. Yesterday, I had made two large Baileys cheesecakes that were still resting in my refrigerator, and Colleen was bringing two loaves of her famous Irish soda bread. Nearly everyone invited had offered to bring something to share at the party, and for that I was grateful. I turned from the stove and said to Rory, "I thought he might have mentioned the leprechaun. Mind you, I'm not entirely certain it was a leprechaun we saw, but while Welly and I were driving back from Peggy's pet salon, someone ran right into the side of the Jeep. For one terrifying moment I thought I had hit a child. I jumped right out to make sure they were okay. That's when I saw a smallish person dressed as a leprechaun running across the street where he disappeared between two buildings. I was just trying to make sense of that when Mrs. Hinkle came running out of Village Hall, waving her hands at me. According to her, she had heard a commotion coming from Fred Landry's office, and when she went to investigate, she thought she saw a leprechaun running away. Obviously, this was the same leprechaun that ran into my Jeep."

Rory narrowed his eyes at me. "You don't really believe that you saw a leprechaun, do you, babe? Because it was obviously some person dressed up as one to throw you both off. After all, the Leprechaun Parade was going on at the same time. I bet that whoever this person was, planned to blend in with the kids. Maybe he was even somehow connected to the parade?"

"Like a parent or a teacher?" I asked.

"Exactly." He gave a nod as he added cutlery to the tray.

"It's a good theory," I agreed. "But this person I saw wasn't what you would term *adult sized*."

"You think it was a kid?" This thought concerned him. After all, the parade was for the grade-school children. I was quick to set him at ease.

"No. It wasn't a child, Rory. What fourth- or fifth-grader could possibly have a beef with the village treasurer?"

"Good point. At that age, most kids don't even know what a treasurer is. So, what you're telling me is that this person you and Mrs. Hinkle saw was the size of a child, dressed like a leprechaun, and had a vendetta against the village treasurer."

"Exactly. Oh, I almost forgot. Peggy O'Leary saw him too. He was peeking in the window of her pet salon. She told me Wellington was barking at the window, and when she turned to look, she saw a terrifying sight."

"You think she saw the same leprechaun?" There was a heavy dose of suspicion in his voice as he asked this.

"She said that it couldn't possibly be a child, Rory. His costume was too good, too authentic—as if he'd come right out of the history books."

"History books?" he questioned as a sardonic look crossed his face.

"Okay, old books on folklore then," I corrected, wrinkling my nose at him. "Peggy described him as wearing an old-fashioned green suit, knee breeches, with a matching top hat. He had bright orange hair and a long orange beard, and he had beady little eyes. The person who ran into my Jeep and attacked Fred Landry fit her description to a tee."

Rory stared at me a long moment with his compelling, light blue gaze, not sure what to make of my story. At last, he let out his breath. "I see. So, you, Peggy, and Mrs. Hinkle believe you saw a leprechaun."

"We *saw* a leprechaun," I agreed. "But even I know that there must be some logical explanation for it. The real question is why did someone attack Fred Landry?"

Rory shrugged. "That is the question, and it's worth looking into. I'll do my best to pick Tuck's brain about it."

"But not tonight," I warned. "Not at dinner. I don't want any mention of the attack or a discussion on leprechauns."

"Agreed. But on one condition. Next time you hit a leprechaun or stumble across a person who's just been attacked by one, call me. Okay? Look, babe, I'm concerned about you." Forgetting his tray of plates and cutlery, he came over to wrap me in his arms. Rory had strong, comforting arms. They were arms that a girl could just melt into, which is exactly what I did. "You have a way of stumbling into trouble."

"I do, don't I? I'm sorry for not calling you. I was just trying to make it back to the Beacon before the children did."

"I know. I forgive you, Bakewell." He convinced me further with a long, passionate kiss.

His ardent kisses filled me with new confidence. When I finally pulled away, I said, "About Tuck. I forgot to tell him that Kennedy is back in town."

"What?" His reaction to this was akin to a man who'd just been jabbed with a hot poker. His arms fell away as he stared at me. "Lindsey! You never told him? He'll be here in fifteen minutes."

"Fifteen minutes?" I looked at my watch just to make sure. "We don't have time to discuss this. We need to set the table! Let's just put them as far away from each other as we can."

"We can try," he agreed, "but I doubt it'll do any good. Kennedy's back in town, babe, and we all know that whenever she's here, trouble follows."

CHAPTER 5

When Kennedy left Beacon Harbor last November, Rory had come up with the great idea to renovate the old boathouse on the lighthouse property. His plan was partially meant to keep me occupied so that I wouldn't pester him with my concerns about my best friend, and partially to make use of the spacious building that I used as a garage. Honestly, it had been a good plan.

Since we were always hosting parties at the lighthouse, and I was always complaining how I needed more space in my dining room for our expanding list of family and friends, Rory had proposed renovating the boathouse into two distinct areas, using a third of the building for a proper two-car garage for me, while turning the larger part into a rustic yet elegant entertaining space. I had loved the idea so much that I instantly called my friend Christy Parks, owner of Bayside Boutiques and Interiors, to advise me on the interior design of the building. Anders Jorgenson had handled the build-out with the help of Rory and Beacon Bakeshop regular, the semiretired Bill Morgan and his son, Roger. After three months of hard work, the boat-house was finally ready to host its first party, our pre–St. Patrick's Day celebration, and I was burst-ing with excitement to finally get to show off the gorgeous space.

The once solid wall facing the backyard of the lighthouse and lake, had been replaced by a window-wall system that allowed for spectacular views. In the cold months the wall would be closed, but in the warm months an entire section could be opened, allowing the space to feel like an elegant covered patio. In the spring I had plans to create an actual patio for more entertaining, but for now, with snow still on the ground, a shoveled trail from the lighthouse through the lawn would have to do.

At Christy's suggestion, the interior walls of the building had been covered with white shiplap to match the interior of the bakeshop and lighthouse. The wood plank ceiling had also been painted white while the long back wall had been made into a staging area for entertaining. Since I already had a kitchen in the lighthouse and a professional kitchen in the bakery, I didn't feel that I needed another one here. However, Christy convinced me that a farmhouse sink flanked by two lengths of butcherblock countertops, and various cabinets would be a welcome addition. There were also two wine and beer refrigerators installed on either side of the dishwasher, and lots of empty cabinets I had yet to fill. On the shorter exterior wall, a large stone fireplace had been built with a beautiful live-edge oak mantel that Rory had made. I felt that it gave the large space a touch of coziness. Because it was so cozy, I had placed two loveseats and a few comfortable chairs around the fireplace to create an intimate sitting area.

As much as I loved this new space, I felt its best feature was the long, rustic wooden dining table placed in the center of the room. Two large, round iron chandeliers hung over the table, providing soft light. If I had listened to Rory, the chandeliers would be made of antlers. He could put all the antlers he wanted to in his house, I had told him in no uncertain terms (antlers were definitely not my style!), but this boathouse was mine. I wanted guests to enjoy it, and so I had won that battle.

Tonight, instead of using a white tablecloth, I decided to go with a green runner down the center of the table, allowing the beauty of the rustic wood to be on display. Embracing the St. Patrick's Day theme, I had also splurged on a set of white bowls with little shamrocks on them that dressed up my plain white dinnerware for the occasion. For the centerpiece I had filled a black cauldron with sand, then topped it with chocolate coins covered in gold foil. I sprinkled extra coins all down the green runner, skirting the medium-sized pillar candles placed there as well, then added some cutout shamrocks to the mix. When I was finished, I turned to Rory.

"What do you think?"

He put the empty tray under his arm, and grinned. "A pot of gold! I love it, and Uncle Finn and Colleen will too when they see this. It's very festive, babe."

Intrigued by the smell of forbidden chocolate, Welly popped his head on the table for a peek. He aimed his tongue at a chocolate coin. "Off the table, Welly!" I chided, thwarting his efforts. To Rory, I said, "We need to keep a vigilant eye on him or he's likely to eat one of those chocolate coins, foil and all."

"Welly, is this true?" Apparently it was, due to the mournful-eyed look he gave Rory. A moment later the pitiful whining began. The predictable nature of my food-loving Newfie made him grin. "You're better than that, Wellington," Rory told him. "She"—he pointed to me—"thinks you'd eat foil if it was wrapped around chocolate. You know that chocolate's not good for you." A challenging look was delivered my way, as Rory showered a little love on my dog. Welly loved the attention. "Besides, you've just eaten." These last words fell on deaf ears. Welly, spying something more intriguing than chocolate coins, barked as he ran to the window-wall.

I honestly hadn't thought about the slobber until after the window-wall had been installed. I cringed as a strand of drool hit and slowly gave way to gravity. With a sorry shake of my head, I silently acknowledged that I was a glutton for punishment. However, the onslaught of drool couldn't be helped. That was because Welly's third favorite human in the world, my best friend, Kennedy Kapoor, was peering through the window. She grinned and waved at Wellington. The tall, dashing man beside her had to be Niall Fitzhugh, I thought, spying the gorgeous bouquet of green and white flowers in his hand.

Just then behind the couple another man came into view. He was as handsome as the first man, and only an inch or two shorter. Kennedy must have heard him coming because she spun around to face him. The moment she did an incandescent smile appeared on the newcomer's face. The smile vanished the moment Niall Fitzhugh turned as well.

"Quick!" I hiss-whispered to Rory. "Get the door. Tuck has arrived."

CHAPTER 6

"Welcome to our St. Patrick's Day party!" I declared in an overly cheerful voice. I then took Kennedy by the arm and ushered her into the newly renovated boathouse, while Rory, with Welly on his heels, went out to have a word with Tuck McAllister.

I gave Kennedy a firm hug, noting that behind her near the door came a barrage of some not-so-happy hand gestures from Beacon Harbor's hottest man in uniform, only he wasn't in uniform, thank goodness. He had come dressed for a St. Patrick's Day party, and I felt like a great big idiot for not telling him that Kennedy was in town. Taking a deep breath to steel my nerves, I then turned to Niall. "And you must be Niall Fitzhugh." Channeling my inner Ellie Montague Bakewell, I gave him a smile Mom would be proud of. "I've heard so much about you."

"You've invited *Tucker*?" Kennedy hiss-whispered between clenched teeth. "Is this your idea of a joke?" She punctuated this with one of her signature looks—raising a perfectly shaped eyebrow at me. Truthfully, I had missed that look. Yet before I could reply, Niall presented me with the beautiful bouquet of flowers he'd been holding.

"A great pleasure to meet you, Lindsey," he said in an English accent that was a tad more cultured than Kennedy's. I didn't think it possible, but my ears weren't lying. My other senses weren't lying either as Niall took my hand and kissed the back of it. The man was definitely giving off a strong *Bond* vibe, that subtle yet heady mixture of etiquette, intelligence, and sartorial excellence wrapped in a hint of danger. I had to hand it to Kennedy, there wasn't anything remotely boyish about Niall Fitzhugh.

"Umm . . . for me as well, Niall," was my awkward reply. I cleared my throat, adding, "A pleasure, that is. And thank you for the flowers. I'll just put them in a vase."

"What a lovely room," he remarked, studying his surroundings.

"Yes, it is," Kennedy added, eyeing me just as intently.

"Niall, there's a rack down that hall for the coats, and you can help yourself to a drink on the back counter," I told him. "Kennedy's going to help me find a vase."

Kennedy left her coat with Niall and followed as I walked along the back counter to the other side of the room. I opened a cabinet where I knew I had a vase, and told her, "I'm sorry that I forgot to mention Tuck would be here for dinner, but he *is* our friend, Ken."

"I understand. But from the look on his face, it

was apparent that he didn't know I was going to be here either . . . with my new boyfriend! That's bloody negligent of you, Linds."

"I agree," I said, working to put the lovely flowers in the vase. "I got busy, and it slipped my mind. Please be civil to him. This dinner isn't about you and Niall, it's in honor of Rory's uncle, Finn, and his cousin, Colleen, who are opening their new Irish gift shop and micro-pub tomorrow. Betty and Doc will be here, and so will Teddy and his wife, Jesse. The Jorgensons are coming as well, along with Christy Parks and Molly Butterfield. Remember Molly? It should be a lively dinner. How's this look?" I gestured to the vase, then began filling it with water from the sink.

Kennedy shrugged. "I don't remember Molly, and how dare you? Of course, I'll be civil! I'm not angry with Tucker. If you'll recall, I'm the one who broke it off with him. I'm the one who needed to move on. I'm simply concerned that he won't be able to handle seeing me so happy with Niall, that's all. It's only been a wee bit over four months since I left, and he was very attached, as most men I date are. The flowers look lovely," she finally remarked. Giving the newly renovated room an appreciative look, she added, "I see you've used your time wisely. I love what you've done with this place."

"Thank you. I had a lot of help from Rory and our friends. This is our first party in this room, and I want it to be a success. Therefore, you and Niall are sitting at this end of the table with me. Tuck will be down there with Rory. You and I will talk later," I told her, waving to Anders and Susan Jorgenson, who had just entered the room. "The other guests are starting to arrive, and we have a lot of catching up to do."

"We do," she agreed with a gentle smile. "I bought a bottle of French wine for the occasion. I thought we could pop up to the lightroom tonight and crack it open, like old times."

"Oh, how I've missed you, Ken."

Aside from the slight buzz of tension that traversed the length of the table from Tuck McAllister at one end to Kennedy Kapoor at the other, I'd say my festive St. Patrick's Day dinner party was going quite well. I had never made a traditional Irish beef and Guinness stew before, choosing instead the traditional favorite, corned beef and cabbage. However, the thick, robust-flavored stew, blending savory chunks of beef, diced bacon, carrots, parsnips, and potatoes with various spices and a pint of Guinness Extra Stout, was positively heavenly. I had stepped away from tradition by adding sliced mushrooms to the mix as well. I loved mushrooms in stew and couldn't help myself from adding them. However, I was relieved when everyone agreed that the mushrooms were a welcome addition. Colleen's Irish soda bread was positively delicious, especially when slathered with Irish butter made from the milk of grass-fed cows. Betty had made a yummy, old-fashioned lime-green Jell-O salad, using lime Jell-O, a carton of Cool Whip, cream cheese, 7-Up, and canned pineapple chunks. It not only looked festive but was surprisingly delicious. It was so good, in fact, Uncle Finn had two helpings, claiming that from now on Betty's green

Jell-O salad ought to be an Irish tradition. That made us all laugh.

Once the dinner plates were removed, Rory helped me serve coffee with the Baileys Irish Cream cheesecakes I had made earlier. Uncle Finn, having had more than a few Guinness beers in him already, kept drinking them as he began regaling the table with tales from Ireland. With a soft fire crackling in the background, and with the full March moon visible through the wall of windows as it hovered over the dark lake, everyone fell silent and leaned in to hear what Finnigan O'Connor had to say.

"See that moon out there?" he asked, pointing out the window-wall. "'Tis the last full moon of winter. The ancient Celts called it the Plough Moon, due to it being that time of the year. 'Tis also referred to as a Worm Moon, because the soil will be warmin', and the worms will be coming out." Finn paused to take another sip of his beer before asking, "D'ye know what I call it?" All eyes were on him as he said, "I call it a Leprechaun Moon. There's a wee blessin' we say in Ireland. *May the leprechauns be near ye to spread luck along yer way. An' may all the Irish angels smile upon you St. Patrick's Day,*" Uncle Finn recited, eliciting smiles from his rapt audience. "But make no mistake," he cautioned. "Although people think that leprechauns are the bringers o' luck itself, they are not. 'Tis near St. Patrick's Day, under the Leprechaun Moon, when the wee green folk are particularly aggressive, emerging from their fairy world into ours. The leprechaun race is far older than the dear saint, sure. Everyone knows they emerge to eat the green stuff growin' in the forest, but once they took a taste of green beer, because that's what we drink on St. Patrick's Day, everything changed. Ye see, 'tis the beer they're after, and they'll do feck-all to get it."

"Ahem, Uncle?" Rory cast his uncle a cautioning look.

"What I meant was, they'll go to great lengths to get it," Finn corrected.

"Ooh, this is quite a tale, Finn," Betty said with a giggle. "I don't think leprechauns drink beer. They're too young."

"Betty, m'dear, pardon me French, but ye know willy-wanker about leprechauns. Have ye ever caught one? No? Because I have, and let me tell you, I'm still sufferin' for it."

"Caught one?" Kennedy asked, casting the Irishman a doubtful look. "Not possible. Everyone knows that leprechauns are a whimsey of Irish folklore."

"Well, ye being English, I expect as much. But I did catch one. Isn't that right, Colleen?"

"Aye, he did," Colleen offered in a passing manner, shaking her head. She was clearly the only one at the table not entertained by talk of leprechauns.

After a few more questions about leprechauns, Niall let out a hearty laugh. "Old man, the tall tales you tell! You did not catch a leprechaun, because they're not real. You were obviously drunk."

"Ye callin' me father a drunk now?" Colleen's fair face darkened, as her light gray eyes shot daggers at the Englishman.

To his credit, Niall didn't flinch. Instead, he offered, "Maybe not drunk, but I wouldn't call him sober."

"Oy!" Finn exclaimed. "No need to defend me, m' dear." He cast his daughter a loving, fatherly look. Turning to Niall, he said, "I'll not deny having a long, illustrious history with drink, just as I will not deny having a long, illustrious history with leprechauns. I owned a pub in Ireland, boy. Every year on St. Pat's Day we dyed the beer green. With the green beer flowin' strange things would start to happen. Money would go missing. Kegs of beer would go missing as well. In the morning I'd come in and things would be all a-hoo."

"Did you ever consider, sir, that you had a thief?" Tuck asked. I noticed that once he asked Finn the question, he glanced at Colleen. She cast him a grin, which made the young man flush bright red. Kennedy, unfortunately, had seen it too. For some reason my friend didn't look happy about the way Colleen O'Connor was boldly staring at Tuck McAllister.

"Aye, Mr. McAllister. I did have a thief," Finn admitted, bringing all eyes back on him. "I caught him once, and he tricked me into letting him go. The trouble is"—Finn's voice suddenly became very serious—"I think the wee man has followed me here."

"What?" I blurted, nearly choking on my coffee. The moment I spoke, Welly picked up his head and stared at me. I gave him a pat, then motioned for him to lie back down under the table. However, the thought that a *wee man*, as Uncle Finn put it, was here in town wasn't sitting too well with me. "By wee man, are you referring to a leprechaun?" I chanced a look at Rory as I asked this. As expected, Rory closed his eyes and slowly shook his head, as if the thought was the height of lunacy.

"Aye, a leprechaun," Finn confirmed, casting a challenging look at Niall. "I saw him myself today, peepin' in the window of the Blarney Stone, he was. I thought I saw him again—"

"Father, now's not the time," Colleen warned with a patronizing smile. She then took a bite of her cheesecake. "Lindsey, this Irish cream cheesecake is delightful." She was hoping, no doubt, to change the subject. However, as fate would have it, my dinner guests were enthralled with the direction the conversation had taken.

"What did this leprechaun look like, Finn?" Molly Butterfield, sitting next to him, asked. Molly, a friend of Betty's, owned Butterfield's Floral Artistry. She and her assistant, Lisa, were designing a special floral arrangement for the grand opening of the Blarney Stone. Molly, a vivacious woman in her mid-fifties who looked as if she'd stepped out of a fashion magazine from the '60s, with her dark brown hair cut in a short bob and long bangs that highlighted her large brown eyes, had admitted to finding Rory's Irish uncle very attractive. The fact that he was single was a bonus. Molly set down her dessert fork and smiled up at him, batting her thick, fake eyelashes a few times too many.

"Small," he said, "red hair and beard, beady eyes, and a face, m'darlin', that would frighten the devil himself."

"Oh, Finn!" she exclaimed with a wave of her hand and a melodious giggle. "You're pulling our legs!"

I wasn't laughing. In fact, my heart clenched painfully at Finn's description. Although I knew that leprechauns were mere mythical fairy folk, the trouble was, I also knew what I had seen. Mrs. Hinkle had seen the leprechaun too. And Finn's description fit Peggy's to a tee. What in the name of St. Patrick was going on in this town? I looked down the table to Rory for support. Unfortunately, he looked just as troubled as I felt. Tuck, sitting to his right, was looking a bit pale as well. After all, he had gotten an earful about leprechauns from Mrs. Hinkle and me regarding Fred Landry's attacker.

"He is joking, isn't he?" Molly directed the question at me, before addressing the table at large.

Finnegan O'Connor pulled her attention back to him, by saying, "Molly, m'darlin', I wish that I was, but I thought I saw the wee devil again today, hidin' in the parade with the kids."

"Oy! Da!" Colleen was issuing a not-so-subtle warning to her father. But Finn O'Connor loved an audience as much as he loved his Guinness.

"Colleen, m'dear, they must hear it for their own good," he warned. "'Tis St. Patrick's Day tomorrow and we've thrown everything we have into our dear Blarney Stone. This village has embraced us, but you and I both know that luck comes dear to the O'Connors of Derry, and the old ways are hard to shake. A clean start we thought we had, but maybe 'tis not as we had wished." Finn looked up and down the table, making sure he had everyone's attention, before he advised, "Lock your doors tightly this night, and all through St. Patrick's Day. Sure, if Finnigan O'Connor won't catch his leprechaun yet."

CHAPTER 7

St. Patrick's Day morning came much earlier than I had wished, partially because I'd gotten to bed so late after the dinner party we'd thrown, and partially because I wasn't looking forward to any more talk of leprechauns. Uncle Finn was certainly a character. He thought he'd caught a leprechaun in Ireland, and he thought that same leprechaun had followed him all the way to Beacon Harbor. I honestly didn't know what the heck was going on, but I was sorry to admit that I believed him. I felt crazy even admitting that to myself, but there it was. The small fellow in clothing of green had run smack-dab into the side of my Jeep. Mrs. Hinkle was certain that this same—dare I say leprechaun?—had attacked Fred Landry.

Poor Fred Landry. Doc Riggles had told me last night that things weren't looking good for Fred. He was in the ICU at Memorial Hospital and was still in a coma. His wife was beside herself with worry. Tuck, after taking our statements at Village Hall, admitted to me after the pre–St. Patrick's

Day dinner, that without being able to question Fred, he was having a hard time following up on any lead. Obviously, the description Mrs. Hinkle and I had given him of the leprechaun in question wasn't helping any. Tuck was also miffed at me for not giving him a heads-up on the fact that Kennedy was not only in town, but that she had come to dinner with her new boyfriend. I had apologized for that. The only saving grace was that the lovely Colleen O'Connor had taken an interest in him. She was the same age as Tuck, lived in the same town, and she had an alluring Irish accent. With any luck, in a few weeks' time he'd be thanking me.

Due to the success of my pre–St. Patrick's Day dinner, and all the cleanup involved, I had to take a raincheck from Kennedy on her bottle of French wine and a chat in the lightroom. Ken had understood. I believed that by the end of the meal all she cared about was getting out of my newly renovated boathouse. I could tell that her anxiousness had something to do with the way Colleen was hanging on Tuck's every word and the attention she was giving him. Yes, it had been a tad awkward, but as I reminded Kennedy, much of the awkwardness was of her own making. Niall, for his part, had seemed perfectly happy to sip Irish whiskey by the fire while talking American sports with Rory, Teddy, and Anders.

My only goal as I pulled myself out of bed at three thirty in the morning was getting through St. Patrick's Day without incident. Angry, aggressive leprechauns aside, I had a big day ahead of me. The Beacon Bakeshop would be open until eleven, after which my staff and I would head over to the Blarney Stone for the grand opening, which everyone was referring to by now as the Blarney Bash. I couldn't wait to see all the finishing touches Colleen and Finn had put into their beautiful shop and micro-pub. I knew the good people of Beacon Harbor and beyond couldn't either. It was going to be a St. Patrick's Day for the record books!

I tiptoed to the bathroom, got dressed, then tiptoed out of the bedroom with Wellington on my heels, being careful not to wake Rory. Rory was letting his uncle and cousin live in his beautiful lakefront log home until they got the Blarney Stone up and running. He knew that they appreciated the rent-free accommodations. Finn had told him that they'd start looking for a house in the late spring, which was fine with Rory. With his house so crowded, he was spending more time at the lighthouse with Wellington and me. It was an arrangement that pleased everyone involved.

After a short walk with Welly along the snowy, open dunes near the lakeshore, and after giving my dog his dental chew along with his breakfast, I brought him back inside the lighthouse with me, then entered the bakery through my private door that led to the café. I was ready to start my busy day.

"Happy St. Patrick's Day!" Teddy greeted me with a big smile the moment I came into the kitchen. It was already warm and buzzing with the morning baking. Wendy was there too, wearing a green turtleneck beneath her red apron, and a leprechaun hat on her head. The hat looked adorable on her as she stirred a bowl of green icing.

"Teddy's been telling me all about your interesting dinner party last night, Lindsey. I hear that

Finn O'Connor said he caught a leprechaun." She made a face indicating that she thought he was crazy. I didn't disagree.

"Happy St. Patrick's Day to both of you," I replied in greeting. "And to answer your question, Wendy, he believes that he did."

"It's just a ploy to drum up business," she declared with certainty. "It's the Blarney Bash today, and he's made it clear he's an expert on leprechauns. Everyone will be flocking to the Blarney Stone to hear more about it."

I cast her a grin as I put on my apron. "You know something? I think you might be right. I never thought about it, but your theory makes sense." It really did, and I hoped my wise, very capable apprentice baker was correct. I looked at Teddy for support and got a thoughtful nod from him. It was then I noticed the bowl of filling he'd just pulled off the stove. It smelled of warm milk, sugar, eggs, vanilla bean, and butter. However, it was a shade of green one didn't normally find in nature. "Is that green custard you're making?"

"Isn't it beautiful?" Teddy smiled with delight as he scooped a spoonful of the silky green mixture then let it plop back into the saucepan. "Wendy and I thought it would be fun to make some shamrock donuts for the bakeshop. It's basically going to be a cream-filled donut with green vanilla cream, basic white frosting on the top, then Wendy will pipe on a green shamrock. We're nearly ready to begin assembling them."

"They sound perfect, you two. I knew you'd come up with something special. I'm making ham and asparagus mini quiches, glazed apple-oat muffins, and Irish currant scones to add to our standard morning offerings. Then, once the bakery cases are filled, Teddy and I will finish the rest of the baking for the Blarney Bash, while you and Elizabeth man the bakery counter. Remember that we're closing at eleven this morning."

"Sounds great, Lindsey." Wendy flicked her long, blond ponytail off her shoulder. "Save me one of those quiches. This donut we're making is certain to give anyone who eats one a green tongue!"

CHAPTER 8

The morning flew by quickly. As my crew handled the bakery counter and café, Teddy and I finished baking and packing all the delicious, bite-sized St. Patrick's Day treats we were bringing to the Blarney Stone. We had made dozens of smaller shamrock sugar cookies and delicious traditional Irish shortbread cookies. We had also made dozens of mini Guinness chocolate cupcakes topped with either a chocolate ganache or a Baileys buttercream frosting, and white cupcakes topped with light green shamrock-shake frosting or Baileys buttercream, as well. We had finger-sized fudge brownies with a minty, crème de menthe filling and a chocolate ganache frosting. They were to die for! And, of course, mini Baileys cheesecake bites with a chocolate ganache drizzle. I truly believed that the pull of free baked goods, green punch, and three-dollar green beer was going to be too much for the townspeople to resist!

As my team closed the Beacon for the day, I let Welly out of the lighthouse and began loading up

my Jeep. Welly had been invited to come to the
Blarney Bash too, although he and Bailey would
spend most of the day playing out back in the
fenced-in yard or sleeping in Colleen's warm office.

"Ryan and I'll be along in a minute with the bev-
erages," Teddy informed me.

"Wear your green so you don't get pinched!" I
replied with a grin.

The lovely, spacious, red-brick ranch house the
O'Connors had purchased on the corner of Main
Street and Forest Ave. had been transformed into
a charming Irish-style cottage. The brick had been
painted white, all the wood trim had been painted
black, and the front door had been painted a welcoming shade of hunter green. It looked so
charming and inviting, I thought, that it truly was
the perfect spot to house an Irish gift shop. Finn's
much-anticipated micro-pub was conveniently located in the attached, oversized two-car garage ac-
cessible through a little breezeway in the gift shop.
The pub was a vision of cozy Irish hospitality, I
thought, tickled at seeing such an establishment in
a transformed garage. Before leaving Ireland, Finn
had disassembled his old pub and had shipped the
heavy oak bar, heavy oak woodwork, and four tidy
oak booths upholstered in red leather to his new
address in Beacon Harbor. Although one would be
hard-pressed to tell that the pub resided in a con-
verted garage, the one giveaway that wasn't totally
authentic was the cement floor. Although, to be
fair, most of the oil stains were now covered with
area rugs in shades of red and tan.

"Lindsey, I'm so glad you're here," Colleen said,
welcoming us at the door. "You too, Welly, boy. I
was getting worried. I know we don't open our

doors for another half hour yet, but I'm sorry to say I'm nervous."

The banner advertising the grand opening was displayed across the front of the house. Inside, Molly Butterfield and her assistant, Lisa Baxter, were already hard at work, placing their beautiful flower arrangements on the front counter with two smaller matching arrangements on the refreshment table near the bay window. That was where I would be setting up the St. Patrick's Day treats and shamrock punch.

"Our complimentary floral arrangements from the Beacon Harbor Welcoming Committee," Molly explained, doing a last-minute adjustment on a beautiful white rose. After a little tweak, she graced me with her bright smile once again. "Which is basically just me and Lisa. We absolutely love bringing a little touch of cheer to our new businesses." Lisa punctuated her boss's statement with a shrug and a shy grin.

"I didn't realize that we had a welcoming committee in this town," I told her. "But I'm impressed. Ladies, Colleen, this place looks amazing. Your grand opening is going to be the hottest St. Patrick's Day party in town."

"I agree," said Molly. "Once I purchase the lovely claddagh ring I've had my eyes on, I know where I'll be spending the rest of the day." Without waiting for anyone to question this, she blurted with a chuckle, "In the pub! With Finn. You say he's divorced?"

Colleen nodded. "Three times now."

"So, your father's a man not opposed to marriage?" Molly's heavily lashed brown eyes glittered at the thought.

"'Twould appear not," Colleen replied prosaically.

"Perhaps he hasn't met the right woman yet?" Molly looked hopeful. Colleen looked amused, and Lisa just looked embarrassed.

"According to him he's met her three times now. The first one, me mother, died. The second one ran off with the vicar, and the last one took him for all he was worth, the hoor."

"Well, you know what they say, the fourth time's the charm. Bet he's never married an American."

I was sure the fourth time wasn't the charm, but I kept my mouth shut. Colleen plucked the box of brownies from my hands, indicating her annoyance with the direction the conversation had taken. With one last look at Molly, she replied, "I cannot say that he has. Come this way, Lindsey. I'll help you set up the refreshment table."

As Colleen and I worked to put the finishing touches on the refreshment table, she uttered, "Curse me father and his Irish charm. He'll flirt with her, sure. He loves the attention. Thank the sweet Lord Rory's helpin' in the pub today, or there'll be a line all the way into the gift shop."

"Well, he's happy to be helping out," I told her, regarding Rory. "Plus, I think he's really looking forward to sampling some green beer."

Colleen wrinkled her nose at this. "I've cautioned Da against it, due to the leprechaun he thinks is following him. But Finnigan O'Connor cannot part with tradition."

"Do you really think there is a leprechaun?"

"I'm Celtic," was her whimsical reply. "I've seen things, and in ten minutes I'll be running a gift shop that trades in the legend of the leprechaun as well as the magic of kissin' the Blarney Stone. We're selling replicas of the Blarney Stone for convenience. Plus, we have some grand books on Celtic mythology, and lucky-shamrock charms galore."

"So, are you telling me that you do? If so, I won't judge you." This I added because I was beginning to believe in leprechauns too, although I was loath to openly admit it.

She cast a quick glance at the door before answering. Betty Vanhoosen, I noted, was at the front of the line, peering through the windows in anticipation. Felicity Stewart, owner of the Tannenbaum Shoppe, was right beside her, jostling for a better position in line. Her husband, Stanley, was there too, but I had a feeling that he'd be making a beeline for the pub the moment Colleen opened the doors. It was heartwarming to see so many familiar faces and fellow shop owners rallying around the grand opening of the Blarney Stone.

"I do not," Colleen whispered in reply. "But I did hear about the attack on that man, Fred Landry, from that fit cop friend of yours and Rory's. By the way, he's coming to dinner tonight, too. I've invited him."

"Good," I told her. "I'm glad you've invited Tuck. It'll be a cozy group tonight, and I'm really looking forward to it. However, regarding leprechauns, there's definitely something very odd going on in this town."

"I agree," she said as a look of fear flashed across her face. Her light gray eyes narrowed in displeasure as she shook her head. "The attack has me frightened, and Da has been acting strangely since the Leprechaun Parade. Those people out there"—

she bent her head to the door—"they'll have heard about this leprechaun as well, I imagine. I've picked a fine time to open an Irish gift shop."

"And micro-pub," I added.

"Thanks for reminding me," she replied with a dark grin.

Just then Rory appeared in the gift shop with Welly and Bailey prancing behind him like royal pages. We'd been so busy in the gift shop that I hadn't realized the dogs had disappeared.

"I've been in the pub brushing up on my bartending skills," he said by way of greeting.

"We're about ready to open," Colleen told him. "Are ye ready in the pub?"

"We are. I'll just put these two out in the yard. They were behind the bar begging for pickled quail eggs."

"Yuck!" I scrunched up my nose at the thought.

"Lindsey," Rory admonished. "At least these two appreciate a delicacy when they smell one."

"Those two eat deer scat," I reminded him, casting a knowing look at my dog. Welly merely looked pleased with himself.

"You two are like children," Colleen admonished, teasingly. "Go." She shooed Rory as she walked behind the sales counter. A moment later a beautiful, haunting Irish melody filled the gift shop, setting the mood. "Ready?" she asked, as much to herself as to me as she walked to the front door. She then turned the closed sign to open, and flung the door wide, declaring to all within earshot, "Welcome to the Blarney Stone. Let the Blarney Bash begin!"

CHAPTER 9

With Ryan helping me at the refreshment table as excited shoppers came by for a treat, I couldn't help glancing around the beautiful gift shop. Eye-catching Irish goods filled every nook and cranny. On the front counter was a basket of shamrock charms that would be given to the kids from the Leprechaun Parade. There were cases of handcrafted Celtic jewelry on display along with Irish Belleek china and Waterford crystal. Irish art filled the walls, from bucolic Irish prints to hand-painted original works, as well as a boggling variety of Celtic crosses one could purchase. There were scented candles, imported foods, and beautiful clothing. The thick wool sweaters looked warm and comfy, as did the socks. There were sweat-shirts, and T-shirts, and many varieties of hats. There were books, and maps, and leather belts, and hand-made shillelaghs, just like the one Finn carried. My eyes, however, instantly went to the rack of Irish walking capes. They were all so lovely. I promised myself that by the end of the day one of them would be mine.

"This dessert table looks positively fabulous, darling."

I'd been talking with Felicity Stewart and hadn't even noticed Kennedy come in. Niall was standing next to her, plucking a mint brownie from the table.

"Ken, you made it! Thank you for coming."

"I wouldn't miss this grand opening for the world. I hear Sir Hunts-a-Lot is bartending with his uncle. How charming." The way she was smiling I honestly couldn't tell if she meant it as a compliment or not.

"They're serving green beer. The pub is very quaint and authentically Irish. I think you'd love it."

"I know I'll love it," Niall remarked.

"In a minute," Kennedy told him sweetly. "We've just arrived. I'd like to look around."

Niall forced a smile and plucked a piece of cheesecake from the table as well.

"With all that talk of leprechauns last night I was half expecting to see one in here today," Kennedy remarked.

"Haven't seen one yet," Ryan told her, offering Kennedy and Niall a cup of green punch. "But there is an awesome Blarney Stone in the corner over there. It's way cooler than a leprechaun."

Kennedy craned her neck to see what the young man was pointing at.

"Over there, luv." Niall directed her attention to a large stone in a far corner of the shop, visible every now and then as the crowd shifted. The large hunk of unremarkable stone was perched on a pedestal. Etched on the gold plate beneath it were the words, BLARNEY STONE.

"The mascot," Kennedy remarked. "You do know the legend of the Blarney Stone, don't you, Linds?" As Kennedy talked, Niall picked up a mini Guinness chocolate cupcake, peeled the wrapper, and popped it into his mouth, all the while scanning the goods inside the gift shop. I silently wondered what he was thinking.

"I know that it's a legendary stone in Ireland."

"Well, you have the gist of it, anyway. It's a block of limestone on the battlements of Blarney Castle," she told Ryan and me. "Bet Hunts-a-Lot's uncle has kissed it a time or two, the way he can carry on. In fact, I'd go so far as to say he's bloody made out with the thing after listening to all that rubbish about leprechauns last night. Kissing the Blarney Stone, darling, is said to give one the gift of gab."

Niall leaned in, adding, "A skill with flattery. A way of spinning a yarn. The pickled Irishman certainly has it." He plucked another treat from the table and popped it into his mouth. I wasn't counting or anything, but it was his fifth one. He eyed the green punch in his hand, then set it back on the table, untouched. "Where's the beer?"

"Right through there, Mr. Fitzhugh." Ryan pointed to a doorway outlined in green-painted trim.

"Good man. Lord knows you can't celebrate the saint's day without a pint or two of green beer. I hear he's got Guinness Stout, Harp Lager, and Smithwick's Red Ale on tap," he said by way of excusing himself, and headed for the green-framed hallway.

After a quick glance around the crowded gift shop, I noted that there was a distinct lack of men. I shrugged and brought my attention back to Kennedy.

"Well, Niall certainly is a fine-looking man. You look happy, Ken. You never did tell me how you two met."

"Quite by accident, darling. You see, Niall Fitz-hugh is the president of Bespoke Textiles, a high-end clothing manufacturer based in London. After a week home, my family was driving me mental. I forgot how loud and overbearing they all are. Dad is still overworked. Mum's still a raving nutter, and Pippa is dating a man with so many piercings and tattoos, it's hard to know what to stare at when talking to him. Hence the reason Mum's a raving nutter. So much for a holiday. While at home I decided to scout out a clothing manufacturer that could make an exclusive line for Ellie & Company. The United Kingdom is known for its high-end clothing manufacturers, Linds, and Bespoke Textiles is one of the top rated among them. I went there to discuss an exclusive clothing line and met Niall. I had no idea he was the president of the company. It was love at first sight," she informed me as her chin lifted to the ceiling. For some reason, I didn't quite believe her love at first sight story.

"That explains his fine clothes and good manners."

"Thanks to me, I've convinced him to cut us a deal. I can't wait to show Ellie some of the fine pieces we're working on for next fall."

"I'm sure Mom will love it. She never mentioned anything to me about it, though." I cast my friend a puzzled look.

"That's because we're keeping it a secret, darling." As Kennedy spoke, she turned her head to the far wall. Her head stilled as all expression left her pretty face. Kennedy, I noticed, was staring at the rack of Irish walking capes.

"You've finally spotted the walking capes!" I was so excited I was ready to run over to the rack, push everyone aside, and grab the walking cape I'd been eyeing ever since arriving at the Blarney Stone. "Aren't they just to die for? I've got to have one. I've decided, having helped with this successful grand opening, that I'm going to treat myself."

"They're gorgeous," she said through narrowed eyes. She then proceeded to walk over to the rack. Since Ryan had everything covered, I followed her.

"Nope, not that one," I said to Kennedy, grabbing the long walking cape in moss-green Donegal tweed from her hands. "I'm sorry, but we've been in a relationship all morning. I'm finally ready to make a commitment."

"Have you seen the price?" She pursed her lips at me.

"Yes. But can't you just picture me hiking on the wild Irish moors in this cape?"

"Actually, I can. It suits you to a tee, Linds. Let me just see something first." Kennedy inspected the coat with the same tenacious fervor as a drug-sniffing dog. At last, she looked up with her face pinched in either anger or indignation, I couldn't tell which.

"What's wrong?"

"This is what's wrong," she hissed, holding out the manufacturer's tag. "I commissioned a line of British walking capes that look just like this, as an exclusive product line for Ellie and Company. I chose that pattern of contrasting plaid! These capes were made by Bespoke Textiles! They look exactly like the ones I ordered! Niall promised me that they would be an Ellie and Company exclusive, but it appears they're not. They're being sold here! In the same bloody village! Two blocks down from our boutique! Wait until I get ahold of that man!" Kennedy threw the cape at me and stormed off for the pub.

"I . . . um, guess I'll just put this back for now," I told the woman standing next to me who was also browsing for capes, and hung it back on the rack.

"What's the matter with Kennedy?" Ryan asked the moment I returned to the refreshment table.

"She just found out that her boyfriend lied to her."

Ryan grimaced as he finished refreshing the cupcake tray. "In the immortal words of Mr. T, *I pity the fool.*"

CHAPTER 10

Kennedy had created a scene after discovering that her handsome and urbane boyfriend, Niall Fitzhugh, had sold her an exclusive textile line that wasn't quite so exclusive after all. Colleen, hearing the kerfuffle by the rack of walking capes, told Kennedy in no uncertain terms that Bespoke Textiles was known for their beautiful, authentic line of Irish, English, and Scottish textile goods. They were one of the largest suppliers, and every shop that desired to sell such items turned to them first. It was her own fault for not reading up on the company beforehand.

Kennedy didn't take kindly to criticism. I could tell that she found it particularly grating coming from Colleen. This, I believed, was partly because Colleen had been flirting with Tuck the night before, and partly because Colleen was correct. Kennedy had let her guard down regarding the handsome Niall Fitzhugh. She had taken him at his word over a business deal without doing her homework, which wasn't at all like her. I felt a pang of sadness watching as Colleen rounded on my friend with a string of stern words. Ever since the Halloween debacle at the lighthouse, Kennedy's confidence had been shattered. Thank goodness she was still feisty and proud, which was a good sign. But confidence was Kennedy's defining trait. She needed it. She needed to get it back, and I was hoping she'd find it again during her short visit to Beacon Harbor.

"This is a place of business," Colleen reminded her. "If you are going to continue to create a disturbance, Ms. Kapoor, I'm going to have to ask you to leave."

"You'll get no disturbance from me," Niall told Colleen with a slight lift of his chin. "It's always good to see that our products are appreciated. And for the record, luv," he added, shifting his hooded gaze to Kennedy, "I never lied to you. I told you that we offered a superior product. I thought you understood that it is exclusive by its very nature. Only the finest domestic and import clothiers can afford us. Did you really believe that Ellie and Company was the only clothier to carry our line of authentic Irish walking capes?"

"No!" She squinted her eyes at him and raised a finger. "You'll not gaslight me, Niall Fitzhugh. You lied."

A slight smile played at the corner of his lips as he said, "I omitted the truth. You were enthralled with our capes, and I wanted to take you to dinner. Forgive me. I see the error of my ways."

"Excuse me. Is there a problem here?" Kennedy and I both turned toward the familiar voice of Tuck McAllister. The young man had entered the gift shop from the pub, wearing a pair of nice-fitting blue jeans and a green hoodie with the Notre Dame Fighting Irish logo on it. The worn hoodie was clearly the only thing green he had in his closet. He must have started his Blarney Bash celebration in the pub.

"No problem at all," Kennedy told him.

"Those two are creating a scene in a public space, Officer," Colleen called to him from the sales counter in her soft, lilting Irish accent. Everyone lingering in the gift shop appeared delighted by this. "I think 'tis a crime in America?"

"I'm not on duty today, Miss O'Connor," Tuck reminded her with a shy smile. "And it's not a crime, it's just rude." This last remark was directed at Niall.

"Stay out of it, Tucker!" Kennedy, losing her patience, exhaled loudly before stomping off toward the door. She stopped, turned, and demanded, "Are you coming, Fitzhugh?"

Niall leaned in and whispered, "Thank goodness I have a bottle of sparkling wine in the room. A little wine, a little caviar, and a dollop of crème fraîche on a biscuit, and she'll be right as rain." With a sly grin, he added, "Excuse me," and sauntered toward the door.

"What a D-bag," Tuck uttered.

"Totally," Ryan added, with crossed arms.

"Boys, I don't know what a D-bag is," I told them truthfully. "But if it's derogatory, then I agree. Mr. Fitzhugh is a shifty, calculating man."

Colleen had declared the grand opening of the Blarney Stone a roaring success, and I had to agree. I was beaming with pride; for the village of

Beacon Harbor had welcomed the new shop with open arms and open pocketbooks. Shoppers couldn't get enough of the Irish goods or the imported beer on tap, which was a fitting end to a stressful opening day.

Before heading over to Rory's house for dinner, Welly and I had to make a stop back at the lighthouse to unload the Jeep, clean and put away the empty trays, and to pack up a box or two of the remaining mini desserts. I was going to bring them to Rory's house for Colleen's traditional St. Patrick's Day supper. I was also going to feed Welly. It was seven o'clock, and his anticipatory drooling was becoming a nuisance.

"Here you go, Welly," I told him as I placed his huge food bowl in the elevated feeding dish. Being a giant dog, Welly ate a lot of dog food. Although he was wolfing down his dinner with relish, I was certain it wouldn't stop him from begging for corned beef. Hopefully, he wouldn't be too obnoxious. We were still trying to make a good impression on Rory's family.

"Ready?" I asked him, once his bowl had been licked clean. I was finished as well and had carried a red bakery box filled with mini desserts into the lighthouse kitchen with me. Welly sat at my feet and began swishing his bushy tail as his soulful brown eyes met mine. I didn't even have to tell him that we were going to Rory's. Somehow, I believed he just understood. Although it was cold and dark outside, Rory's house was only a short walk through a path in the woods. Walking would afford Welly a potty break, and it would give me a chance to clear my head after a busy day. With my winter coat on, and my flashlight in hand, Welly and I headed out the lighthouse door.

I was nearly across the backyard, my flashlight pointing at the snowy pathway at the edge of the woods, when I suddenly saw my own shadow flash on the ground before me. The light above the back door was on, I knew, having just turned it on before we left. This was different. It was a soft light with a tinge of green coming from a much higher place than my back door. The fact that Wellington had stopped short of the woods and had turned back around, made the hair on the back of my neck stand on end. I turned off my flashlight just to make sure.

Yep, I thought with a sinking feeling, cursing softly to myself. I could almost feel the soft green light on my back as it cast its fuzzy halo around me, recognizing it for the harbinger of danger that it was. I didn't have to turn around to acknowledge it, but I did anyway.

"Dear heavens," I uttered. "Not again." I then did what any sane person would do after seeing the Ghost Lights of Beacon Harbor. I gripped the bakery box tighter, turned my flashlight back on, and ran for the woods, knowing that Welly would lead the way.

CHAPTER 11

"**B**abe." Rory greeted us from the kitchen as Welly and I came through the door. Welly made a beeline for Rory and the kitchen, because that's where the food was. Colleen and Tuck were there as well, working to get dinner on the table. I waved to them in greeting, then struggled to get out of my coat. By the time it was off, Rory was standing in the short hallway right in front of me. "I was just about to get you," he whispered, taking my coat, and giving me a kiss.

"I was running late," I apologized. "Can I have a word?" Although I could see Colleen and Tuck, there was no sign of Finn or Bailey.

"Sure." After hanging my coat in the closet, he turned to face me. "What's wrong? You look as if you've just seen a ghost." Yet as soon as the words were out of his mouth, he realized his mistake.

"I have," I whispered. "That damn green light popped on in the lightroom again, just as I was walking across the back lawn."

"You saw the ghost lights?" He looked as unsettled by this as I felt.

"Honestly, I feel a bit sick at the thought that someone is in danger tonight." As I stared at him, an image, not a good one, popped into my head. "Fred Landry!" I hiss-whispered, recalling the gruesome scene, glitter and all. "Rory, what if he's died?"

"That would be a tragedy," he agreed. "I'll call the hospital in the morning. Lindsey, you know there's nothing we can do about Fred, right? What happened to him is not your fault."

"I know that. But I can't help thinking about my bizarre encounter with that . . . leprechaun, or whatever it was that ran into me. You know what happens when the lights appear. I was hoping we would never see them again."

"Me too," he admitted. Then, voicing another thought, he offered, "Have you considered that Kennedy is back in town?" I wouldn't go so far as to call his remark sarcastic, but Rory and Kennedy had the type of relationship that only two feral, territorial cats could appreciate. They collided when necessary.

"What are you saying? Do you think she's in danger?"

"Hardly. However, after her shenanigans last Halloween, maybe the ghostly captain is the one who feels threatened. She has that effect on people, both living and dead."

I shook my head at the ridiculousness of his suggestion but had to admit that there might be a touch of truth in it. "I don't know. It sounds far-fetched," I told him. He gave a noncommittal shrug in response.

"If you'll recall, babe, the lights have come on before without anyone having died. And, to my point, her selfish antics nearly cast him out of the lighthouse and into the great beyond for good, the poor ghost."

"True," I said, taking hold of his hand. I marveled at how the mere touch of him was a balm to my prickling nerves. "I hope you're right. Poor Captain Willy. It looks like dinner is on the table."

Rory cast a glance behind him. A truly delicious looking St. Patrick's Day feast awaited. "Look, just try to forget about the ghost lights, Linds. I'm sure it's nothing, but that dinner is something." He raised his eyebrows in appreciation. "Corned beef and cabbage. It smells just like it did when my mom used to make it."

I was about to take a seat at the table, joining Tuck and Colleen, when I noticed the extra place setting. "Where's Uncle Finn?"

"He'll be at the Blarney Stone with Bailey," Colleen replied with a resigned look. "We're to start dinner without them." For some reason, call it his obsession with leprechauns—dangerous, aggressive, St. Patrick's Day leprechauns—my nerves fired up again.

"Is that a wise idea?" I questioned.

"Not wise at all," she replied, passing the heavy platter of corned beef and cabbage to Tuck. "But it is typical Finnigan O'Connor behavior. The man takes St. Patrick's Day very seriously. He said that he was staying behind to clean the pub, but it was already clean when I left, so he's not doin' that. If

I know me da, he's more like settin' a trap for the leprechaun he thinks is stalkin' him."

This wasn't good! Even Tuck agreed by nearly spitting out the swig of beer he'd just taken.

"Really?" he said, staring at Colleen with his piercing blue eyes. "He really thinks a leprechaun is stalking him?" Unfortunately, Tuck chose that moment to look at me. After all, I'd been the second one on the scene of Fred Landry's unorthodox assault. I gave him my deer-in-the-headlights stare in reply.

"I'm afraid so," Colleen added breezily, as if talk of leprechauns was perfectly sane. "He'll busy himself by settin' out his special leprechaun bait on the front steps, which is essentially a mug o' green beer and a dish of the candied pub mix he makes to go with it. He's convinced himself that leprechauns take to it like cats to catnip, the eejit. Then he'll pull up a chair by the window and wait. Bailey will be right beside him, the dear, until me father's convinced himself it was just the beer talkin'. Only then will he be ready to come home." Colleen shook her head. "That dog has the patience of a saint."

After Colleen said a traditional Irish blessing over the meal, we all dug into the impossibly tender corned beef, the buttery soft cabbage, and the boiled carrots and potatoes, like a pack of starved wolves. With a slice of warm, buttered soda bread on the side, it was perfection. The meal did wonders to calm my nerves. I'd almost forgotten all about ghost lights and leprechauns. In fact, the conversation flowed so easily between the four of us, including plenty of laughter from Rory's tales from the micro-pub, that it was well after the dessert plates had been removed before Rory pointed out that Finn and Bailey still hadn't returned home. I checked my watch.

"I don't mean to alarm anybody," I began, pulling my eyes from my watch, "but it's eleven forty. I had no idea it was getting so late." Noting the late hour had made us all nervous.

"'Tis late even for him," Colleen stated, wringing her hands. That sent the cold fingers of fear up my spine. I flashed a pointed look at Rory, which, I'll admit, didn't help the situation any.

"It's cold and damp out there," Tuck added, getting up from his chair. "No offense, Colleen, but your dad isn't a young man anymore."

"Sure, if I don't know it," she agreed. Then, with a pinched look, she added, "What could he be playing at?"

"Uncle Finn was far from sober when we left. Can't imagine his condition's improved since then." Rory's handsome face was marred by worry lines as he talked. He then glanced at Tuck, and without another word the two men stood from their chairs and headed for the door.

"He's likely fallen asleep at the pub," Colleen called after them with a hopeful tone in her voice. Bless her, I hoped she was right. We both left the table as well and followed the men. "Best check there. I'm sure he and Bailey will be fast asleep on the settee in the office."

Thoughts of the hazy green ghost light plagued me.

With the swift, concise movements common to men of action, Tuck and Rory had donned their winter gear, held flashlights in their hands, and had pulled the first aid kit from the closet. Rory, knowing that Welly was about to bolt out the door with them, had also grabbed the leash. There was no way Welly was going to let his second favorite human leave the house so late at night without him. Rory was ready to slip out the door when Welly started barking.

"That's odd," I said. "There's an echoing bark coming from out there." I pointed at the door.

"'Tis no echo. That'll be Bailey!" Colleen's eyes were wide as saucers as she spoke.

Rory, feeling the call to action, threw open the door and bolted . . . right into his uncle. "What the . . . ?" he said, taking a step back as his hands grasped the older man's shoulders to steady him. Uncle Finn was still swaying a bit as Bailey, seizing her opportunity for warmth and food, pushed her way inside, causing Rory to work even harder to get his uncle on firm footing.

My nerves were still pinging from the shock of seeing Finn standing in the doorway, appearing like a drunken apparition. But he was no apparition. He was as real as the unseemly grin on his face, and the old black pot cradled in his arms. Not only did I find the fact that he was carrying a dirty black pot suspicious, but the rag covering the pot was a touch puzzling as well. However, two thumping heartbeats later he cheerfully cleared all that up for us.

"I did it!" he declared. "I finally did it! I found that wee bugger's pot o' gold!"

CHAPTER 12

"Explain wee bugger, Uncle?" There was a healthy amount of skepticism on Rory's face as he asked this. Both men were still breathing heavily from their sudden encounter, although Rory had taken a few steps back to better look at his relative. Then, like the wolf that is helpless to resist the pull of the full moon, Rory's eyes dropped to the black iron pot held tight as a baby in the crook of his uncle's arm. The weighty skepticism morphed into fear, the type that sneaks up on you unexpectedly; the type you loathe the most. From where I stood, Rory looked frightened of the answer his uncle was about to give him. To be fair, Colleen did too, whereas Tuck was still one step behind, bless him. His guileless blue eyes looked merely curious. As for me, now that my heart was nearly back to normal, I was grateful Finn was alive. After all, I had seen the ghost lights. Whatever Irish flight-of-fancy came out of his mouth next, I felt it paled in comparison to the impending nature of the ghost lights.

Uncle Finn, standing in the entryway with his forest-green Barbour coat slick with freezing rain and his hat dripping on the welcome mat, was still fighting to catch his breath. Either he was being a tad dramatic, or the pot was heavier than its modest size suggested. My guess was a little of both. As the two men locked eyes in a manner reminiscent of a spaghetti-western standoff, Finn, throwing caution to the wind, lifted his head and drew first. "A right nasty leprechaun!" he shot out at his nephew with the speed of a misshapen bullet. I say misshapen because his delivery was a tad wobbly, due to a slight slurring of his speech. I don't know why, but his reckless defiance made me grin. Honestly, we all saw it coming.

"Did you just say *leprechaun?*" Rory delivered a warning in his question, as if he had the power to stop his uncle from saying the word. His stern tone, however, wiped the grin from my face.

"*Auch,*" Uncle Finn made a dismissive sound at him. "'Tis been a long, nasty night and I'm starvin'. That wee bugger, nay that *leprechaun*, Rory," he added defiantly, "led me on a merry chase. I hope the lot o' ye saved me some supper." Finn adjusted the heavy-looking pot in his arms and marched toward the kitchen table, dripping coat and all. Rory's misgivings aside, the Irishman had flair, even when drunk.

Colleen, her lovely porcelain skin flushing bright red, followed him. "You are a terrible man, Father, making us worry about you so!" she scolded. Her large, pale eyes looked even larger as she addressed his retreating back. "Rory and Tuck . . . Officer McAllister," she corrected, "were just about to go hunt you down in this nasty weather, and now you show up here so late with a fake pot of gold in your arms. For shame!" She shook her finger at him, adding, "If ye have a pot of coins they're chocolate ones, for sure—just like at Lindsey's fine dinner. *Your* dinner, I'm afraid, is cold, as cold as the stupid pot you are carrying!"

Once beside the table, Finn turned to address his daughter. "Well now, ye have so little faith in me, I should be sorry. But I am not. Why would I carry a fake pot o' gold all this way?" He set the pot on the table. I had to admit that it made an impressive thud. Then, with a flourish, he removed the dirty cloth, revealing his treasure. I gasped at the sight of it.

"What the . . . ?" Rory appeared dumbfounded as well. I had expected Finn to talk of leprechauns, but he had really outdone himself with this stunt. Although the black pot was dirty, the gold within glittered under the light of the chandelier. I was far from an expert on gold, but from where I stood, the coins looked real enough.

"The pot is a fake and you are drunk!" Colleen, embracing her defiant anger, yelled at her dad. Her eyes refused to look at the pot on the table. I silently applauded her discipline.

"Go on, Colleen. Have a look, m'dear."

"I will not. Leprechauns are not real, Da!" Seeing the tears springing to her eyes, I realized that I had misjudged the passion with which she spoke. Like me, Colleen adored her father. However, it became clear that Finnigan O'Connor was far from the level-headed, dependable, trustworthy man that James Bakewell was. My heart went out to her as she continued. "You have snapped this time! I know things have been tough for you, first with the divorce from Eileen then losing the pub, but this talk of leprechauns has gone too far. I trusted you to make a new start here, but ye've ruined it, Da. We should ha' stayed in Ireland."

"Colleen, m'dear. I have had me a few beers as we waited, sure. Leprechauns don't pop around to nip their green beer unless they believe they're alone." He said this with a remarkable amount of confidence, making me wonder again about the leprechaun sighting I had witnessed.

"THERE ARE NO LEPRECHAUNS!" she yelled at him.

"THEN HOW DO YE EXPLAIN THIS?" he yelled back just as loudly, plucking a coin from the pot.

As he expected, Colleen's jaw dropped at the sight of the glittering coin in his hand. Yet instead of joy, as I believed Finn was expecting to see, Colleen looked frightened instead.

"What have ye done, Father?" she breathed, and crossed herself.

"It can't be real," Tuck uttered, standing beside her. He plucked a coin from the pot and inspected it. "Leprechauns aren't real, are they?" he questioned, very likely hoping that someone had a better explanation for where the gold had come from. He looked to Rory for assurance, but for once my stoic and very capable boyfriend looked just as confused as Tuck did. "I mean, this coin sure feels real. It's heavy enough."

"That's because it is real, boy. Now, is there coffee in the pot?" Finn asked as we all gawked at his treasure. "A coffee would be grand, and some food as well. I don't have to tell you 'tis bone-chillin' business, chasing leprechauns on such a night."

Before anybody could reply, I cheerfully offered, "I'd be happy to make some for you, Uncle Finn, and I'll heat up some dinner for you and Bailey as well." Then, pretending I didn't see the furrowed brow on Rory's face, I left the table and headed for the relative safety of the kitchen, which was virtually in the same great room. In my defense, the situation was getting tense, and I needed to give my fidgety hands something to do. Also, poor Finn looked starving. Once the coffee was brewing (I always regarded coffee a priority), I fixed a plate for Finn and warmed it in the microwave.

"Thank you, m'dear," he said appreciatively, tucking into his meal. I then headed back to the kitchen for the coffee. I wouldn't have any, since I needed to fall right to sleep the moment my head hit my pillow, but the others were all clamoring for a cup as well. With coffee served, I turned to Bailey with a smile. The dog, I knew, was the only one who could corroborate Finn's wild tale, if only she could talk. She couldn't, of course, but she was a noble, loyal pooch in my book. She also deserved a good meal.

"Did you see a leprechaun too, Bailey?" I asked her as I fixed her a bowl of kibble. She was sitting so prettily, looking up at me with her bright brown eyes as her fluffy white tail swished the floor like a happy mop. Noting that Bailey was getting all my attention, Welly, in a flash of tail-wagging jealousy, came into the kitchen as well and placed himself in the tight space between Bailey and me. It was so shameless that it made me laugh. Leave it to Welly to ease the tension that had taken hold of me. I gave both dogs a chunk of boiled carrot, then put Bailey's meal on the floor. I then took Welly by the collar and brought him to the table with me. This I did because if Bailey decided to take a break from eating, Welly would swoop right in and finish it for her.

"Where in God's name did you get this?" I heard Rory ask his uncle. With a solid grip on my dog, I focused my attention on the dining table.

Finn delayed his answer with a bite of cabbage sandwiched between two chunks of corned beef. I could tell that he was relishing the tasty, warm meal as he chewed thoughtfully. Finishing the bite with a swig of hot coffee, he offered, "For a former military man, ye are awfully dense, Rory, m'boy."

"Not dense. I'm just not buying your leprechaun story, Uncle."

"Pity that, for I have no other to tell. And here's the truth of me tale. A leprechaun came by the Blarney Stone at half past ten. He drank the beer, he downed a handful of the leprechaun bait, and then he took off down the street. Bailey and I followed him at a distance. We followed him for some time, careful to not be seen. He then finally stops and gets on his knees. We watched him work a moment until I saw him pull a tiny sack from his pocket. There was a wee bit o' glitter that fell from his pocket as well. Whatever was in this sack, he then dumped into the ground. Me heart began beating quick then, because I had a feelin' I'd caught him in the act. We waited until the wee man left before we went to see what he'd done. Sure enough, that's when we found this pot o' gold."

"Sir," Tuck began in a soft yet professional voice, "with all due respect, what you've just told us sounds an awful lot like stealing. You just admitted to following a man. You said that you watched this man deposit something into the ground. Then once the man left, you went to retrieve it. In this country stealing is a crime, sir. No need to get worried just yet. There's obviously been some mix-up. However, I'm going to need to know where you came by all this gold so we can return it."

"I am not a thief, young man! And I'm certainly not returning this gold, because 'tis mine! I bested the canny wee leprechaun fairly and squarely. He led me right to his gold, he did."

"And where was this, sir?" Tuck tilted his blond head, waiting for an answer.

Finn huffed. "You are a clever one, Officer, but I'm not sayin'. 'Tis a secret I'll take to the grave with me, boy. That gold is mine. Me luck has finally changed." At this, Tuck looked to Rory for support. Rory clearly had no idea what to do.

"Colleen, gentlemen," I broke in, having watched this lunacy go on long enough. It was late and clearly Finn was sticking to his leprechaun gold story. The rational part of me (that was now admittedly punch-drunk with lack of sleep) knew that leprechauns firmly lived in the realm of folktales, and nowhere else. There had to be some sane explanation for what was going on in our village, but I was too tired to think of what it might be. I also had a bakery to open in a few short hours and longed for an hour or two of sleep. "Why don't we sit on this gold business a while and see if anyone reports theirs missing. I don't know if anyone else caught this, but there's dried mud on the bottom of that iron pot." I walked over to the pot in question and picked off the offending dirt with my finger. "See?" I showed them. "And there's more caked around here too. I think this pot was buried, which, unless you're a pirate, you must admit is odd."

"Wait." Rory held me in that look I was beginning to dislike. "You actually believe him?"

"I believe his story," I replied. "He clearly dug up this pot of gold from somewhere." For this I was graced with a beaming smile from Uncle Finn.

"She's a keeper, Rory, m'boy," he declared with a nod. "I knew I liked you the moment we met."

"Thank you, Uncle Finn," I said, but my smile was cut short by Rory.

"Lindsey's tired," he told Finn. "We all are. It's been a long day, and I don't think any of us quite know what to make of this gold or your story. That being said, you have a pot of gold sitting on your table, Uncle. In my experience, money hidden in such a manner indicates that a crime has been committed. This person you witnessed was obviously up to no good."

"I know it, boy! That's what I've been tellin' you!" He didn't, thank goodness, mention the word *leprechaun*.

"Oh, Da," Colleen wailed, shaking her head. "Rory's right. What have you done?"

"I've committed no crime, Colleen. I found a pot o' gold," he declared. "An' that's the story I'm stickin' to!"

CHAPTER 13

Morning came early at the Beacon Bakeshop. Thanks to four cups of black coffee, I was able to pull my weight in the bakery kitchen as I worked beside Teddy. I was making our usual giant cinnamon rolls and pecan rolls while Teddy frosted the donuts he'd made. Although St. Patrick's Day was technically over, we decided to finish the week out strong with our holiday offerings, which meant another batch of green-and-white shamrock donuts with green custard filling. The ham and asparagus quiches were also a big hit, so those would be staying on the menu for a while as well. I also had two batches of delicious oatmeal-raisin muffins baking in the oven. They were quite yummy on their own and would go well with the quiches.

Teddy, realizing I'd be tired after my late night, had gotten in early and had baked his big heart out. Elizabeth had also come in early to ready the bakery cases and to start brewing the self-serve coffee. As I stood across from Teddy, frosting the cinnamon rolls and getting them ready to go into the bakery case, I asked him, "You're a man who's in-vestigated your share of myths and legends." This was because he had. Before becoming a baker, Teddy had worked as a cameraman for a flurry of paranormal shows on Travel Channel. "What's your take on leprechauns?"

The question threw my happy-go-lucky assistant baker. "I hope you're not asking me if I believe in leprechauns."

"I am."

"You're joking. Of course, they're not real, Lind-sey." He looked at me as if I was crazy, then in a twist, he grinned, adding, "I've never seen one, therefore they don't exist." It was just the kind of answer Teddy was known for, playfully unhelpful. I watched as he frosted four donuts at a time, hold-ing two on each hand as he dunked them in frost-ing, then flipped them upright, before placing them on the parchment-lined bakery trays. The man was efficient.

"You might not believe in them, Teddy, but Finn O'Conner sure does."

"Well, for one, he's Irish, so I imagine it comes with the territory. Then there's the fact that be-cause he's Irish, he wants you to believe in them too. Nobody wants to be singled out as crazy be-cause they believe in something that, for all intents and purposes, is unconventional. For instance, I believe in Sasquatch. I don't have a picture of me standing with one, but I'm going to try my best to get you to believe in them too."

"Wait, you really believe in Sasquatch?" Teddy had once worked on a documentary-style cable show dedicated to finding Sasquatch but admitted that they never caught one on camera.

He hit me with his round blue eyes and answered, "Yes. But not leprechauns. People don't report seeing them often, unlike Sasquatch. There are a lot of Squatch sightings in this state." I didn't know if that was true, but I found it a little unsettling. However, this leprechaun business was really bothering me.

"Finn saw a leprechaun last night," I blurted. I had his attention. "He came home late last night carrying a pot of gold."

"What? *No!*" Teddy appeared delightfully scandalized by this. I could also see that he loved it. "More details. I need more details, Lindsey!"

As we baked, I explained the whole situation to him, hoping to get his take on things. Unfortunately, Elizabeth had popped into the kitchen just in time to hear my tale of Finn's leprechaun gold.

"Are you certain the gold is real?" she asked. The way she tilted her head in disbelief caused her long brown ponytail to flop over her shoulder. When I told her that it looked like it was, her large eyes opened even wider. "That's so weird. Cool for him, though." And with that, Elizabeth walked out of the kitchen, presumably to open the front door. The Beacon Bakeshop was open for business.

The Beacon had been a favorite morning gathering place for the locals ever since our grand opening. Yet as the morning progressed, the crowd seemed larger than usual for the off season. Then around ten, I had an inkling of why that might have been. That's when Finn sauntered up to the counter with the air of a newly made Irish lord. Molly Butterfield was right beside him, linking her arm through his as a flow of excited chatter flitted between the pair. If she had found him attractive before his windfall of gold, I could only imagine what she thought of him now.

"I'll have what they're having," Betty said, grinning at Finn.

"I'd love to help with that, Betty," I told her. "But you're in front of them in line. They haven't ordered yet."

"Good point," she said. "I'll just step aside." Then, thinking again, she stayed put. "But while I'm here, Tom, I'll have a shamrock latte." This she called out to my stoic barista with a wiggle of her fingers, as if she was reaching out to tickle his chin. Only Betty Vanhoosen could get away with such an endearment, I mused, as Tom rolled his eyes at me. Tom, the Beacon's head barista and resident ladies' man, was going to be splitting his time between the Beacon Bakeshop and Rory's aquatic adventure center come late spring. He had graduated with a degree in history, and I knew that the pull of wreck-diving and hanging around fishing boats was too much for him. Besides, he looked up to Rory like an older brother. I knew that it was only a matter of time before he abandoned the Beacon Bakeshop entirely, but for now I was happy to accommodate his busy schedule.

"Betty," Tom addressed her as he pulled a shot of espresso for the vanilla latte Felicity Stewart had ordered, "you do realize that St. Patrick's Day is over?"

"Make her a shamrock latte, boy," Finn told him with a grin. "I'm buyin' for Betty, Molly, Lisa," he said, waving to Molly's assistant who'd just walked through the door, "and everyone else here who wants one. Call it spreadin' the luck o' the Irish."

"Finn, that's so generous of you." Betty held

him in a look of pure adoration. Although she had plenty of money of her own, being the local real estate mogul and owner of the only realty office in town, she loved a bargain. She also loved anything that was free.

"Why, Finn, what a nice surprise." Lisa Baxter cast a shy smile at the Irishman as she walked up to the counter. "And it's not even St. Patrick's Day anymore. But you really don't have to buy my coffee."

"I don't have to, Lisa, m'dear. I want to," he told her with a twinkle in his eye.

"Aren't we lucky to have him in our village?" Molly peeked around Finn to look at Lisa, who was standing on his other side. "Finn O'Connor is the soul of generosity."

I wouldn't go so far as to say that Finn was the soul of generosity, but he was Rory's only living uncle and he meant a lot to the man I loved.

"Tom," Felicity Stewart broke in. She slapped the granite counter to get his attention. "Change that vanilla latte to a shamrock one." Tom's eyes nearly bulged out of his head as she asked this. After a dark look at Finn, Tom fake-smiled at Felicity then dumped her vanilla latte in the sink. He then went back to the espresso machine, cleaned out the old grounds, packed the portafilter with a new shot of espresso, pulled out the green shamrock syrup, and then began steaming the milk. Making a good latte was a process.

As if offering to buy everyone in the bakeshop a shamrock latte wasn't enough, Finn had to go and declare, "No. I'm the lucky one, Molly. I have me some leprechaun gold!"

"Well, there it is," Elizabeth whispered to me.

"The cat's out of the bag. I'm going to tell Teddy!" A devilish grin split her face before she disappeared into the bakery kitchen. A pan dropped. I heard laughing. I chanced a look at Tom and saw that he was ready to join them. I grabbed his hand.

"Do we have enough shamrock-flavored syrup?" His curt nod told me we did, thank goodness.

I turned back to Betty. Finn, Molly, and Lisa were standing next to her. Felicity was waiting anxiously for her free shamrock latte.

"You're picking this up, Finn, correct?" she ventured with a winning smile.

"Felicity, m'dear, as the owner of the Blarney Stone, 'tis me duty to spread the luck o' the Irish."

"It's just like Christmas cheer," Betty informed Felicity. "Only it's green and it tastes like a shamrock shake. Isn't that right, Finn?"

"Betty, yer off the mark, and ye are missin' the point. I found a pot o' gold at the end of the rainbow, I did. Now what are ye havin'?"

Betty giggled. "You are a terrible tease," she told him.

"I'm tellin' the truth. I found a pot o' gold last night."

Oddly enough, conversation in the bakeshop ground to a halt. It was so quiet that all one could hear was the hiss and drip of the espresso machine.

The tale of Finn's leprechaun gold spread though the village like wildfire, thanks to Betty Vanhoosen and Felicity Stewart, the latter having adopted the role of Betty's holiday hype-woman. Armed with green shamrock lattes, the ladies bolted out the door with visions of marketing Beacon Harbor as the home of real gold-hiding leprechauns. It was lunacy. Harmless, profitable lunacy, but somehow the mere thought of them spreading Finn's tale of leprechaun gold sparked a storm of prickling fear within me.

As the story of Finn's gold spread, the morning orders came in fast and furious. In a matter of minutes, we sold out of green-custard-filled donuts, shamrock lattes, cinnamon rolls, pecan rolls, and oatmeal-raisin muffins. Teddy was bringing out another tray of Danish when Rory walked into the bakeshop.

I hadn't spoken to Rory since last night, and the mere sight of my very attractive boyfriend still made me go weak in the knees. Yes, I was smitten. I had never imagined that by moving to an old lighthouse on the shores of Lake Michigan I would find the man of my dreams, but I had. We were still trying to figure our relationship out, having two homes and two businesses between us, but I knew we'd find our way eventually. I also knew, from past experience, that a man like Rory was worth fighting for. Knowing that my boyfriend was a black-coffee purist, I handed him a red bakeshop mug and a ham and asparagus quiche.

"Thanks, babe," he said with a grin. He then leaned over the counter and added softly, "Regarding that other matter, I've checked on Fred. He's still in critical condition, yet stable."

"That's good news." I exhaled, not realizing I'd been holding my breath. I thought a moment, then offered, "Maybe you were right about the ghost lights. Maybe seeing them last night really was about Kennedy? After all, I'm sure the captain, being a ghost, knows she's here."

"Take my word for it, babe, Captain Will Riggs was once a man. He can sense her. He can feel the way she sucks the energy from a room the moment she enters it, or the entire town for that matter. Dear Lord," he gasped. "It's happening now." Rory backed away from the bakery counter, as if bracing for a cold wind.

"Stop it," I chided. "You're horrible." But the grin on my lips faded as the bell above the door jingled. It was swiftly followed by a familiar voice.

"Yoo-hoo, darlings, what's all this malarky I hear about leprechaun gold?"

I looked at Rory, mouthing, *How did you know?* He just shrugged, which I found a bit irksome.

My attention shifted to Kennedy. She looked so glamorous and beautiful, I thought, watching her saunter into the bakeshop, wrapped in a stunning Irish walking cape of mossy green, heather purple, and indigo blue. Damnit! I really needed to get one of those capes! Knowing that she didn't buy one yesterday at the Blarney Stone, I realized that Niall had something to do with it. He was beside her, looking both distant and amused.

"Is it true?" Kennedy asked me.

"The bit about the leprechauns?" Rory eagerly asked, attempting to wind her up.

"No." Niall tossed him a look of extreme displeasure. "The gold. Is it true the Irishman found some?"

"It's obviously a sham," Kennedy said, removing her black kid gloves, one finger at a time. "He's a showman, a nutter, trying to drum up more business for his pokey little shop. Luck of the Irish, my granny's bum! I'll bet the gold was his all along."

Rory, leaning an elbow on the counter, turned to face her. "And how much are you willing to bet on that?"

"My, my, Hunts-a-Lot. Don't get your flannel pants in a bunch. It's a logical guess."

"Your logic, I'm afraid, is faulty as usual. My uncle is not a rich man. I can attest to the fact that he didn't bring any gold from Ireland with him. However, last night both Lindsey and I were there when he came through the door with an entire pot of it." He delivered this statement with a touch of pride.

Kennedy looked intrigued. Niall looked confounded. "I find your story very troubling, Rory. Where did your uncle say he found this gold?"

"He didn't say."

"And you don't find that troubling?" the Englishman asked.

"I do. I find it very troubling."

While the men further discussed the troubling nature of Finn's discovery, I prepared Kennedy and Niall's order. No green shamrock lattes for them. Niall wanted an espresso with his orange chocolate chip scone, and Kennedy wanted a mug for tea with her quiche. I was just heating up her quiche when the bell over the door jingled again.

"We've been so busy all morning," I told her. That's when I chanced a look at the door. For some odd reason the hair on the back of my neck began to prickle while my stomach felt like it had been hit with a bowling ball. It was Sergeant Stacy Murdock. Although she was a Beacon Bakeshop regular, and a person whom I think was beginning to like me, she didn't look like she had come to the bakeshop for a friendly cup of coffee and the latest gossip. Nope, she was in her full, albeit tight-fitting, uniform. The fact that she was having a good hair day jumped out at me, but her face was all business as she strode up to the counter.

"Good morning, Sergeant. I like what you've done with your hair." I always thought it best to start conversations with Sergeant Murdock on a positive note. However, the smile I expected never appeared. Ignoring me and my flattery, she turned to Rory instead.

"I'm looking for Finnigan O'Connor. Is he here?"

At the mention of Finn, a lightbulb went off in my head, causing me to blurt excitedly, "You must have heard about the free shamrock lattes!"

The sergeant snapped her head around so fast to look at me that her neatly trimmed hair fluttered before falling back into place. It was the mark of a good haircut. The sergeant finally found herself a decent stylist, I mused. Good for her. While I had her attention, I smiled as I explained, "We're out of shamrock lattes, but we have some shamrock donuts left. Finn's not here, but the offer's still good until noon."

"Ms. Bakewell," she said, acknowledging me with her level tone. "Mr. Campbell. Ms. Kapoor, I see you've returned. And who might you be?"

"Niall Fitzhugh," Niall replied with a hint of hauteur.

"Bakewell, I didn't come here for shamrock treats. I came here because I'm looking for Finn O'Connor. Betty told me he was in the bakeshop."

"He was," I acknowledged. "But he's left."

"What's he done?" Rory asked, holding her in his pointed gaze.

"Well, Mr. Campbell, it appears that your uncle, Finnigan O'Connor, is wanted in connection with the murder of a leprechaun."

CHAPTER 14

While my mind was reeling, Niall rounded on the sergeant. "A leprechaun?" he blurted, his patrician features pinched with incredulity. "Are you mad? Are you all mad?" His head swiveled back and forth like a garden gate in a gale as he stared at each of us. "I feel like I've just landed in crazy town! Pots of gold! Dead leprechauns! Listen to yourselves."

Murdock was not amused. "You have an English accent, Mr. Fitzhugh. I take it you're not from around here?"

"I am not, thank heavens!"

"Do you have a passport to be in this country?" Murdock questioned.

"Of course I have a passport!" he cried. "I'm an international man of business! All my papers are in order."

"Good. Then you won't mind showing me your passport."

"Sorry, but I don't have it with me."

"Interesting. I'm going to ask you to bring it down to the station."

Niall regarded the sergeant like a piece of irksome gum on his shoe. "Are you joking? You ignorant woman. You can't arrest me. That's unlawful."

"I'm not arresting you . . . yet, Mr. Fitzhugh. But I am in the middle of a murder investigation. Miss Kapoor," she said, looking at Kennedy, "will you see that Mr. Fitzhugh brings his passport to the police station?"

Kennedy flashed Niall a look that told him she wasn't pleased with his outburst, before nodding to the sergeant. Honestly, it wasn't like her to put up with such behavior, I thought. I didn't know much about Niall and, quite frankly, I really didn't see what she saw in him, other than the obvious handsome face and money thing. We were definitely going to need our lightroom girl chat, and soon. Rory, I could tell, wasn't a fan either.

"Excuse me, Sergeant. Can you elaborate on this murdered leprechaun?" Rory asked. "For instance, why do you believe this person is a leprechaun, and what makes you believe he was murdered?"

"Good question, Campbell. The body of a man, a small man of middle age, dressed as a leprechaun, was found this morning on the open dunes near the lakeshore. The cause of death appears to be a blow to the head. Doc Riggles was called in to confirm this."

My hand flew over my mouth. "Oh, my goodness!" I breathed, as my heart began racing. Sergeant Murdock's description of the victim was nearly identical to the man I had seen the day of the Leprechaun Parade. I hadn't gotten a good look at his face, but he did run headlong into my

Jeep right after bludgeoning poor Fred Landry with a shillelagh, according to Mrs. Hinkle. This same man dressed as a leprechaun was undoubtedly the person Uncle Finn had seen as well. My heart sank at the thought.

"Do . . . you really think that this man is a leprechaun?" I asked the sergeant. Murdock closed her eyes and took a deep breath before answering me.

"Bakewell, I appreciate the question, but you and I both know that leprechauns do not exist. However, I will concede that the crime scene is a puzzling one. This unfortunate person, convincingly dressed as a leprechaun, had no identification on his body. The ME, Doc Riggles, is looking into it, and forensics have been called in to take control of the crime scene."

"Do you have any idea of the murder weapon?" Rory asked.

"As a matter of fact, we do, Campbell. There was a fancy, hand-carved walking stick found near the body with what we believe to be the victim's blood on it. The walking stick, I'm told, is called a *shillelagh*. It's an old Irish weapon that has its origins in fighting or dueling. Of course, it's also a walking stick. It's the type of thing that would appeal to an Irish gentleman, I imagine, or someone wanting to be an Irish gentleman. We believe it belongs to your uncle. Now, you'd be doing me a great favor if you would call him."

"Well, that makes more sense," Niall reasoned, then paused to take a sip of his espresso. "Why didn't she just say that it was a small man to begin with and not go full-out leprechaun on us?"

After Rory had made the difficult call to his uncle, Sergeant Murdock, on a mission, had gone to get him. Reeling from the news, I had closed the bakeshop behind her. Rory was dumfounded, and I didn't want a pack of gossipers descending on the Beacon, demanding details about the body found on the open dunes. They'd been celebrating the pot of gold. How would they take the news of a dead leprechaun? I banished the thought.

Once the Beacon had been closed, I brewed a fresh pot of coffee, let Welly into the café, and motioned for Rory to take a seat at the table. The poor man was still trying to wrap his head around the fact that his uncle had been taken into police custody regarding a murder. Kennedy and Niall, in no hurry to leave, had joined us.

I could tell that Niall was still miffed that he would have to go to the police station and present his passport, but at least he had calmed down enough to enjoy his espresso. Kennedy, for her part, wasn't too keen on visiting the police station either, but that, I believed, had more to do with a certain smoking-hot police officer she had dumped, rather than a passport issue.

"Drama." Kennedy answered Niall's question. "Everybody loves it, only some of us are better at wielding it than others. I say it was a brilliant delivery on Murdock's part. Kudos to scary Sergeant Stacy for using the name *Finnigan O'Connor* and *murdered leprechaun* in the same sentence. That really got the heart pumping, didn't it? Not to mention that it cleared up the mystery of Finn's leprechaun gold. The secret's out of the bag, I'm afraid. *Over my dead body*, the silly man probably told Finn. No doubt your sauced uncle believed he was confronting a leprechaun." Kennedy held my boyfriend in a guileless, doe-like gaze as she continued.

"Rory, darling. I know that you and I go on a bit, we like to torque each other up, and it's all in good fun. However, I am truly sorry that you had to learn about your uncle being a murderer in this way. That's a black mark on any family. I suppose your poor cousin will have little choice but to return to the home country with her tail between her legs."

Rory plastered on a smile as he looked at my friend across the café table. "First off, Kennedy, with all due respect, *stuff it*! Secondly, my uncle Finn may be many things, but he's not a murderer. Thirdly," he said, holding up three fingers and thrusting them in front of her face, "Colleen is not moving back to Ireland, so don't get your hopes up there. She's going to keep selling those stupid walking capes you three keep yammering on about, plus she's got a new boyfriend." This last statement was delivered like a shot to the heart from the bow of a hunter. In other words, Rory had gone in for the metaphorical kill.

Kennedy's sharp, scandalized inhale at the word *boyfriend* was so loud that it echoed off the bakeshop walls and woke Welly. Bless her, she tried to hide her faux pas with a fit of coughing, but Niall had caught it. He was looking confused. I knew how he felt. I was still stuck on the fact that Rory had called the gorgeous walking capes *stupid*.

"Walking capes? I don't know what you're talking about." Kennedy recovered, skipping right over the boyfriend comment. "Niall and I might have had a little disagreement yesterday at the Blarney

Stone, but it was pure business. Niall instantly saw the error of his ways." According to the look on Niall's face, this might have been an overstatement. Kennedy continued. "I'm getting the capes for half of what I originally paid, plus, I got this gorgeous gift from Niall this morning."

"The least I could do." Niall set down his espresso cup and took her hand. "It suits you, my dear."

"Right. Capes," Rory said, narrowing his eyes in an almost menacing way. "Back to my fourth point, which is the gold. Why are we connecting the two? Simply because there's an unidentified man dressed as a leprechaun and Finn has a pot of gold?"

"Absolutely!" Niall said. "If we're parsing folklore here, the two go hand in hand."

"I agree," I said. "Also, dear, there's the matter of the shillelagh. Every time I've seen your uncle out and about, he's got his shillelagh with him. Last night he had that pot of gold in his arms. He wasn't carrying his shillelagh."

"I realize that," Rory said. "But, Linds, you pointed out something last night that doesn't fit the crime scene, at least not the one Murdock loosely described to us."

"What was that?" I honestly had no idea what he was talking about. "It was late, and I was tired," I admitted. "I remember spending a lot of time in the kitchen with the dogs. Finn was drunk, and Colleen was very angry with him."

"Murdock said that the body was found this morning on the open dunes, which are sand. They're also covered with snow and ice. Last night you pointed out that the cauldron, or pot, Uncle Finn was carrying had mud caked on it."

"You're right," I said, suddenly recalling the pot of gold. It had been covered with a dirty cloth, and the black pot had a bit of mud on the rim and the bottom of it, indicating that it had been buried.

"Right, mud," Niall said. "That could easily be explained by your uncle hunting down the poor man, clocking him with his shillelagh, then retrieving the buried gold." Niall appeared satisfied by this, but even as he offered this scenario, I felt it was wrong.

"No," I said, as I thought on this. "Finn told us that he and Bailey followed this person at a distance. He then said that he watched as this man put something into the ground. He was careful that this person, whom he believed was a leprechaun, didn't see him."

"That's right," Rory agreed. "This all sounds crazy, I know, but if my uncle took the gold that this person was hiding, which he did, and he brought the gold home with him without this person knowing, then someone else must have been looking for the gold too. I'll wager that the spot where my uncle found his treasure was nowhere near where the body was found."

"Well, that sounds like a plan," Kennedy told him with a smirk. "Only one thing, Hunts-a-Lot. Your uncle has been thrown in jail."

"He also vowed, if I remember correctly, to take the secret of where he found the gold to the grave with him." I crossed my arms, frowned, and looked at Rory.

"He did," Rory agreed. "I heard him too. However, there are strange things going on in this town, and I'm going to get to the bottom of them. Anyone else care to join me?"

I glanced at Kennedy, then shot my hand into the air like an excited schoolgirl. Kennedy, with a determined grimace, did too.

Niall, looking both smug and curious, said, "I don't know what you three believe you can do about any of this, but count me in. When in Rome, you know."

CHAPTER 15

We had no sooner agreed to stick our noses in where Sergeant Murdock fervently believed they didn't belong, when a pounding knock on the bakeshop door shattered our focus. Welly, snoozing behind my chair, sprang to attention and started barking. Niall flinched at the sound and nearly spilled all the coffee he had poured into his tiny espresso cup.

"Bloody hell!" he uttered, staring at my dog with displeasure.

I ignored him and followed Wellington to the door. Colleen O'Connor was standing on the other side with Bailey, both woman and dog looking troubled, and with good reason.

"Rory!" Colleen cried the moment I had let them in. "Oh, Rory, it's just terrible! Da was in the Blarney Stone with all his new friends, celebrating his good fortune about the gold, an' all, when a gruff policewoman stormed in and took him away in cuffs! He's been brought to jail!" she sobbed.

"She thinks he murdered a man! I have no idea what's goin' on."

Rory stood from the table and wrapped Colleen in his arms. Her large, gray eyes looked even larger from the onslaught of watery tears as they dripped unchecked onto her cousin's shoulder. Bailey, feeling much the same, I imagined, plopped on the floor near Wellington and rested her head on her paws. Her big brown eyes looked as sad as Colleen's, and it broke my heart. It seemed that Wellington had sensed his friend's sullen mood, although being a dog, I doubted he understood why. I watched as he gave Bailey a few well-meaning nuzzles in the ear. Seeing that they had little effect, he then decided on mimicking her, by plopping his large head on his paws. Welly knew how to look sad. Extreme sadness was one of his begging strategies and it brought him great success. However, the sight of the two giant, fluffy dogs on the floor, one black as night, the other white as snow, and both looking like the sorriest pair of pups in the world, caused me to take action. "Excuse me," I said, and went behind the front counter. Once there I grabbed a handful of apple cinnamon Beacon Bites and attempted to change the prevailing canine mood. After the dog treats had been eaten, I was able to console myself with the fact that at least one dog looked much happier for having eaten them. I then returned to my seat at the table and turned my attention to Colleen.

"Colleen, I'm so sorry," I gently told her. She released Rory, took a step back, and dried her eyes.

"I didn't mean to come here cryin' all over you, but I'm scared."

"We saw the sergeant earlier. She heard Finn

was here and came looking for him. Rory then made a call to your dad, who was at the pub, explaining the situation to him. He knew the sergeant was coming," I gently explained to her. "He's just been brought in for questioning."

"You called him?" She delivered a frown as she looked at Rory. "He never said a word about it."

"Colleen," Rory began, and placed a steadying arm on her shoulder, "Uncle Finn is in denial. This morning the body of a man was found near the lakeshore, dressed as a leprechaun. There likely isn't a person in all of Beacon Harbor who hasn't heard about your dad and his pot of gold by now. The sergeant simply connected the two."

"What?" she cried. "Did ye just say *leprechaun*, Rory Campbell? Because I thought I heard that you did."

"Dressed as a leprechaun," Kennedy clarified for her, twisting the proverbial knife a little deeper. She was regarding Colleen with a hefty amount of suspicion which, from my vantage point, smacked of jealousy. Not a good look, under the circumstances. Kennedy then added, because she couldn't help herself, "There are no such creatures as leprechauns, although your father obviously bought into the deception. He's the one with the gold, after all."

"Jesus, Mary, an' Joseph!" Colleen uttered before crossing herself. "The policewoman never said a thing about the man being dressed as a leprechaun. Oh, Rory! Da is in a heap o' trouble, isn't he?"

"Darling, I've met your father," Kennedy told her. "He's the type of man who'll keep digging, hoping to come out the other side."

Colleen ignored her, choosing instead to focus

on Rory. "You must do something about it, Rory! Da might be fond of his Guinness, and he might even believe in leprechauns too, but he's no murderer!" She wrung her hands nervously, then snatched Niall's tiny espresso mug from its saucer— the one he'd just refilled—and sipped it down with the same gusto as a thirsty desert camel. Her hand was shaking so violently after the shot of coffee that it sounded like she was tapping out a jingle instead of trying to land the little cup back in its saucer.

"What about his shillelagh?" Rory asked. Colleen looked at him and dropped the cup.

"What do ye mean *about his shillelagh?*"

"Where is it?"

"How should I know? 'Tis his shillelagh."

"We know where it is," Kennedy offered, casting a knowing look at Niall.

Niall pulled his sneering gaze from his recently debauched espresso cup long enough to offer, "Correction, luv. We know where it *was*." He turned his head and graced Colleen with his cultured smile, before offering, "Next to the body of the man dressed as a leprechaun. It is now undoubtedly in custody as the murder weapon."

"What?" Colleen looked fit to be tied at that, and I dare say that I didn't blame her. "His shillelagh was next to the body? I don't understand what's going on here."

Before Kennedy could enlighten her, Rory shot my friend a look that even a rabid dog would recognize as a no-go zone. He then took his seat, pulled another chair next to him, and motioned for his cousin to sit. The moment she was in the chair, Rory gave her the rest of the news. "The shillelagh is believed to be the murder weapon. It's also believed to be the one belonging to Uncle Finn. Brace yourself, Colleen. It's not looking too good for him. However, Lindsey and I are going to do everything in our power to get to the bottom of what really happened on St. Patrick's Day night. We've been known to investigate murders before around here."

"And are there many murders?" she asked, looking rather frightened at this. "I was under the impression that this was a friendly village."

"It's the friendliest of villages," I was quick to reply. "But sometimes there's just no escaping trouble. However, Rory is right. He, Kennedy, and I have helped the police before, and we will again. I don't believe that Uncle Finn murdered that man either."

"Well, I suppose that does make me feel a bit better. But if you all are going to help investigate this, I'm going to be right there with you. After all, he is me da."

"Fair enough. Welcome aboard," Rory told her. "Now, let's go see what Finn has to say for himself."

CHAPTER 16

Tuck met us at the police station. Dressed in his police blues, and owning every inch of the pet name Officer Cutie Pie, as the women of Beacon Harbor liked to call him behind his back, he nonetheless was at a loss for words when he saw our little cadre walk through the station doors. This was because Kennedy and Colleen were walking next to one another. They made a striking pair, and I could tell that Tuck was uncomfortable seeing them together. As his face turned a deep shade of red, he decided that addressing Rory was the safest course of action.

"I don't mind telling you, Rory, that your uncle is being difficult," Tuck said, offering a frustrated shake of his head. "He's refusing to give up his pot of gold as evidence. He's refusing to tell us where he's hidden it, and he's refusing to tell us where he found it in the first place." He chanced a look at Colleen as he said, "Your father is a very stubborn man."

"He is," she agreed. "Can't tell him anything he

doesn't want to know. Maybe if we had a word with him, Officer?" Their eyes met and held for a beat too long. Kennedy, noticing it too, and growing uncomfortable, loudly cleared her throat.

"That . . . would be a good idea. But I can only allow you three in to see him," he said, indicating to Colleen, Rory, and me. He then turned to Kennedy and Niall. "I'm told Mr. Fitzhugh has a passport to show me."

"Are we back to that bloody passport?" Niall said. "I flew here. Customs have seen it."

"We'd like to see it too," he informed the Englishman.

"It's back at the hotel," Niall fumed, and headed for the door.

"I'll wait right here for you, Niall," Kennedy informed him.

"Why don't you take a seat in the waiting room, Kennedy. I'll be back to handle Niall's passport issue when I'm done with Mr. O'Connor."

While Kennedy headed for the waiting room, Tuck brought us back to a small room off the main hallway. I'd been in this room before. It was the interrogation room. As he opened the door, he addressed Colleen. "You must get him to cooperate with us, Colleen. If he doesn't, he's going to spend the night in jail."

"Da!" Colleen exclaimed the moment Finn was brought into the room. She gave him a fierce hug, as if he'd been gone longer than the hour he had.

As we all took a seat at the little table, Finn leaned back in his chair, crossed his arms, and held us with a hardened look that a lifetime inmate would be envious of. He gave a short, disgruntled, cough-like noise before addressing us.

"You all think I'm a murderer, don't you? 'Tis the reason you're all here, I bet. Well, let me clear the wee matter up for the lot of you, then. I did not kill anyone, especially not a leprechaun. That would be lunacy, not to mention a lifetime o' bad luck."

"Da, again with the leprechauns!" Colleen, clearly rethinking her decision to go into business with her leprechaun-loving father, glared at him and shook her head so hard it appeared she was trying to dispel a demon. "A man was murdered last night, the same night you found that feckin' pot o' gold. It is not a coincidence! You told us that the gold belonged to him, a leprechaun, only he's not, and now he's dead! What are we to make of it?"

"Then explain to me this, m'dear. Why would a man, if he were not a leprechaun, bury a pot o' gold?"

"That is a good question." I jumped in, attempting to break the tension. What I did not expect were the twin looks of disapproval from the "cousins grim." "I mean," I began, backpedaling a tad as I smiled at Rory, "let me rephrase that. Why would a person *dress as a leprechaun* and bury a pot of gold? Very suspicious behavior."

"Uncle, clearly something criminal is going on here," Rory said, obviously drawing on his years of military service as well as his disbelief of magical beings. "You very likely stepped in the middle of something much bigger."

"Like more gold? There's an old saying in the old country, Rory, me boy. Where there is one leprechaun there are twenty. And since they're all a pack o' gold-hoarding devils, you can bet there's more out there to be found." There was an avaricious twinkle in his eyes as he said this.

Rory, choosing the safer road of ignore and divert, told his uncle, "We're here, Uncle Finn, because we're worried about you, and we'd like to clear your name. None of us at this table believe that you killed a man last night to get that gold—" I'll admit that I was straddling the fence on this one. Rory continued, "But only you know the truth of what happened last night. We need some help from you to prove your innocence and to clear your name."

"Rory, m'boy," Finn began, smiling broadly at his nephew, "I shall do all I can. But I've already told ye the truth. I told it to ye last night, but here it is again." Finn took a deep breath, folded his hands, and softened his pleasant features to appear nearly angelic. He then repeated his story.

"After everyone left the Blarney Stone, it went just as I told you. I baited the leprechaun with green beer and a sweet, salty pub mix I call me leprechaun bait. That brought the wee bugger in like nuts to squirrels, it did. I watched him greedily drink the green beer, which he relished. He next ate the bait, gobbling it right up before he skipped away into the night. Bailey had watched the whole thing as well. She has a nose for leprechauns, she does." Finn touched the side of his nose as he said this. "We waited until he was just out of view and then Bailey tracked him all the way to his hideyhole."

"By hidey-hole, are you referring to his home or the place he hid the gold?" I asked, just to be clear.

"The gold."

Rory leaned in. "And where was this hidey-hole located, Uncle?"

"I'm not sayin'. But I will say that I never touched

the wee man. In fact, he never knew we were there
a'tall."

"Da, he wasn't a leprechaun, he was just a small
man."

"That's what they're sayin'. But answer me this,
m'darlin'. Why was he dressed as a leprechaun?
Why was he hoarding gold? And why haven't they
been able to identify him yet?"

The man had a point.

"We can't answer any of those questions yet,"
Rory told him. "But whoever this man was, somebody murdered him last night, after you and Bailey
followed him, and they're placing the blame on
you. Maybe you can explain to us why your shillelagh was found next to the body?"

"'Twas not my shillelagh," he said with the same
angelic look. "I never took it with me."

"Whyever not, Father? 'Tis your prized posses-
sion. That shillelagh is practically attached to your
hand."

"Well, not last night, it wasn't. I left her behind
in the pub. Bailey and I were in a hurry."

"So, if what you are saying is true, Father, it
should still be there."

"Indeed," he said, yet as he spoke, I detected a
slight lack of conviction in his voice. I got the feeling that Finn was more hopeful of this misplaced
walking stick being there, than positive. However,
that might have been just me. Colleen seemed
convinced.

"That would be grand, Da," she said, her lovely
bright eyes sparking with hope. "That would help
matters greatly, I should think."

"Uncle," Rory said, leaning across the table and
giving the older man a stern look, "I need you to

understand that a real person has been murdered, not a leprechaun. I need you to tell us where you found the hidden pot of gold so that we can prove you were nowhere near the man when he was murdered."

"I have a better idea," Finn replied. He leaned across the table, nearly coming nose-to-nose with his nephew. I marveled at the striking similarity between the two men, particularly how stubborn they could be in their own way. Finn then commanded, "Find me shillelagh, boy. Prove me innocent!"

CHAPTER 17

"That sounds simple enough," I said as we walked down the back hallway of the police station to the waiting room. "All we have to do is go to the Blarney Stone, find his shillelagh, then Finn gets his get-out-of-jail-free card."

"I hope it is that easy," Colleen said, crossing her fingers on both hands. "Yet he didn't seem very certain about it, did he?"

"Could be because he was drinking all day. He might very well have forgotten to bring it, like he said, or maybe he's not sure where it is. However, he's still suspect number one," Rory reminded us. "Although finding his shillelagh, if it's not covered with blood, will definitely help matters." Colleen and I both cast him a nose-scrunching look for the blood comment.

As we came out the door that separates the police offices from the waiting room, I noticed that Kennedy and Niall were still there, perched on the uncomfortable plastic chairs as they stared at their respective smartphones. Thank heavens for smartphones, I thought, because they'd likely be waiting there a bit longer. Murdock had put Tuck in charge of verifying Niall's passport. In other words, clever Sergeant Murdock had given him the task of making sure his ex-girlfriend's boyfriend was legally allowed to be in the country. Obviously, the jilted ex-lover was in no rush to handle the matter. Sure, we all knew that the whole *Niall and his passport* issue was a load of bull-doody, but those were the risks one ran when belittling scary Sergeant Stacy on her home turf. The mere thought of being on her bad side sent a shiver of fear down my spine. There were just some people you didn't want to offend, and Sergeant Murdock was at the top of my list. As Rory and Colleen headed for the door, I took a quick detour to have a word with my friend.

"Hey," I said, walking over to the couple. At the sound of my voice, Kennedy looked up from her phone. Niall was either ignoring me or the article he was reading was more interesting. It was likely a little of both. "Looks like you two are going to be here a while longer, so why don't we meet back at the lighthouse later for dinner. Sound good?"

Kennedy's expression told me that she wanted nothing more than to bolt out the police station door and join us, but she refrained. Instead, she pouted. "You three are clearly having all the fun. What happened in there? What did Finn say? Where are they going?" She gestured to the door as she asked this.

"I'll tell you all about it tonight. Hopefully this leprechaun business will be sorted out by then. And in answer to your last question, we're heading over to the Blarney Stone to pick up Finn's shillelagh. He claims that he left it back at the pub."

"Well, have fun with that. We shall just sit here twiddling our thumbs until Tucker decides to see us. This whole ridiculous situation should take no more than one whole minute, but since he's lording his civic power over us, we will likely be here until dinner. I don't mind," she quickly added, turning her pout into a saintly smile. "It's the price one pays for true love." My eyes were locked on hers, issuing her a silent challenge. Accepting it with a smile, Kennedy then reached for Niall's hand, eventually found it attached to the phone he was still holding and gave both a vigorous squeeze. The phone popped out of his grip like a slippery watermelon seed. Without uttering a word she'd gotten his attention. I was impressed.

"My phone!" he snapped, glaring at her. Kennedy was unfazed.

"It fell, darling. Why don't you pick it up." She wiggled her beringed fingers at the floor, then rolled her eyes, mouthing to me, *men!* As if they were the most ridiculous creatures in the world. I wanted to laugh but didn't dare.

"Where are you three going?" Niall asked, suddenly realizing I was standing there. "And where's that young officer?"

"Tuck's busy," I lied. "And you definitely should not have insulted the sergeant in my bakeshop. She's a good woman with a tough job. Look, I've got to run. I'll text you when we're back home."

Colleen, practically bursting with anxiety, was just pulling out of the parking lot as I walked out the police station door. I'd only been a few minutes, but I didn't blame her. Rory and Wellington were waiting patiently for me in the Jeep. I gave Welly, who was sitting up in the back seat, a pat on the head before buckling my seat belt. The moment I did, Rory drove out of the parking lot heading for the Blarney Stone as well.

Colleen was in the process of unlocking the back door when we pulled into the little parking lot on the side of the gift shop. Noticing that we were right behind her, Colleen paused on the back step to wait for us. We jogged the short distance, knowing that every second was taking a toll on her nerves.

With a hand on the doorknob, she forced a smile. "Da seemed rather certain he left it behind the bar last night, so we best start there."

The two large dogs, ignorant of the enormity of our task, dashed ahead of us into the gift shop as if it was a playground—a very fragile playground full of imported goods. "I'll let them play out back," I told her as she and Rory headed for the breezeway that led to the micro-pub.

Once the dogs were safely in the backyard, chasing and wrestling one another, I could breathe a bit easier. The gift shop was no place for such big, and in Welly's case, drooly, dogs. As I glanced around the shop, I felt a pang of regret for Colleen having to close the gift shop early, especially after such a successful grand opening the day before. The village had embraced the beautiful gift shop, and now there was further evidence that their excitement had continued this morning before Colleen had to abruptly close her doors for the day. A pair of shamrock earrings and a claddagh ring littered the floor by the jewelry display rack. T-shirts and hoodies with Irish symbols and

slogans on them were strewn across a table where
they had been neatly stacked the day before. The
racks of the more expensive Irish clothing, including the beautiful walking capes I so admired,
looked as if they'd been riffled through, tried on,
and sloppily returned to the rack. There were piles
of books on the table in the sitting area by the
bookcase, and a string of small Blarney Stone sou-
venirs and keepsakes placed neatly in a line on the
floor near the large replica stone of the same
name, as if some child had busied themself while
their parent was shopping. I swept my gaze a little
further down the wall and came to rest on a beautiful wooden display rack filled with hand-carved
Irish shillelaghs. Each expertly carved walking
stick was different from the next, and I couldn't
help noticing that quite a few were missing.

I spied Colleen then. She was emerging from
the connecting hallway with a pensive look on her
face as she nervously twirled a lock of her lovely
black hair between her fingers. Since there wasn't
a shillelagh in her other hand, my best guess was
that Rory had relieved her of the task and was now
digging a bit deeper in the pub to find it.

"Colleen," I said, grabbing her attention. She
looked up at me with a distracted smile. "I noticed
that you've sold quite a few shillelaghs."

"We did," she said, walking over to me. "Given
their hefty price tag, I was surprised to find that
they were such a hot item yesterday. I'm not complaining, mind you."

"I bet not," I agreed. "I've just noticed that there
aren't any two alike on this rack."

"That's because every true shillelagh is a work
of art. They're made of blackthorn wood, the

knobbier the better. All the knots and knobs of the branch chosen for a shillelagh give it its unique look. Think of the shillelagh like a wand in the Harry Potter books. 'Tis a tool, a weapon should you need it, and every one of them is unique. Back in Ireland, Da knew a man who was a famous shillelagh maker. He made Da's shillelagh, and when we planned to open this store, Da commissioned him to make thirty more of his famous shillelaghs for us to sell. We are lucky to carry such authentic ones here. As for me father, he always carries his when walking, especially when walking Bailey, which is why I'm so puzzled that he told us he left it here last night."

"It's not on that rack by any chance, is it?" This I asked thinking that maybe Finn hung his there, along with the others. After all, he was quite tipsy after his day in the pub. I felt it was worth a look. But after inspecting the shillelagh rack, Colleen shook her head. I could see the panic rising in her fair cheeks.

"Let's go check on Rory, shall we?" I took her hand and led her back to the micro-pub.

"Any luck?" I asked hopefully. Rory lifted his head above the bar, peering at me.

"Not yet. I'm moving all the bottles and glassware down here, hoping he hid it behind them, but he hasn't. I've searched all the booths and all the corners. There aren't many places it could be back here. Uncle Finn said that he'd left his walking stick in the pub, but it's clearly not here."

"Have you checked the storeroom?" Colleen pointed to a door at the far end on the wall behind the bar. The nondescript door was largely hidden from public view by a partitioning wall that had been built to separate the working area of the bar area from customer seating. Rory nodded, then opened a drawer and pulled out a key. As he began to check the storeroom, I followed Colleen back through the gift shop, and through another door that led to the office. I was in this room earlier, because just off the office was the door to the backyard. I peered out the window to check on the dogs before joining Colleen.

Unlike the slightly disheveled nature of the gift shop, the office was immaculately clean. As Colleen inspected the coat closet, I checked beneath both desks. Nothing.

"The man was mistaken," she finally said, her chin quivering as she fought to hold her emotions in check. "His shillelagh isn't here. He's lied to us!" But the thought was too much. Tears began filling her large, light gray eyes. "Oh, Lindsey, what has that man done?"

While I had to admit that it wasn't looking too good for Finn, I wasn't quite ready to throw in the towel regarding the missing shillelagh. I went to Colleen and placed a hand on her arm, offering support as her fears were slowly spiraling out of control. She heaved a great sob, releasing the flow of tears that had been gathering in her eyes like a storm. My heart went out to the poor young woman. I pulled a tissue from the box on the desk, then offered, "I realize how frightening this must be for you, Colleen. However, I don't believe that your father is a murderer any more than you do. He seemed very certain that he left his shillelagh here last night, and I'm still willing to give him the benefit of the doubt. The first thought that comes to my mind regarding the shillelagh is that we never saw a picture of the one that was found next to the victim's body. Sergeant Murdock told us that it appears to be the murder weapon, and that it belonged to Finn, likely because he carries one and he's been spreading his tale of leprechaun gold around the village. However, Colleen, if you think about it, your father makes a convenient fall guy for whoever committed this heinous crime."

That got her attention. She dried her eyes, tossed the tissue in the garbage can, then looked at me. "What are you sayin', Lindsey?"

"Look, crazy as this sounds, I also saw a leprechaun yesterday." Noting her look of surprise, I pushed on. "I didn't mention it because, well . . . you know . . . crazy," I said, rolling my eyes. She got the point. I continued. "However, I was picking Wellington up from the groomer's and while I was driving back to the lighthouse someone ran right into the side of my Jeep. At first, I thought I'd hit a child because the grade-school Leprechaun Parade had started. I felt terrible and jumped out to see if the child I thought I'd hit was okay. However, when I walked around to investigate, I saw this person who was the size of a child, running across the street with alarming speed. He was dressed as a leprechaun, and he was carrying a shillelagh. I found out moments later that this man had attacked Fred Landry, the village treasurer, bashing the poor man's head in with the same shillelagh he was carrying."

"He was carrying a shillelagh?"

"He was, but he didn't purchase it from you. He couldn't have. This was the day before your grand opening."

"I see." Colleen narrowed her eyes at me as she

asked, "So, you really saw this leprechaun as well."
I nodded.

"We, meaning me and Mrs. Hinkle," I explained, "told Tuck about it. He was the officer called to investigate the attack on Mr. Landry at Village Hall."

"What? Are you telling me that you and another woman—this Mrs. Hinkle person—saw this leprechaun, and you told Tuck about it?" I could see that she found this very troubling. I quickly nodded.

"Tuck didn't believe us, of course. I mean, it sounded crazy. Also, I didn't get a good look at this person. Neither did Mrs. Hinkle. She briefly saw the back of this person as he was running out of Mr. Landry's office. We honestly didn't know what to make of it. But he clearly had a shillelagh with him."

"I don't think I find that as comforting as you do," she said before crossing her arms. She leaned a hip against her desk and thought a moment. "Who else saw this leprechaun?"

I shrugged. "I'm not entirely certain, but Peggy O'Leary—you know, of Peggy's pet salon?—she mentioned seeing him. According to her, he was peering through her window, which, supposedly, sent Wellington into a barking fit. Her story was so outlandish that I didn't believe her . . . until . . . I hit the man."

"Mary Mother and Joseph," she breathed and crossed herself. "Why didn't you speak up about this last night when me father had lugged that pot o' gold through the door?"

I shrugged again, then offered, "Fear?"

"Of sounding like an idiot?" She glared at me, hitting at the truth. "Me father has no such fears, I'm afraid."

"Well, it was a long day, and I was very tired. I also wasn't entirely certain of what I had seen. However, back to my point about this shillelagh," I said, skillfully trying to bring the focus back on the matter at hand. "Clearly, there is more than one in this village. Also, I know for a fact that the shillelagh this leprechaun fellow was carrying had blood on it—Fred Landry's blood. Therefore, I suggest that we try to get a picture of the shillelagh found beside the victim's body. One way or the other, we need to find your father's shillelagh."

"I agree."

"No luck," Rory said, popping into the office. He then walked to the back door and called the dogs inside. A moment later they appeared, one on either side of him, and both begging for a cookie. Thankfully, I had plenty of dog cookies in my purse for emergencies like this. With the dogs appeased, Colleen looked at her cousin and shook her head. "It's not here, Rory. It appears that Da will be spending the night in jail."

CHAPTER 18

I put both dogs in the back seat of my Jeep and took them to the lighthouse with me while Rory and Colleen drove to the police station. I didn't envy them their task. They had to deliver the news to Finn about his missing shillelagh. The trouble I was having was that Finn had seemed rather ambivalent regarding where he'd put the dang thing. Stating that he had left it in the pub because he was too excited to get it, having spotted the leprechaun drinking the green beer, seemed reasonable enough, although Colleen claimed differently. She had said that Finn always carried it with him, especially when walking with Bailey. So why didn't he carry it with him on St. Patrick's Day night? Unfortunately, the way I saw it there were only two possibilities: either Finn was lying, or someone took his shillelagh, and he couldn't find it.

I truly adored Rory's uncle. He was such a charmer, and yet still so much of an enigma to me. I mean, what grown man believes in leprechauns? I'd like to think that the whole pot-of-gold fiasco last night was purely a marketing stunt, or an act meant to solidify Finn as the foremost expert on leprechauns in Beacon Harbor. Yet the gold was real. Finn had been elated by having found it. He truly believed that his luck had changed, and now he was in jail without his shillelagh or his pot of gold. I shook my head at the thought. Poor Finn. It was going to be a long night for him.

It was getting late, and I knew that everyone would be starving by the time they arrived at the lighthouse. The fact that we were also investigating a murder weighed into my decision regarding dinner. The lightroom was calling to me. Not literally, but I was feeling the need to go up there. I felt like a habitual runner who had taken the week off. There was something in my body that needed the cathartic release of climbing up the spiraling stairs, taking a seat in one of the cushioned wicker chairs, and staring out at the endless lake, preferably with a glass of wine in my hand. The lightroom was my happy place. In the past, whenever facing a troubling murder, Rory, Kennedy, Tuck, and I also made the lightroom, or the lantern room as it was also known back in the day, our headquarters. It was the place we'd go to put our heads together regarding a troubling situation, or to ruminate over puzzling clues. Just sitting in that majestic tower that had once housed the great rotating light, and where all the past keepers had worked, not only felt historic, but inspiring. Tonight, with Rory's uncle in jail and a man dressed as a leprechaun found murdered on the beach with a shillelagh, I believed we all needed a dose of inspiration. We also needed comfort food as well. But first, the dogs.

While I whipped up two large bowls of top-quality kibble, adding some homemade chicken stock in for good measure, I made a quick call to my parents. They were snowbirds who spent the colder months at their lovely home in south Florida to avoid donning winter coats and shoveling, the lucky kids. However, James and Ellie Bakewell were making the most of their retirement by spending two weeks in Maui. I hated calling when they were lounging in paradise, but I felt that I should. This was because my parents were good friends with Betty Vanhoosen and Doc Riggles, Beacon Harbor's middle-aged power couple. Due to the lack of phone calls and messages from Mom, I believed I would be the first person to break the news about the troubling murder. Knowing Betty and her penchant for spreading scandalous local news far and wide, I thought it best to get ahead of the situation. Maui, after all, was still within the bounds of the Beacon Harbor gossip mill. Knowing that Dad would take the news of a murdered leprechaun with nary a hiccough in his golf swing, Mom, on the other hand, would be all-in on it. Fancying herself a gracefully aging super-sleuth with her Realtor sidekick, Betty, she would, at the very least, pester me with questions and phone calls until the murderer was brought to justice. Hopefully, it wouldn't be Rory's uncle, Finn.

In the thick of multitasking mode, I made the call to Mom and Dad while slicing onions and shaping three-ounce balls of ground beef for the smash burgers I was making. I had decided on smash burgers, which are the most delicious of all the hamburgers because they are smashed flat on a hot grill so the juicy meat will fry faster while creating a slightly crispy edge. I made them smaller so that two, or, in the case of hungry men, three patties would be placed on one buttered and perfectly toasted bun. When covered with melted cheddar cheese, grilled onions, and with the toasted bun generously slathered with a mix of ketchup and mayonnaise, it was, in my humble opinion, the ultimate comfort food. Greasy, tasty, and portable, the smash burger was swiftly becoming a favorite go-to of Rory's and mine. Welly, of course, believed he loved them too, and often got a patty for being so adorable. Tonight, Bailey would get one as well, but not before the adults headed into the light tower.

In addition to the delectable smash burgers, I was going all in on the whole portable finger food meal by serving the burgers with crispy, baked Tater Tots and a fresh veggie tray with ranch dip. The relish tray, if I was being honest, was put together purely out of guilt.

Working with my EarPods in, Mom's voice came over on the other end. I had to admit that even though she was in Maui, the call was crystal clear.

"Dear, we've heard," Mom told me, although I wasn't as shocked as I should have been. Mom, after all, was on Betty's favorites list on her phone. "I was just waiting for you to call. I know that you've been so busy with St. Patrick's Day at the bakery and the grand opening of the new Irish gift shop. I heard it went very well. So, what's the scoop?" she asked in a hushed voice. "Betty told me about the pot of gold, and that Finn is now suspect number one, due to the gold, of course. Do you think it's true?" Mom, as expected, wanted details. Dad was listening but taking his usual backseat approach. Before I was able to give any details, Mom added, "I honestly can't understand why a man would dress as a leprechaun and hide a pot of gold."

"That is the question, Mom," I agreed, giving both Welly and Bailey a piece of the cheese I was cutting. Since a three-ounce smash burger wasn't very big, I was cutting the cheese slices in quarters, so they'd fit. "We're all dumbfounded. A shillelagh seems to be the murder weapon, and since Finn is known to carry one, and his is missing, it's not looking too good."

"I suppose they'll be testing the one they found near the body for fingerprints and blood samples," Dad said. "According to Betty, the shillelagh was sent to Bob's office. Something to do with matching the weapon to the wound."

"I'd love to see what it looks like," I told them. "According to Colleen, Rory's cousin, each shillelagh is unique. If the shillelagh is Finn's, Colleen would know."

"Ask Bob Riggles," Dad suggested. "He might let you see the shillelagh in question, or maybe even send you a picture." I thanked Dad for the suggestion. Mom then offered that she also had a knack for investigating murders but was currently on vacation. I had to smile at that.

"Also," Mom chimed in, "I heard that Rod Jeffers found the body early this morning on his walk. Poor Rod. As if being mayor isn't stressful enough! Betty told me that he thought it was a prank at first, you know, finding a little leprechaun like that, sprawled on the snow. But then he saw the blood. Disturbing is what it was."

I hadn't known that the mayor discovered the

body. Mayor Jeffers was a regular at the Beacon Bakeshop. I guess I'd been so busy that I hadn't noticed he didn't come in this morning to get his coffee and his favorite pastry.

We talked a little longer about the curious case of the murdered leprechaun, as Mom was now calling it. As I peeled and cut carrots into thin strips, I promised my parents that I'd keep them posted regarding the investigation.

"Please do," Mom said. "You know I'm going to be on pins and needles, waiting to hear, Lindsey. Please be careful. I know how focused you can get. And give my love to Rory and Kennedy."

"Will do. Love you, Mom. Love you, Dad. Have a great vacation." I smiled at the phone as I ended the call. I wanted them to enjoy themselves, not worry about me and this troubling leprechaun business.

With all the food warming in the oven, Rory and Colleen came in through the back door. It was perfect timing.

"Look who we found at the police station," Rory said with a grin. Kennedy and Niall appeared behind them, both looking tired and, if I was reading their expressions correctly, relieved to be at the lighthouse.

"Lindsey, darling, something smells fabulous." Kennedy left Niall's side to breeze into the kitchen. She then opened the fridge and spun around with a grin on her face and a bottle of wine in her hand. "Don't judge me. After the day we've had I need this." The Kennedy I knew and loved was back!

"Is there another one in there for me?" Colleen asked, making her way to the fridge as well. "I won't judge you, m'dear, if you don't judge me.

Me father's in jail." Coleen punctuated this sorry statement with an ironic grin that for some reason made Kennedy and me giggle.

"What a ghastly day," Ken agreed and placed another bottle in Colleen's hands. I gently reminded the ladies that we had wineglasses. No need to drink straight from the bottle.

"At least he's found himself some gold," Colleen added, twisting the bottle opener deep into the cork. As she heaved on the handle, popping the cork out of the bottle, she declared, " 'Tis the silver lining in this sorry tale. Cheers!"

Rory, ignoring the ladies and their excitement over two bottles of wine, was stuck on the meat.

"You made smash burgers!" he exclaimed, gracing me with a loving look. If ever there was a truer statement than *the way to a man's heart is though his stomach*, I didn't know what it was.

"I don't presume to know what a smash burger is, but I'm game," Niall added, casting me a nod of approval.

"Glad you're all here," I told everybody, setting out plates, napkins, and personal dining trays. There was no need for flatware with this meal. "We're having smash burgers, Tater Tots, and fresh veggies. Take what you want and fix yourselves a drink. There's been a murder in Beacon Harbor. Therefore, we're eating in the lightroom tonight."

CHAPTER 19

"You think this is a good idea?" Rory questioned in a whisper as he shot a concerning glance at the light tower stairs. Kennedy had been so excited to show Niall the lightroom, arguably the most awesome room in the entire lighthouse, that she had pulled him and his heavily loaded food tray right up there with her. Colleen, carrying her own tray, had gingerly followed. To Kennedy's credit, given her past lighthouse antics, and the fact that the lightroom was the domain of the resident ghost, Captain Willy Riggs, she seemed game enough to venture up the stairs again. After all, it offered the most spectacular 360-degree view of Lake Michigan and the village.

The moment I had purchased the old place on the internet, sight unseen—a risky move, I'll admit—I had fallen in love with the lightroom. It sat at the top of the three-story light tower, which was attached to the lighthouse proper by a hallway that could be accessed through a doorway just off my entryway. The light tower could also be ac-

cessed through an outside door that led to that
same hallway. That door was for the assistant
keeper, an underling who didn't have access to the
tower from the comfort of his warm house. He
had to walk around and use the outside door. I was
privileged to live in, and own, the keeper's house.
The moment I realized what a gem the old lantern
room was, I had scrubbed it down, covered the
floor with a series of small area rugs, put comfy
chairs and blankets up there, and had hung some
decorative Edison lights. It was now the coolest she
shed around. However, unbeknownst to me at the
time of my impulsive purchase, the lightroom was
also the nocturnal domain of the first keeper,
Captain Willy Riggs. Yes, he was a ghost, but he didn't
bother me. I also believed that he didn't mind the
slightly feminine lake-house nautical decor either.
However, as Rory and I had discussed earlier, we
didn't think the ghostly captain was too keen on
Kennedy. After all, last October she had tried to
smudge him out of his tower.

"Look, we were wrong about the ghost lights," I
reasoned to Rory as we stood at the bottom of the
stairs. "They really were a warning. A leprechaun-
ish man," I added, noting the look in his eyes, "was
murdered. I must admit that your Kennedy theory
had merit, but you and I were wrong about that
one. I honestly think he likes her."

Rory looked puzzled. "Babe, I'm not talking
about your friend. I'm talking about *her* friend."
Once he emphasized the word *her*, I finally regis-
tered what he was saying.

"Niall, you mean? What about him?"

"I don't trust him. And now we're bringing him

in on our private murder investigation. I don't think that's a good idea."

"Go on," I said, curious about his mistrust. Rory had good instincts. Admittedly, I wasn't a fan of Niall's either. He was smug, arrogant, and I didn't think he was right for Kennedy. Although to be fair, she could be just as smug and arrogant. All that aside, if Rory didn't trust Niall, there had to be a reason more substantial than a friend's intuition.

"The first note of interest is that he and Kennedy show up two days before St. Patrick's Day. Coincidentally, that's when the leprechaun sightings began. Another note of interest is that Niall owns a textile company that produces and exports pricy British textiles. Importing and exporting goods can be an easy way to smuggle illegal substances into the country. Is it mere coincidence that he has a business relationship with the Blarney Stone, as well as with Ellie and Company? Two shops in the same small town?"

"That is odd," I agreed.

"Thanks to Kennedy and her volatile moods, everyone in the Blarney Stone during the grand opening learned that she was promised an exclusive product line, yet clearly that was a lie. If Niall is smuggling something into this village, then this unknown person acting as a leprechaun—who, according to Uncle Finn, was burying gold—might be working for, with, or even against Niall. What I'm saying, babe, is that there's a good chance the two are connected."

"When you put it like that, I see what you mean. It is suspicious. So, what you're saying is that one

wealthy businessman from England, aka Niall Fitzhugh, and one small man who clearly identified
with being Irish, aka Mr. Leprechaun, could possibly be working together in a smuggling ring?"

Rory shrugged. "I'm just throwing it out there
as a possibility. Maybe somehow the shipments of
the tweed capes, hats, and sports coats that Colleen ordered for the Blarney Stone were packed
with illegal goods that Mr. Leprechaun was inter-
cepting, selling, then turning the cash profit into
gold? After all, Finn reported seeing the leprechaun on several occasions."

"Good point. But how does Fred Landry fit into
all of this? He was, after all, beaten to a pulp by
Mr. Leprechaun."

Rory blew out a breath as he thought on this.
"Maybe Fred caught them?"

"Okay. That's worth checking out. What about
Finn's missing shillelagh?"

"I'm not sure yet. But Niall was in the pub for
quite a long time with us, and so was Uncle Finn's
shillelagh, according to him."

"Do you think Niall could have taken the shillelagh?" This thought sent the cold fingers of fear
gripping my heart. If Rory was right and Niall, for
whatever reason, took Finn's shillelagh and murdered the leprechaun, that meant I had a murderer in the lightroom! What would Captain Willy
make of that?

"I didn't see him with it," Rory admitted. "I'm
just speculating. But my point is, Linds, I don't
trust Mr. Niall Fitzhugh."

"I don't either. Unfortunately, Kennedy does.
I'll try to get her alone at some point and ask her a
few questions, the most important being, did Niall

leave her sight at any point last night after eleven p.m. I'm using that time frame because, if Finn is to be believed, he told us that the leprechaun came by the Blarney Stone around ten thirty, so we know he was still alive then. An hour and ten minutes later, Finn arrived at your cabin with the gold, that was eleven forty. Presumably, Mr. Leprechaun was still alive, but we don't know that for sure. Doc Riggles will be able to narrow down the time of death, but until he does, I think we can safely assume that Mr. Leprechaun was killed sometime after eleven on St. Patrick's Day night."

Rory graced me with a smile. "Good thinking, Bakewell. That's a good place to start. However, it would help if we knew where the gold was found. Then we could figure out how long it would have taken Uncle Finn to get back to the cabin. Mr. Leprechaun could have been murdered any time after Finn found the gold. Until we know more, it's best we keep Niall close to us so we can monitor his movements."

"Okay. Well, here goes nothing," I said, and raised my loaded food tray to him ever-so-slightly. Appreciating the gesture, I received a wink before we both climbed up the circular stairs to join our friends.

It never fails to take my breath away, that first step onto the lightroom landing. Greeted by the warm glow of the Edison lights, a luminous full moon, and the mouthwatering scents of juicy hamburgers and crisply baked potato nuggets, the cozy space—for it was cozy being a snug 144 square-ish feet—had a lofty, bird's nest feel to it provided by the great circular window. There was a modest desk and chair tucked behind the railing of the staircase where the keeper once sat to observe ship traffic. I sat there from time to time, but mostly used it as a place where I kept my fake logbook that, I was sorry to admit, held lists of recent murder suspects. The leather-bound logbook was now referred to as the suspect journal. Aside from this small desk, I'd put four comfy, cushioned, white wicker chairs across the room, facing the window, with a pair of tables in between for drinks and whatnot. Tonight, the tables had been pushed out to make space for a fifth chair that had been brought up for Colleen. It felt a little tight as Rory and I gingerly made our way to the empty chairs furthest from the stairway. Then I heard the dogs barking from below (Welly refused to navigate the narrow light-tower stairs, so neither would Bailey!), followed a moment later by a familiar voice.

"Hey, guys, mind if I come up? I'm just going to grab some food first." It was Tuck. Being a good friend of ours, he was told to make himself at home at the lighthouse whenever he pleased, which he did often. Tuck was off duty, it was dinnertime, and he knew that we'd be in the lightroom discussing the murder. What he likely didn't know was that Kennedy and Niall had joined us.

Rory cast me a look before setting his food tray on his chair. "I'll just jump down there and lug another chair up for Tuck."

"Good thinking." I cast him a loving smile.

"It's quite a marvelous view from up here," Niall admitted, staring out the window at the full moon. It was a clear, crisp night. The large, full moon was perched in the sky a mere handbreadth above the black horizon. The shimmering moonglow tickling the glossy black waves was mesmerizing. From this view, with the lake and the sky nearly indiscernible, I imagined that Lake Michigan went on for an eternity.

"It's one of the perks of owning a lighthouse," I told Niall. "Did Kennedy mention that it's haunted?"

Niall emitted a snickering laugh. "She did, but it's all nonsense. I don't believe in such things. Kennedy has also mentioned your reputation for crime-solving. She's claimed that when the three of you put your noggins together you get results."

"I did. I told him that," Kennedy said, right before popping a Tater Tot into her mouth. She chewed, swallowed, then asked, "Was that Tucker I heard calling up the stairs?" It certainly wasn't the wind, I thought, and refused to answer her.

Colleen wasn't about to answer either. Instead, she cast me a sly grin over the lip of her wineglass, then covered that grin with a sip.

Niall ignored Kennedy completely. "Well, I, for one, am anxious to join you in this hunt for a leprechaun killer and match wits against the rozzers. I think I'd be quite good at it."

Just then the fluffy, handsome blond head of Officer Tuck McAllister poked above the lightroom landing. "Rozzers?" he questioned. "Isn't that British slang for police?" He cleared the lightroom landing with his food tray in hand, containing two smash burgers, a preposterous mound of tots, three cans of beer, and absolutely no veggies. He looked at Kennedy, blanched, and stuttered, "I . . . I . . . didn't expect to see you two here."

"And we didn't expect to waste the entire day at the police station, either," Kennedy snapped, be-

fore haughtily flipping her gorgeous, silky black
hair over one shoulder. I'd always gotten the impression that it was her haughtiness he found irre-
sistible. Go figure?

"What are you doing here?" Niall asked, frown-
ing so intensely at Tuck, one might be inclined to
think he'd eaten a bite of goat poop instead of a
Tater Tot.

"I live here," Tuck shot back, looking utterly territorial. If Tuck was a dog, I'd say his hackles were
not only up, but they were ready to shoot out like
porcupine spines. Then, noticing the confused
look on Niall's face, Tuck corrected, "I mean, not
right here . . . not exactly in this lighthouse, but in
this town. Just . . . down the way."

"I've saved you a seat, Officer," Colleen purred,
thankfully grabbing the young man's attention
while removing Rory's tray from the chair he had
claimed. She handed the tray to me, and I dumbly
took it. Thank goodness Rory appeared then, carrying another chair with him. I slid my chair back
from the tight line, waved for the others to do the
same, and made just enough room for Rory to add
this new seat to the party, right next to mine. It was
now officially cramped in the lightroom. It was
also, if I was being honest, thick with flaring testos-
terone and estrogen-fueled snark.

Knowing that I had to do something, but not exactly sure what that something was, I decided to do
the easy thing and raise my wineglass in the air.
"Friends, excuse me. May I have your attention? As
I was saying, tonight we are gathered in this auspi-
cious and iconic room for one purpose, and one
purpose only: to shed some light on the troubling
matter of the St. Patrick's Day murder. Over the

past two days one man has been attacked, one man has been killed, and one man has been—dare I say, wrongly?—accused of perpetrating that murder. I realize that some of us have our differences, but I ask you to put them aside for the sake of our task. It's not going to be easy, and it might get dangerous. But if you are willing to join Rory and me, then raise your glass." Nearly everyone raised their glass or beer can, everyone except Tuck.

"Look, you guys are my friends," he said, "but I'm the professional. You're not supposed to get involved in police business."

"We know," I offered a bit too cheerfully. "We're just going to write down some names. People of interest, that sort of thing."

Tuck grimaced. Then he relented. "Right. I can't stop you. I know that. Also, we're a bit over our heads on this one, I'm afraid."

"You need help," Rory told him. "Very little about Finn's gold and this leprechaun murder makes sense."

"Nothing like a good brainstorming session to see things more clearly," I added helpfully, holding up my fake lighthouse logbook. Rory, Kennedy, and I had used the logbook before to write down possible suspects.

"I agree," Tuck said with a grim set to his lips. "Just be careful. And keep me posted if you learn anything of interest."

"Of course," I said, and I meant it.

CHAPTER 20

"Well, that was a slow start," I confided to Rory as we cleaned up the dishes. "At least everyone pretended to get along."

"*Pretend* is the operative word, babe," he said, drying a wineglass. "That was just downright awkward. While you were trying to write names in the fake lighthouse logbook, aka the suspect journal, Colleen was flirting with Tuck. Kennedy was sniping at Colleen, and Niall was strangely focused on the gruesome details of the murder scene. Yet the most disturbing aspect of the evening, in my opinion, was the sexual tension between Kennedy and Tuck. I don't get it. She broke up with him, and he should want nothing to do with her. I was actually hoping Captain Willy would show up, heralded by a hint of pipe smoke and the flickering of the Edison lights, but no. At one point I found myself praying for it, but I think even Captain Willy was scared off by the wonky energy in that room tonight."

"We should just strike out on our own," I offered. "We'd get more done."

"Best idea you've had all night, babe," he agreed and rewarded my flash of brilliance with a knee-weakening kiss.

"But . . ." I began, coming up for air, "we need to keep Tuck in the loop."

"Of course. He's the professional."

"Kennedy will suspect that and push her way in too."

Rory frowned. "Then we're back to square one," he said, and flipped the towel he'd been using over his shoulder.

"Look, we're in the beginning stages. All Tuck could tell us was that the crime scene was not only gruesome but was covered in green and gold glitter as well."

"All the glitter must have come from the pockets of Mr. Leprechaun," I added. "What an odd touch, don't you think?" In my opinion, that glitter had been one of the most unsettling aspects of the attack on Fred Landry.

"If Mr. Leprechaun was a deranged criminal mastermind, the glitter might have been his calling card," Rory offered, shaking his head at the thought. "I bet the Crime Scene Unit had a heyday with that. According to Tuck, Doc Riggles hasn't been able to identify the body either, and the shillelagh has been sent to the lab for testing. Also, did you notice that he wouldn't even tell us where the crime scene was?"

I touched his arm, offering a mischievous grin. "Rory, I might know how to find the crime scene," I told him. "I talked to my mom today. Thanks to

Betty, Mom already knew about the murder. And, thanks to Betty, Mom informed me that Mayor Jeffers was the one who found the body on his morning walk. That was information even Tuck wouldn't tell us."

"Rod Jeffers found the body?"

"Since the bakeshop is closed tomorrow, being Monday, I'll call him in the morning and get the details. I'm also going to have breakfast with Kennedy. We still haven't had our girl talk yet."

"Sounds like a plan. I told Colleen I'd help her with the Blarney Stone tomorrow morning. Sorry I'm going to miss your girl talk breakfast," he teased. "Let's meet up in the afternoon. We need to go back to the police station and talk with Uncle Finn again. Since we can't find his shillelagh, I'm going to make him understand that he must tell us where he found the gold. If we can prove that the body and the hidey-hole, as he called it, are no-where near each other, we might be able to create a plausible timeline of Uncle Finn's movements and get him out of jail."

After a luxurious morning where I slept until nine (which felt like noon!) then lounged in bed for another half hour, drinking coffee with Rory and cuddling Welly, I then got dressed and took my dog on a nice long walk on the icy beach while Rory left for the Blarney Stone. I then fed Welly, took care of some mundane household chores, then made the phone call to the mayor.

Rod Jeffers was still in shock after finding the body of that strange little man dressed as a lepre-chaun. In fact, the terrible image was so ingrained in his head that he kept calling the murder victim a leprechaun. I couldn't blame him. I had the same issue, and I hadn't found the man face down in the snowy, brush-covered dunes with his head bashed in and covered in glitter. Rod, as I had expected, was quite willing to tell me all about it. The mayor had gone for his usual early morning walk along the beach, but since he lived a block from the lake, he took a neighborhood access path to get there. The path cut through an expanse of gently rolling, snow-covered sand dunes before opening onto the shores of Lake Michigan. Although I had never taken that exact pathway, I knew the type. There were many such access trails to the lake, all up and down the west coast of Michigan. However, as Rod was taking his usual route, making his way to the snowy shoreline, he saw something strange out of the corner of his eye that drew his attention. He then cut across the open dunes and found the body. Noticing the time, I thanked the mayor for talking with me, and ended the call. I let Welly out once more, gave him a cookie, and ignored his mournful look.

"I'm late, Welly." I told him before smothering the top of his muzzle with kisses. "I'm having brunch with Kennedy. If you're good, I'll bring you a piece of bacon."

Bacon was one of the few words Welly understood. I believed he recognized far more words and phrases than he let on yet chose to ignore them, often with a direct yet suspiciously blank stare plastered on his adorable face. Welly was stubborn at times. Maybe even prideful. However, he certainly wasn't too proud to wag his tail and start drooling at the word *bacon*. Knowing I'd pull through with a piece of his favorite treat, he escorted me to the door, where I promised him that I'd be back soon.

I had chosen Hoots Diner for our girl chat. I knew that Kennedy loved the home-style diner with its kitschy Northwoods theme, green faux-leather booths, and all the owl pictures gracing the walls. Hoots served the delicious, hearty, stick-to-your-ribs type of food your grandmother would serve you when visiting her house. I wouldn't say it was the type of food my mom used to make me. Being a model, my mom wasn't the best cook. And what she did whip up in the kitchen wasn't what you'd call stick-to-your-ribs food. Nope, Mom's cooking just kinda slid right through you. I once heard my dad refer to it as ghost food, the type of food you don't remember eating, but it still haunts you. I had laughed at that. Back then, Dad and I had perfected the art of covert fast-food runs. Thankfully, now that Mom has given up dieting, her cooking has gotten much better.

Knowing that Kennedy wouldn't admit in public to loving the old diner, and certain that she hadn't taken her snooty, wealthy, cultured boyfriend there yet, I figured that Hoots was the perfect setting for our much-needed girl chat.

"Lindsey!" Kennedy's familiar voice greeted me as I walked through the door. "Surprise-surprise! I beat you here. It's likely the first time in our entire friendship."

Smiling at her comment, I gave her a hug before slipping into the bench across from her. The waitress then poured our coffee, took our order, and headed for the kitchen. Marveling at how I could drink so much coffee yet still be thrilled by the sight of a fresh cup, I cradled the white diner mug between my hands, took a sip, and looked at the woman across from me. "I've missed you, Ken. It has not been the same in Beacon Harbor without you."

Kennedy stared at her own mug of coffee a moment before answering. "I hate to admit it, but now that I'm back here I realize how much I miss this pokey little village. Silly, right? However," she was quick to add, "I must admit that life has been very good since I've left. Living in London again was good for my soul, Lindsey. Being in the hub of all that activity was not only invigorating but inspiring. All the shopping! All the *haute couture*! The influencer and fashionista in me came alive. I now feel closer to my mum and sis. Dad is proud of my accomplishments, and I've finally found a man whom my mum deems an enviable catch. Even Granny Gladstone told me that I've changed. *Matured*, I believe the term was. And I have." I couldn't help noticing that this last remark was said in a manner as if she was trying to convince herself of it. Being her friend, I let my observation slide.

"I'm glad you're doing so well," I told her. "Also, your boyfriend, Niall, is very handsome."

"And rich," she added with a wink. "Don't forget rich." For some reason this remark irked me. Focusing on a love interest's wealth and not character was not only shallow, but it was also a big mistake. Maybe even a red flag. It was also the opening I needed.

"I can only imagine," I said, raising my brows at

this. "However, Niall seems to be a bit distanced or distracted whenever he's with us. Is he like that with you?"

Kennedy shrugged. "He's a very busy man, Lindsey. It comes with the territory."

She took a sip of her coffee then and nearly spit it out when I asked, "Do you trust him?"

She set the mug down, picked up her napkin, and dried off her chin. She then glared at me. "What is that supposed to mean?"

I stared right back into her wide, dark eyes. "It's a simple question, Ken. He's lied to you once about the Irish walking capes he sold you. We're now including him in our murder investigation, and I'm not so sure he's trustworthy."

"Well, I trust him," she added defiantly. "And if I trust him, you should too. That's what friends do. I accepted Sir Hunts-a-Lot, didn't I? Talk about a skulking man with secrets. And he has guns!" She paused to make her point, before adding, "You know who I don't trust? Colleen O'Conner, that's who. I leave town for a few months only to return to find all of you so chummy with the new girl, especially Tucker. Did you notice the way she hangs on his every word? You've certainly welcomed her into your little cadre. Need I remind you that her father is currently in jail for murder?" The way Kennedy's jealousy had flared up at the mention of Colleen told me that her feelings regarding Niall weren't as committed as she'd have me believe. It saddened me a little, but it also meant that I might get her to be more objective where Niall was concerned.

"Finn O'Connor has not been convicted," I reminded her. "He's just being held for questioning.

Regarding Colleen, she's Rory's cousin. Of course we've embraced her and have welcomed her into the community. She's a good person, but there's no way she could ever replace you, Ken."

Her eyes softened at this. "You mean it?" That she could even question the strength of our friendship caused a twinge of pain in my heart.

"Of course, I do," I told her sincerely. "You know that you are as dear to me as a sister. I'm just concerned about you. I know very little about Niall Fitzhugh, and what little I have observed is jaded by my fondness for Tuck. Can you forgive me?"

"Of course." Her voice was as soft and sincere as the look in her eyes.

"Good. There's just one more question I have." Kennedy, intrigued, tilted her head, causing her long, silky black hair to fall to the side as well. "Can you tell me where Niall was St. Patrick's Day night, between the hours of eleven p.m. and five a.m.?"

"What?" The shock in her voice caused heads to turn our way. "I don't believe you!"

Feeling slightly guilty, I explained, "I just want to be sure."

She huffed, snarled at me, then offered in a haughty voice, "He took me to a very posh restaurant in Traverse City."

"Nice," I offered. "What time did you get back to the hotel?"

"You're really doing this?" She huffed a bit more, took an angry sip of coffee, and offered in the manner a gunslinger offers a challenge, "Nine-ish. Maybe ten. Then we proceeded to have a little *adult time.*"

"Nice," I said again. "What time did *adult time* end?"

"Wouldn't you like to know." The fact that she didn't offer up an impressive hour led me to believe that it might not have been very impressive at all. As if reading my mind, she added, "I was too busy to bother with the time, but it was late. Very late."

"Nice. Did you two just stay in the hotel room then?"

"I did. I was exhausted, darling." Although her head was turned as she said this, I caught her glancing at me out of the corner of her eye. She squared to me again, adding, "Niall had to leave to get antacids."

"He left the room?" This caught Ken's attention. Her eyes narrowed at me. I added, "What time was that?"

She thought a moment, then offered a quiet, "Around eleven thirty-ish?"

I didn't know if she heard them, but alarm bells were going off in my head. "Okay, let's say that Niall left the hotel room at eleven thirty. What time did he return?"

If my alarm bells were going off in my head, Ken's were going off behind her eyes. "After midnight. He took the keys. When he returned so late, he told me that he had to drive out to a gas station near the expressway to get them because the hotel didn't have any, and nothing else was open at that hour. It seemed reasonable at the time." Her voice was escalating as she talked. "Bugger all, Linds! I might be dating a leprechaun murderer!"

CHAPTER 21

I'd like to say that my lunch with Kennedy had gone smoothly, but it hadn't. It had gone off the rails, thanks to me. Instead of making her aware of my suspicions regarding Niall, as I had hoped to do, I had instead successfully transferred all my suspicions of him to Kennedy, and the result wasn't nearly as satisfying as I had imagined. After pointing out Niall's connection to the Blarney Stone, and after learning that he didn't have an alibi for that sweet spot of time in which the leprechaun could have been murdered, Kennedy had gone, to use her own term, mental. At one point she had actually cried out over her stuffed veggie omelet, "I've gone from dating a police officer to dating a leprechaun snuffer in one leap. Who does that sort of thing? What's wrong with me, Lindsey? I've not matured, as Granny Gladstone thinks. I've gone and rotted. I should have never left this dodgy little village." After that statement she had dropped her head on the table, cushioned by her folded arms.

I wouldn't use the term *dodgy* to describe beautiful Beacon Harbor, but I did take her point. I then spent the rest of our brunch together talking her down from the proverbial cliff she was teetering on, explaining to her that I was merely suspicious of Niall. I had wanted her to keep her eyes open, not sprung wide and accusatory like some flashing electric road sign monitoring speed. "Look, we don't have any proof Niall's involved, so you have to go on and pretend everything's normal."

"Normal?" she had cried, looking both helpless and hopeless. "I just found out that the man I'm shagging has a penchant for killing leprechauns. They say that extreme wealth warps one's sense of reality, but how warped do you have to be to go around clubbing the fairy folk? I've hit rock bottom."

I then patiently pointed out that Niall, as far as we knew, didn't own a shillelagh, nor did he have a connection to the leprechaun that we knew of. However, it was something we needed to investigate. Kennedy swore that she never saw Niall with a shillelagh, but admitted that one, or possibly even Finn's, could have been hidden in the trunk of their rental car. She would do some snooping around regarding the shillelagh. However, she would have to hide her suspicions of her boyfriend until we had more proof, and I doubted she'd be able to act convincingly. I was then struck with a thought.

"Lillian Finch," I said, looking at her. Lillian Finch was Ken's alter ego, so to speak. She used the fake name to pretend she was a hard-hitting reporter, often getting people to admit to things due to her snappy string of questions. It was a long-shot, but I thought it might help her out in her current situation.

"What about Lillian?"

"What if you pretend that Lillian Finch is dating Niall, and not you? You play her very well, and it might be a way for you to remain close to Niall, while distancing yourself and your emotions from him. He can't know that we're suspicious of him."

She thought on that a moment. "I see. What you are, in fact, suggesting is that I summon Lillian when I'm with Niall, acting as if she was dating him and not me? You just might be on to something there, darling. You realize that my relationship with him then would be an act?"

"That's the point," I had admitted. "For the sake of this investigation and your sanity." I then watched as she rolled the idea around in her head a moment longer. Coming to some conclusion, she hit the table with her fist.

"Brilliant," she had proclaimed. "I'm in. Poor Niall. I don't believe he's strong enough to survive a woman like Lillian Finch."

After having brunch with Kennedy, I met Rory in the parking lot of the police station. He'd just come from the Blarney Stone and looked slightly exhausted. The moment I spied him I got out of my Jeep and went to meet him.

"Babe! How'd the girl chat go with Kennedy?"

"Interesting," I told him, linking my arm through his and walking to the front door of the station. "I found out that Niall left the hotel room around eleven thirty p.m. on St. Patrick's Day night. He didn't return until after midnight."

Rory stopped. "What?" he said, holding me in his bright, questioning gaze. "Did Kennedy know why he left the hotel?"

"Apparently, he needed antacids. He told her that he had to drive to a gas station near the interstate because it was the only place open that late."

Rory shrugged. "It's plausible, yet suspicious all the same. I say we have Tuck check it out just to be safe. If we can get the name of the gas station in question, Tuck can sequester the surveillance tape from that night."

"That should be easy enough," I told him. "Kennedy was pretty upset when she realized that Niall didn't have an alibi for that critical half-hour time slot. Knowing that she was uncomfortable with the thought of sharing a hotel room with a possible murderer, and not wanting her to blow it and make Niall suspicious that we might be on to him, I told her to pretend that Lillian Finch was dating him instead. That way she can act the part even if she can't feel it anymore, if you know what I mean."

The darkly puzzled look Rory held me in suggested that he had no idea what I was talking about. "Bakewell, are you telling me that Kennedy is going to embrace that ridiculous Lillian Finch act of hers?"

"It looks like she might," I admitted. "Whatever she does, it's best to play along. It's Kennedy we're talking about here."

His response was a noncommittal grunt as we entered the police station arm in arm.

Once inside, Sergeant Murdock met us in the waiting room. "Campbell, Bakewell, I'm glad you're here. That uncle of yours is one stubborn man," she added, looking at Rory with her deep-set, brown eyes. When she squinted, I was sorry to think that her eyes reminded me of raisins burrowed deep in the soft, white dough of her face. I knew only too well how that doughy face could harden in a flash, looking tough and menacing. Therefore, I preferred to stay on the sergeant's good side. Murdock continued, "We can't get him to tell us anything regarding the pot of gold or where he found it. Finnigan O'Connor is not doing himself any favors, I'm afraid."

"Don't I know it," Rory concurred. "We'll see if we can get him to crack."

We met Uncle Finn in the same little interrogation room where we'd met him earlier. Finn looked drawn and tired, as if he hadn't slept well. I doubted he had. However, one look at his nephew and the twinkle rose to his eyes once again.

"Rory, me boy," Finn began, taking a seat across from his nephew, "'tis no great secret why ye are here. You want to know where I found it." The word *gold* was never mentioned. It didn't need to be. That pot of gold was the reason Finn was still in jail.

"I do, but only to prove that you're innocent, and get you out of here."

"How do ye plan to do that, now?" Finn leaned across the table to better stare at his nephew.

"Lindsey and I know where the body of the man dressed as a leprechaun was found." Rory cast a look at me before he continued. "We believe that if the crime scene is far enough away from the place where you discovered the pot of gold, we can put together a time line of your movements on St. Patrick's Day night that will help prove you didn't

have time to murder that man. This is because we
know that you were on foot when you and Bailey
followed this supposed leprechaun from the Blarney Stone. We also know the time you arrived back
at my house. Doc Riggles will determine the ap-
proximate time of death of the victim soon. If everything lines up, we might be able to get you out of
here."

"And if it does not?" Finn's eyes narrowed as he
looked at his nephew.

"Then we'll have to think of something else."

Finn forcibly blew out his breath. "You and
Colleen told me about me shillelagh. 'Tis gone
missing from the Blarney Stone. If it was mine
found beside the body, I'm done for."

"It's still being tested," I told Finn. "We're hoping it's not yours." It was then I decided to tell
Finn about my encounter with the unidentified
victim. "I don't know if I've mentioned this to you
before, but the day of the Leprechaun Parade, a
man named Fred Landry was attacked in his office, supposedly by a leprechaun. This leprechaun
hit the side of my Jeep as he was running from Village Hall where the attack had taken place. Welly
and I ran into the building to help Mrs. Hinkle,
and there we found Fred Landry on the floor with
a terrible head wound. Mr. Leprechaun, we realized, had attacked him with a shillelagh. Fred is
still in the hospital in critical condition. But my
point to you is that the leprechaun had one, and
so did you."

"You saw the leprechaun and failed to mention
it until now?" Finn looked almost angry at this.

"I'm sorry," I told him. "It was very traumatic,

and I wasn't quite sure what I had seen at the time."

"Lindsey told me about the attack on Fred," Rory told his uncle. "The police are aware, and they have Lindsey's statement. The point is, Uncle, this Mr. Leprechaun, as Lindsey calls him, attacked a man at Village Hall, nearly killing him. You have his pot of gold, and now Mr. Leprechaun is dead. We don't know what's going on here, but it's not a good situation. I need to know where you found that pot of gold."

"And what if the hidey-hole is close to the crime scene?" Finn held his nephew in a challenging look.

"We won't be able to determine that until you tell us where you found it. Help yourself, Uncle, and tell us. If not for your sake, then for Colleen's. She's worried sick about you. Is that pot of gold worth more to you than your daughter's happiness?"

Upon hearing that, all Finn's bravado deflated. His broad shoulders sagged, and his head dropped to his hands. Rory had hit a nerve. At length, Finn looked at the younger man sitting across the table from him. "When you put it like that, I'm ashamed. I'm also tired." Finn's eyes then darted around the room, making sure we were alone. That was a joke. Although we were alone in the room, everyone knew that interrogation rooms were monitored for safety reasons. Spying the camera in the corner, Finn rested his elbows on the table, folded his hands, and pressed his lips against his fingers. Slyly cupping his fingers around his lips, Finn whispered, "I'll tell ye where I found it, but ye must promise to keep what I tell ye a secret."

"If you've already found the gold, why keep it a secret?" Rory questioned.

"What if there's more?"

"Doubtful it would be in the same place," Rory reasoned. "You should consider yourself lucky you found the one pot."

"Alright. I'll tell you. But keep it to yourselves." Finn raised his brows and gave us a hard look. Then, surprisingly, he let out a little chuckle. "The irony is grand. Just grand, I tell ye. For you see, I found the wee pot sitting at the end of a rainbow."

Rory, failing to see the humor in what his uncle was telling us, leaned back in his chair and crossed his arms. "Impossible, Uncle. You found that pot of gold on a cold, rainy night in March. There aren't any rainbows at night."

"Aye, and that's the genius of it, man." Finn, unable to help himself, chuckled again. "Never underestimate the cunning of a leprechaun."

CHAPTER 22

Armed with the location where Finn had found his pot of gold, we called the group together and asked everyone to dress in warm, dark clothing before meeting at the lighthouse. We had promised Finn that although Colleen and Bailey would be coming with us, we would use caution while checking his story against the location of the crime scene. The leprechaun gold hidey-hole was to be kept a secret. I agreed. I also didn't dare mention to Uncle Finn that Kennedy, aka Lillian Finch, and Niall, were now part of our sleuthing team as well, for better or worse. I was curious to see how Niall would react when we led him to the crime scene. For that matter, I was interested to see what he would make of Finn's secret leprechaun-gold hidey-hole. Kennedy, I knew, would be on pins and needles the entire night.

Welly and I greeted Colleen and Bailey as they came through the lighthouse door. I had to push Welly's big, fluffy body out of the way just so they could enter. "Glad you could make it," I told

Colleen while giving Bailey a big hug. With a look of apology, I offered, "Rory suggested taking two cars to the beach access path where the body was discovered, due to the dogs."

"Grand idea," Colleen agreed. "I'm bundled like a snowman under me black Irish walking cape." *She had two of them? The luck of some people!* "Unfortunately," she continued, "there's little I can do about Bailey. She'll be the only one among us standing out like a fluffy white blanket against the darkness."

"She'll blend in with the snow," I assured her with a grin, admiring the dog's lovely white fur. "Besides, she's been to this secret hiding place that your father told us about. If we lose our way, hopefully Bailey can get us back on track."

Colleen cast me a skeptical look as she pursed her lips. "Ye have a great deal of faith in me dog. Although she's dear as a lamb, she's no bloodhound, I'm afraid."

"Well, we're happy to have her along. You two will ride in the truck with Rory and Welly. I'm taking Kennedy and Niall in the Jeep."

"What about Tuck?" Colleen asked, trying hard not to look excited at the thought of traipsing around in the dark with the attractive young police officer.

Rory descended the stairs in time to hear Colleen's question. I was having a hard time pulling my gaze away from my hunky boyfriend, who was dressed head-to-toe in black, form-fitting, all-weather gear. He looked good, special-ops-on-a-night-raid good! He embodied a heady mix of physical strength, professional confidence, and just a hint of danger, although I hoped there'd be no danger tonight. It also didn't hurt that the dark clothing set his blue eyes off to perfection. Rimmed in thick black lashes, they had the vibrance and intensity of aquamarine crystals. Yes, I was staring. Rory was aware of this too. With a private grin, he cast me a wink before turning his attention to his cousin. Due to the intense heat rushing to my cheeks, I knew I was blushing.

"Sorry, Colleen, but Tuck won't be joining us tonight," he told her, alighting from the last step to join us. "We've promised to keep the location a secret. We can't tell Tuck because he'll inform Sergeant Murdock. It's his duty, and he knows it. However, if we can determine that your father couldn't have murdered Mr. Leprechaun, which is the name we're using for the murdered man," he clarified, "then we'll call Tuck and let him know. Okay?"

Colleen agreed.

Kennedy and Niall arrived a moment later. Both had gotten the dark clothing memo. Apparently, judging from Niall's sour and slightly confused expression, he'd also gotten the memo regarding Kennedy and her alter ego as well.

"We made it, darlings," Kennedy announced, breezing into the room. She paused momentarily to shower Welly with two-handed head-ruffling accompanied by baby coos and air kisses.

"Not without a casualty, I'm afraid. Namely, my patience," Niall quipped. "Kennedy's just informed me that her friends call her Lillian. *Lillian*, for all love! It's the first time I've heard about it."

"Well . . ." I began, jumping to my friend's defense, "you can count yourself lucky, Niall. Lillian's her pet name, reserved only for her closest friends. Rory still hasn't been given the okay to use it. Isn't that right, babe?" Before turning to Rory, I flashed Kennedy a covert, *Don't blow this!* look.

Rory, swiftly losing his patience as well, narrowed his eyes at my friend. "It is. And I'm just fine with it. Besides, I have my own pet name for her. Princess Ridiculous, or PR for short. The way I see it, there's good PR, there's bad PR, and then there's just plain old Princess Ridiculous." Rory punctuated this surprisingly fitting pet name for my friend with a curt, military nod, before heading for the back door. Colleen and I stifled a bout of giggles as we followed with the dogs.

Behind me, I heard Niall exclaim, "I rather like his better than yours, luv. Come along, PR."

Kennedy, seething, called out, "Touché, Hunts-a-Lot, but the battle is far from over."

With Niall and Kennedy bickering in the Jeep, I kept my eyes focused on the red taillights of Rory's black truck and followed at a safe distance as he drove down Main Street through the town, then took a right turn on Inner Harbor Road. The road, following the shoreline of a small, inner coastal lake, known as the Inner Harbor, which connected to Lake Michigan through a manmade channel near the marina, was now flanked by a knee-high wall of plowed snow. Thankfully the road was dry. Once around the lake, Rory made a left on Beach Street and continued until he turned in to the entrance of an established neighborhood. I recognized it as the neighborhood where Mayor Jeffers and his wife lived. The moment Rory pulled onto the snowy shoulder ahead of me, I did the same and parked behind him. We had come to the beach access path that the mayor took every day for his morning walk. Unfortunately for him, it was just off this well-worn path where he'd discovered the body. I watched Rory, Colleen, and the two dogs exit the truck. I turned off the Jeep and addressed my passengers. "Okay, we're here. Look, I'm going to need you two to put a stopper in it for now. Whatever this is," I said, waving a hand between the two of them, "you can continue it later in your hotel room."

"You know very well what this is, Lindsey," Kennedy hiss-whispered at me from the passenger seat. "And it's all your fault." It was just like Kennedy to put the blame on me when she was the one dating the guy! I mean, really! It wasn't my fault he'd gone missing during a critical hour on St. Pat's night. She was just angry I had pointed it out to her. Thankfully, Niall jumped to the rescue.

"No, PR, it's Campbell's fault," Niall corrected, glomming on to Kennedy's new nickname like a coveted bolt of cashmere cloth. "You should be flattered he called you a princess."

I flashed Ken a grin before whispering my suggestion: "Embrace the role. May the great Lillian Finch rest in peace." Thankfully, she got the point.

With my flashlight in hand, we met Rory and Colleen at the head of the beach access path. The dogs, both leashed to prevent them from bolting ahead of us . . . or, heaven forbid, contaminating the crime scene with their curious noses, appeared anxious to be on the move. I took Welly's leash from Rory as he reminded us, "Be careful and try not to touch anything." He then turned to the trail and flicked on his headlamp.

Thanks to Welly, I was pulled up a short yet

steep incline that brought us to the top of the rolling, open dunes. Behind us sat the heavily forested land. Before us, one hundred and fifty yards away, was the icy shore of the fathomless dark lake. Although it was cold, I couldn't deny that it was a beautiful night, crisp and clear with a full moon. Normally, under such a bright moon, Rory wouldn't need to use a flashlight to find his way. However, I knew that he was on the lookout for any signs that might be important or lead us to the crime scene.

Welly and I brought up the rear of the group, following Colleen and Bailey. However, as the group pressed on toward the lake, marching along the trampled footpath, Welly suddenly stopped. Then, before I could register what was happening, he leapt off the path, pulling me with him into the deep snow and bracken.

"Hey!" I called to the group. "I think Welly's found something."

Although my dog wasn't formally trained in the art of search and rescue, he did seem to have a knack for sniffing out danger. I wasn't certain whether it was the faint sound of crime scene tape snapping in the wind, or the scent of human blood that had caught his attention. Whatever it was, my dog was anxious to pull me to an unseen spot in the snow-covered dunes. Deftly skirting the woody skeletons of tenacious beach shrubs and the sizeable clumps of reedy husks poking through the snow, threatening to trip me, I held on for dear life as Welly pulled me along. After trudging a good distance into the forlorn, rolling land, Welly suddenly pulled to a stop as a strip of bright yellow tape snapped him in the nose. He sat on the snow and let out a soft whine.

A moment later the light from Rory's swiftly moving headlamp illuminated the telltale yellow crime-scene tape flapping in the cold breeze, along with an alarmingly large spot of rust-colored snow speckled with glitter.

"Good boy," I told my dog, hugging his thick neck. "You've found it."

CHAPTER 23

"I can't think of anything more dreadful than being murdered out here . . . in this icy wasteland," Kennedy offered, crossing her arms tightly against her chest.

Rory, turning from what had undoubtedly been a violent scene, faced my friend, purposely blinding her with the light on his head. In a voice tinged with impatience, he asked, "Are you complaining about the icy wasteland or the fact that a man was murdered?"

Shielding her offended eyes, Kennedy snapped, "At the moment, I'm complaining about that ridiculous light on your head, Hunts-a-Lot. Why can't you just hold a torch, like Lindsey is doing?"

Knowing that Rory didn't tolerate it very well when ordinary civilians, or in this case, Kennedy, questioned his use of cool, techy gadgets, he turned from her and went back to investigating the crime scene, being careful not to cross the line of yellow tape.

"I think you're right." Colleen addressed Kennedy. Colleen had come beside Kennedy, both women peering over the line of tape with the same grimly terrified expressions one gets when staring into a bottomless pit. "Not about the headlamp," Colleen clarified, "but 'tis quite a dreadful place to be murdered. So much blood! I didn't know glitter could look so sinister. What do you suppose happened here, Rory?" There was a note of anxiousness in her voice as she asked this. And why wouldn't there be, I thought, knowing that her father was sitting in jail on suspicion of having committed this brutal crime.

"Aside from the blood and glitter, which that white dog is licking—" Niall pointed out, much to Colleen's horror. She immediately tightened her grip on Bailey's leash. "I'd say the snow is too trampled to make heads or tails of it."

I had a secure hold on Welly, lest he try to do the same. Rory, who'd been squatting on the ground with his eyes peeled on the trampled snow, suddenly stood. He turned off his headlamp before addressing Niall.

"We're not here to make sense of the crime scene. That's the job of the police. We're here to mark this location." With that said, Rory then reached into his pocket and pulled out a dark, handheld device. "A military grade GPS marking device," he said, answering all our questions. "Your cell phones basically do the same thing. You can drop a pin marking your location for friends. This device does much the same but has pinpoint accuracy, denotes elevation, doesn't rely on cell service, and it's not shared by friends. By mapping the exact coordinates of this crime scene against the spot Finn found the gold, and the location of the Blarney Stone, where he first spotted what he termed *a leprechaun*, I'm hoping to create a convincing argument in Finn's defense."

"How's that again?" A quizzical look appeared on Niall's face as he addressed Rory.

"We know what time Finn came to my cabin on St. Patrick's Day night, carrying the pot of gold. Colleen closed the Blarney Stone at eight o'clock, leaving Finn behind to clean up the pub. We know that Finn stayed there quite a while before spotting the leprechaun. Finn, living under some delusion, told us that he baited the leprechaun with a mug of green beer and some snacks. Apparently, this fellow came by, drank the beer, ate the snacks, and continued on his way. Finn then followed him at a prudent distance, where he claims to have witnessed this leprechaun depositing something into a hole. Once the leprechaun left, Finn uncovered the gold and, according to him, brought it straight back to my house. That was at eleven forty. Finn is an older gentleman. At the very least he was carrying the gold from the location it was found back to my house. I can attest to the fact that the pot was heavy. If we can prove that the scene of the murder is too far away for him to have traveled, especially with a pot of gold, we might be able to help him."

"Sounds plausible, Campbell, but you're asking us to believe Finn's story."

"True," Rory admitted, flashing a grim smile at the other man. "However, at this point, anything helps. Okay," he said, pressing a button on his device. "Got it." He looked up and continued addressing us. "At this point we have a choice to make. We can continue walking down the shoreline to our next location, which is the public beach, or we can head back to the vehicles and drive there."

"What?" Kennedy questioned. Then, catching herself, she stared at Niall's face. "You don't look surprised."

"Why should I look surprised?" Niall, looking both mildly irritated and curious in turns, glared at Kennedy.

"Because we're going to the location where the gold was found. Doesn't it sound ridiculous that it was hidden on the public beach?"

Niall shrugged. "How do we know that we've been told the truth? I know better than to trust an Irishman. No offense, Colleen," he was quick to add.

"Offense taken. But under the circumstances, I'm goin' to let it slide, Englishman." After delivering a pointed look at Niall, Colleen turned to Rory. "It's cold out here, and I don't feel like traipsing back to this horrible place. Let's drive."

Finally, the voice of reason! Kennedy and I were only too happy to follow Colleen as she and Bailey headed back to the trail.

Twenty minutes later we were at the public beach. Tired of the bickering between Niall and Kennedy, I had taken Welly with me instead. Niall had gone with Rory in the truck. We were no sooner out of the car when I saw Bailey dragging Colleen toward the war memorial near the edge of the parking lot. "I'll be darned," I uttered, as Welly, fighting to keep up with his friend, pulled me along with him. It was an odd place to be sure. Spying the very public monument, a wave of disbelief washed through me, chased by a flicker of doubt. I wasn't convinced Finn O'Connor had told his nephew the truth about the gold. However, judging from Bailey, it appeared that the dog seemed familiar with this spot. Either that, or she found the plethora of comingling smells of the frozen public beach too much to ignore.

The war memorial sat on a plot of thick lawn between the park and the beach. In the summer the tall flagpoles, fanning out in a semicircle and denoting the various branches of the armed services, was surrounded by neatly trimmed hedges and lush flower gardens. On a cold March night, it looked as bleak and barren as the fallen men it honored. Then, staring at one flagpole in particular, Rory began to laugh.

"I don't believe this," he said, pointing at the flag in question. Beside the American flag, stood the Army flag, the Air Force flag, the Navy flag, the Marine Corps flag, and the Coast Guard flag; all of those were to be expected. What was unexpected, and quite frankly stood out like a sore thumb, was the Saint Patrick's Day flag proudly flapping on the town's flagpole beside them. It was a colorful flag depicting a shamrock, a rainbow, and a pot of gold. I backed up. *A rainbow?*

"Dear heavens!" I said, staring at Rory. "Your uncle told us that he found the gold at the end of a rainbow."

"I'm stunned," he said with a chuckle. "I thought he was mad. I thought he was lying, but here it is, a rainbow! And what's more, look at this." The moment Rory shined his light on the large memorial brick, I caught the distinctive sparkling of glitter on the snow beside it. "Uncle Finn told us that the man took a sack from his pocket and deposited the contents into a hole. He also mentioned glitter, which must have come from the man's pocket."

"What sane adult carries glitter in their pocket?" Kennedy questioned with an eye roll.

After an ironic shrug, Rory then set about removing the town's large memorial brick in question as we all watched in speechless wonder. It wasn't long before the sizeable brick gave way, revealing a hollowed-out space in the dirt large enough to hide a pot of gold. Rory noted the exact spot on his GPS device.

"Did you know this was here?" Kennedy questioned Niall.

"How in the bloody hell would I know that was there?" He gave her a hard stare before filling his lungs with a sudden and loud inhalation. Just as sharply, he exhaled. "Dear Lord! You don't believe I'm somehow involved in this tomfoolery, do you?"

"It did cross my mind." Ignoring his affronted look, and knowing that she was surrounded by friends, Kennedy dug in her heels and went full disclosure on him. "For instance, Niall, where were you last night between the hours of eleven thirty and midnight?" Brave, I thought. Maybe not the best timing, but *You go, girl!*

"Getting antacids!" Niall snapped. "For the heartburn you gave me by forcing me to drink all that blasted red wine! You know I can't drink red wine, and yet you ordered two bottles of the ruddy stuff."

"It was a specialty of the vineyard. We had to try it."

"Do you want proof? Is that what you're asking me?" As he talked Niall took off a glove and angrily thrust his hand beneath his heavy coat, struggling to retrieve something deep in the pocket of his tight jeans. After a wiggle and a leg-thrust, he pulled his hand free, revealing a half-eaten roll of antacids. "There's your proof! I had to drive all the way out to a dodgy little petrol station by the interstate just to get the bloody things!" Having retrieved the antacids in question—which, honestly, surprised me that Kennedy hadn't seen him eating them—Niall popped two into his mouth and began chewing. With a forceful swallow, and a dagger-eyed look at Kennedy, another thought must have dawned on him. "Bugger all!" he cried. "Is that why you wanted me to call you Lilith?"

"It's Lillian, and yes, that might have had something to do with it. I can tolerate a lot of things, Niall, darling, but I draw the line at dating a murderer."

"Well, I draw the line at insanity, Princess Ridiculous!"

Since shouting on the beach at night was bound to draw attention, I felt it best to intervene. "Look, let's just calm down and sort this all out back at the lighthouse. We can all do with a hot drink. Besides, it's an honest mistake, Niall. Kennedy told me that you went out St. Patrick's Day night around the time the murder might have occurred." Ignoring his look of extreme displeasure, I pressed on. "Anyhow, we found the spot where the gold was hidden. Rory's marked it, which makes the night a success."

"Success?" he cried. "I'm standing under a desecrated American World War II memorial freezing my bollocks off and have just learned that my girlfriend thinks me a murderer! My night has been a bloody hellscape of leprechaun-driven lunacy!"

Kennedy placed a hand on his arm. "My apologies, darling. The imagination is what the imagination is. It made sense at the time." Niall peeled her gloved fingers from his arm.

"Lindsey's right," Colleen piped up, brushing past the bickering couple, and coming to my defense. "The night has been a success. The crime scene appears quite a hike from where me father found the gold. However, a question remains. What numpty thought hidin' a pot o' gold under a rainbow flag was a bright idea?"

"Good question, Colleen." Rory smiled at his cousin. "However, the question we should be asking ourselves is why? Why would someone hide a cache of gold coins under a rainbow flag? When we find the answer to that, I believe we'll find the killer."

CHAPTER 24

Although Niall hadn't quite forgiven Kennedy, and Rory still had his suspicions about the man, I decided it best to placate all our ruffled nerves with a warm fire blazing away in the lighthouse fireplace, while placing a cup of Baileys-laced hot cocoa in everyone's hand. Each mug was topped with a dollop of thick, freshly whipped cream, and a dusting of shaved chocolate. My culinary efforts were appreciated, as was the cozy setting. Although I always found it inspiring when pondering difficult situations up in the lightroom, I felt that, under the circumstances, tonight's gathering would best be served in the coziest room in the lighthouse, my living room. Besides, Bailey and Wellington were with us, and neither one of them could manage the circular light-tower stairs. They weren't exactly giant-dog-breed friendly. As we sipped our Irish cream–laced cocoa and mulled over what we had learned on our nighttime reconnaissance mission, the dogs seemed content to curl up together by the fire, sharing Welly's large dog bed. With a snack in their bellies, they looked so peaceful as they slept in our company, seemingly without a care.

After meticulously marking the locations of the Blarney Stone, the public beach war memorial, the crime scene, and his log home on a map of Beacon Harbor, Rory had traced Finn's movements, as we knew them, on St. Patrick's Day night. The map was spread out on the coffee table for us to study. I had to commend Rory. Seeing all the important places at once, marked with Finn's account of his movements, the time frame we were working with, and the distances between each location, a clearer picture was coming into view regarding what had possibly occurred on that cold, wet night. However, without the medical examiner's report, we only had Finn's account to go on.

Although we had driven the distance from the crime scene to the location of the gold at the war memorial, the route had taken us through the village to access both locations. However, now looking at Rory's map, the actual location of the crime scene was a mile south from of where Finn had found the buried pot of gold, a fact that was pointed out to us by Niall Fitzhugh. I took the fact that he was still willing to sit next to Kennedy to be a good sign.

"Since some of you have basically accused me of being a murderer"—here Niall paused to shoot a dagger-eyed look at Kennedy before continuing—"I'm going to play devil's advocate. While the case has been made that Finnigan O'Connor is an older gentleman in his mid-sixties, he's still spry enough to walk a mile down the beach, with shillelagh in hand, to off the nasty little leprechaun."

Colleen piped in, "I beg to differ. While he is spry enough, me father has great reverence for the fairy folk, of which the leprechaun is one. Daft as it sounds, me father truly believed he was trailing a leprechaun and had outwitted him. 'Tis a long-held dream of his, sure."

"That *is* daft!" Niall proclaimed in no uncertain terms.

"I think it's endearing," I countered, offering a smile to Rory's cousin. "Also, you must consider the location of the Blarney Stone. It's right here," I said, pointing to Colleen's Irish gift shop. "It's located in a cottage on the corner of Main Street and Forest Ave, which is four blocks away from the public beach. My lighthouse is right here." Again, I pointed to the map. "It's located at the far north end of the public beach. The beach ends on the other side here, at the marina. Past the marina, just down here is the inner-harbor bridge, which is the only way you can reach the crime scene from here. The gold was found just to the south of the beach pavilion, which is here. Then, there's Rory's cabin over here." As I touched the location on the map, I couldn't help offering a grin to the man in question.

"And your point is, Lindsey, darling? Or are you merely illustrating how convenient it is for you to sneak out in the dead of night for a romantic interlude? According to this map, Hunts-a-Lot's cabin is just a hop-skip-and-a-jump through the woods."

"No need for sneaking," Colleen offered with a grin worthy of the Cheshire cat. "Rory's livin' here for the time being."

"Can we please bring our focus back on the map?" It came out sterner than I had wished it to, but in my defense, a man's life was on the line. "My point is this. The leprechaun was murdered a mile south of the public beach, which requires crossing the inner-harbor bridge. If Finn followed the leprechaun from the Blarney Stone to the public beach, then dug up the gold, why would he and Bailey take a detour south, walking a mile along the coastline? He already had the gold. From the flagpole at the public beach to Rory's cabin is less than half a mile. Given that Finn already walked that distance to the public beach after a long day at work, I don't see him lugging that heavy pot of gold any further than he'd have to. Looking at this map, it just doesn't make sense."

"My point exactly," Rory agreed. Niall, however, wasn't convinced.

"You do realize that you're basing your entire case on the word of a besotted man. What if Finn saw the leprechaun, chased him all the way to this spot on the beach"—here Niall pointed to the crime scene—"then used his shillelagh in a manner to persuade the little man dressed in green to give up the location of his pot o' gold? If Finn believed him to be a leprechaun, which we know he did, he'd also believe the man had a pot of gold hidden somewhere."

As Niall talked, I realized that Colleen was staring at him, and not in a good way. "You eejit!" she blurted. "Listen to yourself. Me father wouldn't hurt a fly, and he certainly wouldn't crack a man's skull because of some hidden gold, even if he did think him a leprechaun. Of all the stupid things!" Her light gray eyes bore into Niall's with all the intensity of a vaporizing laser.

"Clearly we don't have all the answers," Rory admitted, breaking the tension. "And Niall does bring up a good point. The only hard evidence we have so far is a pot of gold, the location where it might have been hidden, and a crime scene where a man fitting the description of a leprechaun was murdered. There's also the matter of the murder weapon. Finn is missing his shillelagh, which is ironic. Yet let's not forget that this man also might have carried one as well. After all, the murdered leprechaun fits the description of the person accused of attacking Fred Landry the day of the Leprechaun Parade."

At the mention of the word *shillelagh*, Kennedy's eyes glittered with excitement. She sat up straighter, gripped her cocoa mug tighter, and set her lips in a curl of pure delight. "Tucker can help us with that. There isn't a closely held secret that man has which I can't wheedle out of him. What?" She bristled, noticing two sets of eyes glued to her as she spoke. Colleen wasn't pleased, and Niall, to his credit, looked nearly dangerous. Kennedy cleared her throat and leaned back on the couch, snuggling deeper into the puffy leather cushion. "What I meant to say is that we should call him tomorrow. He's bound to have found out by now."

"I was planning on calling him," Rory told her.

"Tuck is well aware of what is riding on the proper identification of the shillelagh."

I asked anyone if they'd like a refill of spiked cocoa. After making another round of the delicious drink and knowing that I, for one, could use a sugar-alcohol boost to help ease the tension of the last hour, I refilled everyone's mug before taking my seat in the old rocking chair. Rory was sitting beside me. I reached across to him and gave his hand a gentle squeeze.

"Thanks to Rory, we now have an idea of Finn's movements on St. Patrick's Day night. But we can all agree that we have many unanswered questions. I have to admit, I feel like we're running in circles here. We still don't know the identity of the murder victim, or why he was in Beacon Harbor on St. Patrick's Day night to begin with. Finn's shillelagh is missing, but anyone could have walked off with it during the grand opening party at the Blarney Stone. Colleen has also sold quite a few of them, so it's imperative the murder weapon is correctly identified. Another thing to remember is that Finn wasn't the only person who saw the leprechaun on or before St. Patrick's Day. Others saw him too, including me. I say that tomorrow we canvas the town, inquiring after anyone who saw this leprechaun and where they spotted him. Rory's made a map of Finn's movements on the night in question, but what if we make another map, this one indicating where and when the leprechaun was sighted on the days leading up to his murder? Maybe a pattern will emerge, one that will help us to understand who this person was, where he might have lived, and why he was hoarding gold. What do you think?"

While the others thought about this, nodding in silent agreement, Niall, projecting an *if you can't beat 'em, join 'em* attitude, raised his cocoa-encrusted mug to me. "You're proposing a leprechaun hunt? Count me in."

CHAPTER 25

"Good morning." I waved at Teddy, who was hard at work in the bakeshop kitchen when Welly and I arrived. I hung up my coat, grabbed a Beacon Bite for Welly, and escorted him to the café door, where my loveable pooch would lounge just outside the doorway while we worked to fill the bakery cases. Even though he couldn't be in the kitchen, he loved being inside the Beacon Bakeshop early in the morning while we baked. The downside was that all the delicious smells wafting his way induced a heavier than normal amount of drool. But that was all part of loving a giant, fluffy dog: shedding and drool. Both could be cleaned. In my opinion it was a small price to pay for the unconditional love Welly showered on those he cared about. Sometimes, embracing his lazier nature, Welly opted to stay with Rory and sleep a little longer. Rory would often take Welly with him to the warehouse he was converting into his new business if it wasn't a day where power tools were involved. Welly wasn't a fan of loud noises. Today, however, Rory was planning to help Colleen by working in his uncle's micro-pub. Sure, he could take Welly with him. After all, Bailey would be there too. But Rory's motivation for opening the pub, aside from the fact that it should have been up and running already, was that he was planning to put my idea to the test. Rory was going to spread the word about the man dressed as a leprechaun and see if anyone visiting the pub had spotted him on or before St. Patrick's Day. During our busy morning at the Beacon, I was planning to do the same.

"Morning, Lindsey," Teddy greeted in return, handing me a steaming mug of black coffee. One of the things I loved about working with Teddy was that he was as addicted to coffee as I was. Like me, he started a pot brewing the moment he came through the kitchen door. "So?" he prodded, staring at me as I sipped the heavenly brew. I flashed him a puzzled look over the rim of my mug.

"What?"

"Oh, I don't know?" he replied sarcastically, rolling his round blue eyes at me. "How about the fact that Finn O'Connor has a pot of gold hidden somewhere, and he's now in jail for murdering a leprechaun? Let's start there. We all know that you and Rory, being Beacon Harbor's power-sleuthing couple, are neck deep in this one. Also, you have your own history with the recently deceased. After all, you hit him with your Jeep during the Leprechaun Parade." Teddy grinned unseemly at this.

I recalled that I did tell him about all that, and poor Fred Landry.

Teddy bent his knees, placed an elbow on the flour-dusted counter, and theatrically rested his chin on his fist, imitating a curious child. "Tell me, Linds, what have you found out, and how can I help?" He grinned and stood up again. Childish antics were a part of Teddy's charm.

Although he'd only been working with me for a little over six months, it never failed to surprise me how well Teddy knew me. He was like the big brother I'd always wanted. "Alright," I said, tying on my apron. "Hand me that tub of flour. Let me get the sweet roll dough started, and then I'll tell you what we know so far, which, for the record, isn't much."

"I'll be the judge of that." Teddy handed me the flour tub and continued to work on his muffin batter.

As I mixed up the yeast dough for the cinnamon rolls and the pecan rolls, a Beacon Bakeshop staple, I brought Teddy up to speed on what we had learned so far, focusing on the location of the crime scene, Finn's missing shillelagh, and the fight between Kennedy and Niall, which, if I was being totally honest, he was most interested in. Of course, I gave him all the sordid details regarding that, including Rory's and my suspicion of Niall.

"Kennedy thinks he's a leprechaun killer and went full metal Lillian Finch on him?" Teddy was delighted to hear it.

"Yeah, well, it backfired when Rory gave her a new nickname. He's calling her PR, which is short for Princess Ridiculous. It's only fair given that she calls him Sir Hunts-a-Lot. Anyhow, Niall glommed on to that in a hurry. They'd been arguing."

At the mention of Ken's new nickname, Teddy inhaled sharply—as if he'd seen a ghost . . . or was extremely impressed. It was the latter in this case.

"You're dating a genius," he told me in no uncertain terms. He shook his head in wonder, uttering, "Rory Campbell. It's short, succinct, and spot-on. I'm going to make sure it sticks." Armed with this new, diabolical mission that Kennedy was sure to hate, Teddy began expertly filling the giant muffin tin with his delicious oatmeal-raisin batter.

While he did that, I transferred the sweet dough into two large metal bowls that had already been coated with butter. I rolled each ball of dough once, then covered them with cheesecloth before placing them on a shelf near the stove for the first rise. Making the sweet dough was second nature to me by now. I had an hour before the dough would double in size. Until then, I set to work on the three types of quiches I had planned for the day, our standard spinach-and-bacon quiche, a ham-and-asparagus quiche, and our meatless option, a tomato, basil, and caramelized onion quiche. Teddy had come up with that one, having made it for his wife. Jesse had loved it.

"So, now that you've been brought up to speed, let me tell you our new plan." Unfortunately, as I talked, I had crossed to the walk-in refrigerator to retrieve the pie crust dough Wendy had made on Saturday. Pie crust was very basic. However, making it every morning for the quiches wasted valuable time. Months ago, Wendy had volunteered to make a week's worth at a time, bless her. It was a brilliant plan, and she was good at it. While in the fridge, I also gathered all the fresh ingredients I'd need for the quiches, including a case of eggs. With my arms full, I popped back out, and continued the conversation right where I'd left off without skipping a beat. That's how conversations went in the Beacon's kitchen—in all their walking, talking, baking, multitasking glory! "Leprechaun sightings," I blurted, as if it was the punchline. "Our goal is to map as many as we can to see if a pattern emerges. We're hoping to find a concentration of sightings that might help us understand what he was doing here in the first place."

Teddy, with muffins in the oven, had taken a tray of recently fried yeast donuts that had been cooling. He was now in the process of loading his pastry bag to begin filling them with our various homemade jellies and custards. "Not a bad idea," he said without looking up from his task. To do so at this point would be disastrous. Filling pastry bags was an art. "How do you propose to do this?"

"Today, when we open, I'm going to start asking customers if they had spotted this leprechaun on or before St. Patrick's Day. Then, if they did see him, I'm going to make a note of where the sighting occurred and mark it on the map of Beacon Harbor Rory made last night. Rory's going to do the same at the pub today. I'm putting all leprechaun sightings in green, noting them with a shamrock." I punctuated this last detail with a prideful smile.

In the time it took me to explain my plan, Teddy had filled a dozen donuts with our Traverse City cherry jelly. The man was more efficient than a machine. He placed the donut he was holding on a parchment-lined bakery tray and looked at me. "Well, well, I can see that you've put some thought behind this. However, would you permit me to propose another idea?"

"If it involves leprechaun sightings, I'm all ears."

"It does." He grinned, changed his pastry bag,

and then set to work on another tray of donuts. "Back in my filming days, I once worked on a show that centered around a group of Sasquatch hunters, called *My Sasquatch Summer*."

"I do recall you mentioning something about that." I offered a grin before returning to my task, fitting the rolled-out pie crust into my mini quiche pans.

"Right. Well, the team would go into a town suspected of Sasquatch action . . . *What?*" He looked up at me, trying hard not to grin. "It's a thing. Anyhow, once there they'd host a town hall meeting, inviting anyone in the area who claimed to have had a Sasquatch encounter to come and tell their story. They always managed to get a crowd. Refreshments were served," he added with a wink. "Then, with the town hall meeting rolling, the team would hear stories and map each sighting, just like you're proposing to do, and find a possible pattern—or, as they say in the biz, a favorite Squatch haunt. That's how they'd pick a spot to investigate."

"Wow, that's a really great idea."

"You can thank the producers of *My Sasquatch Summer* for coming up with that one. Town hall Squatch meetings became a fan favorite. I think it would work perfectly in this case. After all, you're trying to find a mythical creature, a leprechaun. Once word gets out about your town hall meeting, I'm sure people will come out of the woodwork to be part of it and tell their tale. I'll even volunteer to video the event for you. You should probably also offer refreshments. Nothing draws a crowd like the promise of free coffee and cookies."

"Again, great idea."

"This way, Linds, all you have to do is spread the word, and we have our own PR—Princess Ridiculous—to do that for us."

"Heavens, Teddy. You've really thought this one through." Although to those unencumbered with leprechaun issues it likely sounded crazy, I was impressed.

"Yep," he replied with a mock prideful grin. "That's why you pay me the big bucks."

"And you're worth every penny. I'll give Kennedy a call once nine o'clock rolls around. That's the agreed-upon earliest time I'm allowed to call her."

"Perfect! However, I should warn you, that when hosting a town hall like this there are always red herrings thrown into the mix—you know, folks who show up purely to be on film while telling an entirely made-up story. Some folks get their jollies doing stuff like that."

"Forgive my impertinence," I broke in, nearly ready to start filling my quiches, "but how could they tell the stories were made-up? We're talking about Sasquatch sightings here. The entire thing sounds made-up to me."

"Good question." To my great surprise, Teddy actually had an answer. "These guys were experts on Sasquatches. Before you toss one of those quiches at me, Linds—yes, it's also a thing. They had a whole dictionary of Sasquatch terms and behaviors, like a field guide, if you will. Totally made-up, I'm sure, but it looked legit enough, and they used it like a card player uses a *Hoyle's Rules of Games* book. If a sighting fell within the wild realm of possibilities, they'd call it legit, and make a note of it. You should probably have a leprechaun expert on-site for the meeting you're proposing."

Expert on leprechauns? *Ha!* I thought. The victim was a man dressed as a leprechaun. And anyhow, who the heck is an expert on the fairy folk? Then, as if a flash of lightning struck my addled brain, I blurted, "Finn O'Connor! Rory's uncle! He's the closest thing to a leprechaun expert we have. He even has a pot of leprechaun gold to prove it."

"You just might be on to something there." Teddy, having finished the tray of donuts he was filling and frosting, stroked his chin meditatively. "Finn should definitely be involved with this. After all, his love for leprechaun lore has gotten us into this pickle to begin with. However, there's just one problem. How are you going to spring him from jail?"

Good question. Yet the ball was already rolling, and once it was rolling, I knew that, even with the best of intentions, I couldn't get out of my own way. I was going to host a town hall meeting, and come hell or highwater, Finn O'Connor was going to be there!

CHAPTER 26

With PR herself onboard (and really, Kennedy didn't have much of a choice in the matter), and with Teddy and my staff at the Beacon Bakeshop ready to help run the show, my leprechaun town hall meeting scheme was in action. Word had gone out that the Beacon Bakeshop would be hosting the meeting after hours, in our newly renovated boathouse, and, yes, refreshments would be provided in the form of shamrock sugar cookies and green leprechaun punch. Betty Vanhoosen, doing her part for justice and our friendship, had fired up the town gossip mill to spread the word, asking her friends in the chamber of commerce to put out a call, asking that anyone who had spotted a very convincing-looking leprechaun on or before St. Patrick's Day, should come to the Beacon Bakeshop boathouse at seven p.m. and tell their story.

Rory and Colleen had also gone above and beyond by making and handing out flyers at the Blarney Stone the moment the gift shop and micro-

pub had opened for business. Word had gone out.
Interest had been generated (folks were clamoring to get a peek at my renovated boathouse!) and
Betty, bless her, had put the thumbscrews to Bob
aka Doc Riggles, urging him to put a rush on the
blood DNA sample taken from the shillelagh found
at the crime scene. Tuck had stayed behind at the
police station, waiting for word. We knew that we
were taking a gamble on the DNA sample, hoping
the results, when combined with Rory's map of
Finn's movements and the crime scene, would be
enough to cast doubt on Finn's involvement in the
murder and spring him from his jail cell. Crazy as
it sounded, Finn O'Conner was our local leprechaun expert, and we needed him to be present at
our town hall meeting.

Once the Beacon had closed for the day, I let
Welly out of the lighthouse to do his business before bringing him over to the boathouse with me
to start setting up for the town hall meeting. We
were halfway across the back lawn when Welly
spied Elizabeth, Alaina, Tom, and Ryan making
their way to the boathouse as well. They had volunteered to help take the leaves out of my large
table, move it aside, and set up chairs. Like a toy
sword in the hand of a busy child, Welly's tail cut
through the air with gusto as he ran to greet his
friends.

"Welly!" Elizabeth cried. She and Alaina waited
for my giant fluffball of a dog to catch up with
them so they could give him a big hug. Welly was a
sucker for hugs.

"Any word from Doc Riggles yet?" Ryan asked,
opening the door to the boathouse for us.

"Not yet," I said, pulling Welly inside with me.

"I'm on pins and needles. If Finn can't make it to the meeting, Colleen has volunteered to take his place. As Teddy has informed us, there are always those who show up to these things craving attention. In order for this crazy scheme to work, we need to record the legitimate leprechaun sightings and not the made-up ones."

"With the emphasis on crazy," Elizabeth quipped. She flashed a grin before heading for the folding chairs.

As we worked to set up rows of chairs, all facing the fireplace where Rory's map would be displayed on the wall beside it, Teddy and Wendy came in with trays of cookies. Those we set up on the back counter. Satisfied that the gang had the chairs under control, I excused myself to make the leprechaun punch. After all, we had promised refreshments.

With the chairs set up and the refreshments ready and waiting on the back counter, Rory came in with the map. After a quick greeting, he hung it on the wall, where it would be easier to reach when it came time to mark the sightings.

It was another cold, dark night in Beacon Harbor. The boathouse was ready and waiting for the meeting to begin, and yet I was suddenly struck with a near debilitating bout of panic. *What was I doing? Was I really hosting a town hall meeting over possible sightings of a man dressed as a leprechaun . . . who'd been brutally murdered . . . possibly by Rory's uncle? Was I insane? Had I reached rock bottom? Is this what living in a small village on the frozen shores of Lake Michigan did to people?* I was afraid the answer was an unequivocal yes. Then, however, Kennedy entered the room.

"Lindsey, darling, if ever you've doubted my devotion to you, recall that I have spent my day
spreading the word about this leprechaun town
hall meeting of yours." She paused and with a dramatic flourish whirled the gorgeous walking cape
off her shoulders. Niall showed up just in time to
take it from her and hang it on the coatrack.
"Thinking way out of the box on this one, aren't
we, Linds? But I love it. You know that I'm a sucker
for your devious schemes. Let's hope this works."

"Cookie, PR?" Teddy appeared beside her, grinning for all he was worth. He held out one of the
beautifully decorated cookies he'd made. Kennedy glowered at the nickname but couldn't resist
plucking the cookie from his hand. Niall, deriving
some secret pleasure from Kennedy's new nickname, flashed my baker a thumbs-up before catching up to Kennedy as she headed for front row
seating.

At six thirty a string of familiar faces from the
village started to arrive, relieving my nerves. Maybe
I wasn't going insane after all. Either that, or the
good folks of Beacon Harbor were here for the
show. Felicity and Stanley Stewart were the first to
stroll in followed by Ali and Jack Johnson. Felicity
mentioned to me in a whisper that she'd seen a
leprechaun peeping through her office window at
the Tannenbaum Shoppe. Apparently, it had given
her a fright. Molly Butterfield and Lisa Baxter also
strolled in. Lisa indicated to me in a whisper that
she had seen the leprechaun peeking in the front
window of the flower shop. Molly was Lisa's moral
support. She'd also heard that Finn was going to
be at the meeting. Her smile at the thought was incandescent.

The floodgates had opened and soon a deluge of friends and regulars at the Beacon arrived, filling up the seats in the boathouse. I was relieved to see Peggy O'Leary, of Peggy's Pet Shop & Pooch Salon. She came with one of her employees, a young dog groomer, who also claimed to have spotted the leprechaun. Mrs. Hinkle came in right behind her, accompanied by her son and daughter-in-law. She looked ashen and frailer than I remembered. The poor woman had gone through quite a lot the day of the Leprechaun Parade. I greeted her as she walked in and asked how she was doing.

"I'm positively haunted by what occurred that afternoon, Lindsey. Fred could be a royal pain at times, but he didn't deserve what that nasty leprechaun did to him. The leprechaun's dead, and I hear Fred is making progress, but he's still in ICU. I'm not sure how this is going to help you, but I'm here to tell my story." I breathed a sigh of relief for Fred, thanked her, and watched as her son took her by the arm and marched off to find a seat.

By five after seven the room was filled to capacity, with many people standing near the back, nibbling cookies and sipping green punch. I was doubtful that everyone in attendance had spotted the leprechaun, but I was happy to see so many familiar faces, nonetheless. It was time to start my meeting, and yet I waited, checking my phone every minute to see if Doc Riggles had had any luck regarding the shillelagh. Then, to my great surprise, Betty blew into the boathouse on a gust of cold wind, breathing heavily and in high color.

"Hold the meeting!" she cried. "The results from the shillelagh found at the crime scene have come in!" She then collapsed at the waist like a ragdoll, her hands resting on her knees so that she could catch her breath, leaving us all hanging on her next words. Betty, a plump, vivacious woman in her early sixties, certainly took her sweet time, seemingly unaware that she hadn't yet delivered the punchline. After a few minutes of deep breathing, she stood. Unfortunately, she spied the refreshment table. "Punch!" she cried, then began clip-clopping her way toward it on unsteady legs. "I need punch."

Praying that blocking an older woman on her way to the refreshment table wasn't a form of elder abuse, I cut her off at the pass, so to speak, demanding, "Betty. The results, please!"

"Didn't I just say?" Her unblinking, round blue eyes held the same unnerving look as an owl's on the hunt. I shook my head, urging her to continue. "It's not the murder weapon, at least not yet," she added with a troubled look. "The blood on the shillelagh matched Fred Landry's. It's the leprechaun's shillelagh, not Finn's. He's being released now and will be here any minute. I'll just get a cup of that punch while we wait."

It was good news for Finn, but the fact remained that the murder weapon was still missing, along with Finn's shillelagh. Were the two connected, or was the murder weapon another type of club, like a bat or a hammer? The answer was still a mystery, but I offered a silent prayer, hoping that Finn's missing shillelagh was just that, missing.

Finn, having been held under suspicion of murder, hadn't been charged with any crime. The evidence so far had been circumstantial. Getting awfully close to the forty-eight-hour rule, the legal amount of time a suspect can be detained without being charged with a crime, Tuck had waited patiently at the police station. The moment the results had been phoned in, he filled out the paperwork, released Finn, and whisked him over to the boathouse. Obviously, Finn had been briefed regarding his role at the town hall meeting. He was, *ahem*, the leprechaun expert. I had to admit, the man knew how to make an entrance. With two days of salt-and-pepper stubble on his face, a gleam in his eyes, and purpose in his stride, he made his way to the front of the room amongst a chorus of oohs, aahs, some discordant clapping, and a handful of boos. He waved at them all like a hero emerging nearly unscathed from the aftermath of a calamity. Noting his sardonic grin, I was reminded that Finn had survived his ordeal with his leprechaun gold still intact. No one knew where he'd hidden it, including Sergeant Murdock. Kudos to Uncle Finn.

"Good evening, ladies and gentlemen," he began in his lilting Irish brogue. "I've come here fresh from the county jail, an innocent man held in confinement purely on account that I recovered a pot o' gold. You all know the story by now—how I saw this leprechaun with me own eyes, and how I recovered his gold. I am here to state in no uncertain terms, that I did not kill the wee man. What reason would I have to do that? Me folly was that I truly believed he was a leprechaun. In my defense, where I come from the land is thick with such tales. According to the lore, a man has a right to trick a leprechaun into giving up his gold, but not to kill one. To do so brings eternal bad luck. I've been told the wee fellow in green was a man, a mortal man, rest his soul. But his is a curious case, is it not? No fingerprints in the database, no dental records to match, and no one to come forward to claim his poor body. Why was he dressed as a leprechaun, I ask meself? Better yet, why did I see him hiding gold?" The crowd that had gathered was silent, held rapt by Finn's speech. He paused to take a sip of water before continuing.

"We now know that the deceased was Fred Landry's attacker. It creates a compelling mystery, does it not? There has been no mention of a robbery either, just a vicious attack. So where did the gold come from? Well, we are here tonight to help sort out this mystery. It has come to my attention that I was not the only person to lay eyes on that wee man. Others saw him too. Lindsey, here, along with me nephew, Rory, and their friends have come up with this grand plan to mark the places in this village the poor devil was spotted. We ask that if ya have a sighting or a story to share, raise your hand."

Remarkably, judging from the sea of raised hands, it appeared that a quarter of the crowded room had seen a leprechaun.

Chapter 27

I had to hand it to Teddy. His town hall meeting idea had produced results. While I manned the microphone, passing it to whomever had been called upon to tell their story, and while Rory stood ready at the map, marking the location where each credible sighting occurred, Finn hosted the meeting like a man born for the job. He listened intently to each story, calling upon his vast knowledge of leprechaun lore to judge the validity of what he heard. It seemed that most who had come really had seen the leprechaun, on or before St. Patrick's Day. However, a few tricksters had come as well, purely for the purpose of testing Finn's knowledge and having a laugh in the process. Bill Morgan, a semiretired man from the village and a Beacon Bakeshop regular, was one of them. Bill stood and began telling his story.

"I saw him before the Leprechaun Parade when I looked out my back window. I live on Inner Harbor Road," he said to Rory, who was standing at the map with his green marker, ready to place a

shamrock on the site. Rory already knew where
Bill lived. "Just past the boat ramp," Bill added for
good measure. "Well, this little fella looked around
to make sure no one was watching, then he jumped
upon my deck and began dancing a jig. He had a
four-leaf clover clenched in his teeth, like so, and
he was clicking his heels in the air as he wiggled
his arms like this." Here Bill put his fists together
with elbows out and began swinging them from
side to side, wiggling his hips as he did so. He
nearly clocked Roger, his son, in the head. "Soon a
lady leprechaun joined him, and they began
singing about their Lucky Charms, claiming how
they were so magically delicious." The crowd erupted
in laughter. Uncle Finn was not amused.

"Shenanigans!" he cried, thrusting his forefinger
at Bill like a weapon. "Double shenanigans on you,
sir! Leprechauns are dour, singular creatures, with
a mind for trickery and a taste for green beer. The
only tapping they make is when they're cobbling
shoes, deep under the hills where they live. They
are shoemakers by trade, and there are no lady
leprechauns. Only male. Also, they don't eat sugar-
coated cereal with wee stale marshmallows stirred
into the mix. Sit down!"

Bill took a bow as the villagers applauded his
charming yet ridiculous tale. The good news was
that of the credible sightings, a pattern had begun
to emerge.

Once the town hall meeting had come to an
end, and all the villagers had left the boathouse,
Rory removed the map from the wall and brought
it to my much smaller table that had been moved
to the back corner of the building. Due to the
crowd, Welly and Bailey had taken up residence

underneath it and had fallen asleep. They were now both awake and ready for a romp outside. While Colleen, Kennedy, and I took the dogs to do their business in my backyard, Niall, Teddy, and Tuck helped Rory move the table to the middle of the room once again, where the lighting was better. When we came back inside, I was happy to see that most of the folding chairs had been put away as well, and that eight of my stouter dining chairs now circled the table. The ladies and I took a seat, joining the men while the dogs, enlivened by the cold night air, enjoyed a spin at the water bowl before some light wrestling and romping in the now empty space of the room. Two impossibly furry large dogs playing rough was a sight to behold indeed. The vacuum was definitely coming out before I locked up for the night.

"What did I tell you?" Teddy remarked, staring at the map. He looked up and flashed me a grin. "Regarding oddities and folks that see them, they just can't wait to share their stories. Makes them seem less crazy. It's the old *crazy loves company* adage. This place was packed tighter than a sardine can. Great job spreading the word, PR."

Kennedy, with the grace of a princess, gave him a royal wave. "As you know, I'm not a fan of the name, but PR is what I do best. I'm warming to it. And . . . you are welcome." Knowing that her contribution to our plan had been huge, she seemed genuinely pleased by the acknowledgment.

"Back to your *crazy loves company* garbly-gook, I am not flattered," Finn told Teddy with a hard look. "But I cannot argue the results. Looky here." Finn pointed to the plethora of green shamrocks in the vicinity of the village hall building. "There's a large concentration of sightings here on the day of the Leprechaun Parade. Aside from peeping in the windows of a few of the shops surrounding the building, he seemed to be casing Village Hall. It begs the question, why Fred Landry? What was the connection there, I wonder."

"I agree," I said. "Judging from the accounts we've just heard, he seemed to have come into town from the southwest, near the inner harbor. Felicity's sighting would be the first, hers being the first shop one sees when coming into town down Main Street. The Tannenbaum Shoppe is on the south side of the street, and I have to believe either he parked a car somewhere around there, or came through the trees."

"Haven't found an abandoned car in the village," Tuck informed us. So much for that theory.

"Then there's Peggy's sighting," I continued. "Her pet salon is here, on the other side of the street, two blocks away from Village Hall. Both Peggy and her assistant, Ashley, saw him, but at two separate times. Then Lisa from the flower shop saw him back here. Butterfield's Floral Artistry shop sits on Forest Ave, behind city hall. Why would he do that?" Everyone shrugged.

"He could have been a Peeping Tom," Niall offered.

"The creeper," Kennedy remarked with distaste.

"Before Uncle Finn spotted him on St. Patrick's Day night outside of the Blarney Stone, his interest seemed to be Village Hall, hence the attack," Rory said. "My guess is that he knew of the Leprechaun Parade and was trying to blend in with the children. After all, this man was about the size of a fifth grader. He was also likely waiting for the building to clear so that he could confront Fred Landry in his office without notice. As we know, Mrs. Hinkle was still in the building, and Lindsey hit the man as he was running away after doing the deed."

"For the record, he hit my Jeep," I chimed in. Rory nodded, before continuing.

"However, what I'm interested in are these sightings here." Rory pointed to a location on the map that was just south of town, close to the beach where the man in question had been murdered. "This is the neighborhood Mayor Jeffers lives in," he said. "Before this man was murdered, four residents of this neighborhood spotted him, either peering in their windows or, as in the case of Hugh Ingle, he saw the man hiding in the woods. He thought he was going crazy. That was early on the day of the Leprechaun Parade, one day before Mr. Leprechaun was murdered. These markings indicate that he might have had some sort of ties to this neighborhood."

"What about this Mayor Jeffers fellow?" Niall asked. "We know he found the body. We know he lives in this neighborhood. What if he had a connection to this man as well? Do we know what his relationship was like with Fred Landry? Maybe the mayor wasn't paying his property taxes and was about to get publicly excoriated for it. Jeffers could have easily hired the little fellow to make a hit on a local rival, bury the evidence, then take him to task on the dunes, making sure he wouldn't squeal about the dirty deed. Happens all the time in the movies."

"It's plausible," Tuck said, stroking his chin as he thought on it. Colleen, I noted, was hanging on

Tuck's every word like a lovestruck teen. It was adorable. "But I doubt it," Tuck concluded. "The mayor is a stand-up guy. He's also the choir director at the church. Doesn't seem the type to hire a hitman. But maybe somebody else did. This mysterious little fellow who paraded around town as a leprechaun, peering into the windows of mostly female-owned businesses, would fit the bill. He's not even in the system. We can't identify him."

"Maybe he's changed his identity," Kennedy offered. "You know, with plastic surgery—done to make him look ghastly and fairylike?"

"Really, Kennedy, why would anyone want to look like a leprechaun?" I chided.

"Which brings us back to my original point." Finn broke in with a pensive look in his eyes. "Maybe he was a leprechaun. Maybe he really did follow me from the old country, where I first spied him out of the corner of me eye one evening, jumping into an old well behind the pub because he knew that I'd seen him."

"You saw a leprechaun in Ireland jump into an old well?" Tuck questioned, knowing that we were all thinking the same thing. "Aren't those old wells pretty deep?"

"That they are. When I went to investigate, thinking he'd be down there, trapped like a fish in a barrel, to my great surprise, the well was empty. The leprechaun had vanished."

"Da," Colleen chided. "You were deep in your cups at the time."

"True that may be, m' dear, but I know what I saw."

"Look, we can argue this all night, but it won't change the fact that Fred Landry was attacked, and another unidentified man was murdered here in Beacon Harbor," Tuck reminded us.

"These are strange happenings," Finn added. "Need I remind everyone that he was hoarding gold, burying it under a rainbow, as all of ye are well aware by now. Not the act of a sane man by any account."

"What?" Tuck questioned, looking at Finn. "I'm not following you. The gold was hidden under a rainbow?"

Realizing our mistake, Rory quickly covered for Uncle Finn. "He's not serious, Tuck. Anyhow, regarding the gold, it's likely stolen."

"We're certain it is," Tuck remarked.

"But until somebody proves it beyond the shadow of a doubt, I'm keeping it safe with me," Finn declared. "After all, I've paid the price for it."

"Very true," I said, offering Rory's uncle a kind smile. After all, the man had been through quite an ordeal since finding the gold on St. Patrick's Day night. I then offered my suggestion. "Mrs. Hinkle told me something interesting tonight, which was that Fred Landry seems to be improving. Since he's the key to all of this, I say that we pay him a visit tomorrow at the hospital."

"Great idea. You kids do that, I'll man the Beacon," Teddy informed us with a grin. He then added, "Hospitals give me the creeps. With so many people expiring in hospitals, I've always felt that they were ground zero for hauntings . . . if you believe in that sort of thing." Teddy apparently did. I then assured him that I'd still be in the bakery kitchen with him in the morning.

"I'm going to cry off on this one as well, I'm afraid," Niall informed us. "I second Teddy's remark about all the deaths that occur in hospitals. Besides, I have some business to attend to. Kennedy, luv, you are welcome to join them should you care to."

"Thank you for finally using my Christian name," she told him as a petulant smile touched her lips. "I believe that I will join them. I'm anxious to hear what Mr. Landry has to say regarding this marauding leprechaun. My hunch? Fred Landry was knee-deep in something he's now regretting. It should be an enlightening visit."

CHAPTER 28

Kennedy, with high expectations of an enlightening visit to the hospital, met Rory and me at the Beacon Bakeshop at ten thirty in the morning, a half hour later than planned. Although I'd been up since four a.m., baking up a storm with Teddy in an effort to fill our bakery cases, I knew that anything before nine o'clock was early for Kennedy, especially since, as she claimed, she was on vacation. That was fine with me. I honestly couldn't have left any sooner with the way the morning had gone in the bakeshop. After the success of last night's crowded town hall meeting, it seemed like everyone in attendance, and then some, planned to continue the fun at the Beacon. After all the free cookies and punch we'd provided, I welcomed the business. Also, if I was being honest, there was something comforting about the fellowship that had descended on the village during this highly unusual time. I was honored that the Beacon Bakeshop was the place to be, not only for a great cup of coffee, a delectable baked good, and the latest gossip, but as a welcoming business where our customers felt comfortable sharing a table and their thoughts with one another. It was no wonder that these strange sightings of the murdered leprechaun had captured the imagination of the village. Then too there was the fact that this same fellow had been linked to a brutal attack as well as hiding a pot of gold. Real gold. No one knew what to make of it, least of all the police.

Speaking of police, Sergeant Murdock had also come in for her morning coffee and sweet roll. "Congratulations, Bakewell," she had said with her usual lack of cheerfulness. "Heard that your town hall meeting last night generated results. Interesting. I'll have to keep that one in my back pocket. Although I doubt we'll have another infestation of leprechauns in the future, but you never know. We now have a real Irish gift shop and pub in town." Although her wispy blond bangs hovered just above her eye lids, I got the feeling that she had pointedly arched a brow at me regarding the Blarney Stone. Just in case I had failed to catch her meaning, she whispered, "I haven't figured out what Finn's involvement is in all of this just yet. Let's just say, he's still on my radar. *Blip. Blip. Blip.* If you know something, I'm counting on you to do the right thing."

"*Ugh!*" The noise escaped me like a punch to the stomach. Murdock had that kind of effect on me. For a woman, I found her awfully intimidating. It was obviously why she was so good at her job. "I know nothing!" I blurted, like a cornered criminal.

"What about his pretty daughter, Colleen, and her relationship with McAllister, what do you know about them?"

"Not much. It's cute. They're cute. She likes him." I shot out the comments at her like a succession of bullets from a pistol, only kinder, and quieter.

"And Ms. Kapoor?"

"My friend." *Duh!* I felt like I was on a game show for simpletons.

"No, Bakewell, how is she handling McAllister's new relationship?"

"Like you'd expect." Again, my obvious game show answer.

Murdock leaned across the counter. "I don't know what that means. But here's what I mean. While Ms. Kapoor is undoubtedly your friend, this sleepy little village seems to run smoother without her—for example, no murders. I'm not saying she's connected to any of this, but McAllister was finally able to concentrate on his job once again. A good thing. But now she's back, and I have the feeling he's cracking. Need I remind you how she destroyed him? In the force, we have a code. We watch out for one another."

I was surprised that the sergeant believed I could control the forces and whims of nature, aka Kennedy and Tuck. I was flattered, but the truth was, the heart wants what the heart wants—even in the face of mutual destruction. After all, my one takeaway from Greek mythology was Troy, Helen of Troy, and, of course, that awesome Trojan horse charade. But my point was that Troy was destroyed over love. It was history, ancient history, and humans aren't the best at learning from it. I shrugged and gave her my kindest smile. "Regarding Tuck and Kennedy, it's out of our hands. Regarding Finn and Colleen, they're at the Blarney Stone. If you have any dating suggestions for Colleen, or pressing questions for Finn, you can find them both there."

"Funny." She didn't smile but instead doubled down. "The only question I have for Finn, he refuses to answer." She was, of course, referring to the pot of gold. "That gold is evidence in this case."

I thought about that a moment as I handed her the latte Tom had just made, and the giant, gooey cinnamon roll Elizabeth had plated for her. "Regarding the law, I believe Finn is still under the finders-keepers rule. Has anyone come forward to claim the gold?" I took her unimpressed gaze to mean no.

"A man posing as a leprechaun was murdered, Bakewell. Finn is still a suspect. The gold he supposedly found is being regarded as evidence."

"Right," I said, placing my hands on the counter. "I saw the gold, so I can tell you it's real. But that's all I know. However, because you and I are friends . . ." Here I paused to see if she'd confirm my bold assumption. Crickets. Not even the ghost of a smile. Thwarted, but not defeated, I added, "If I find out anything else regarding the gold, I'll let you know."

"Thank you, Bakewell. Was that so hard?" Like a sluggish caterpillar on a chilly morning, her lips might or might not have curled slightly before she left the counter. In my mind, it was definitely a smile.

Kennedy, who could be difficult at times, was like a breath of fresh air as she swooped into the bakeshop, late as usual. She was wrapped in her gorgeous walking cape and had a snazzy black leather Gucci purse slung over her shoulder. Her black knee-high boots looked so perfect with her outfit that they sparked a tinge of jealousy in me. Mom would have applauded the look for sure. Kennedy was also carrying a beautiful flower arrangement. We had briefly talked about flowers for our hospital visit, and I was pleased to see that she had pulled through for us on that note. They were gorgeous.

Rory, seeing that she had finally arrived, stood up from the table he was sitting at, excused himself from the other gentlemen, and met her at the bakery counter. He glanced at his watch then looked at her. "Glad you could make it, PR."

"Nice to see you too, Hunts-a-Lot. Hold the flowers." She thrust them into his unsuspecting arms. He had no choice but to take them from her. "And, for the record, I'm running behind because we only have the one rental car, and Niall had to take me to Molly Butterfield's shop before dropping me off here. Lisa made these for me. Didn't she do a lovely job?" She wiggled her fingers in the direction of the flower arrangement. "They're just the thing to perk up a drab hospital room. But I was having a hard time leaving that shop without getting an earful about the amazing Finn O'Connor from Molly. Heavens knows why, but Molly seems infatuated with the man. My guess is that the old goat is keeping the gold to impress her."

"He's keeping the gold for now, because he found it," Rory told her in no uncertain terms.

She tilted her head, allowing her silky black hair to fall to the side like a curtain. The curtain righted,

and she offered, "That's fair. Now, are you two finally ready to go?"

Thanks to Teddy and his previous comment regarding hospitals, death, and ghosts, I had a little
more reverence for the critically ill when walking
through the main doors of Memorial Hospital. For
some, this building would be their last stop, and
that gave me pause. It also sent a shiver up my
spine as well. Hospitals weren't my favorite places,
but they were necessary. I also didn't know how I
felt about visiting a man, who'd recently been in a
coma since the Leprechaun Parade, purely to jog
his memory. It was only because we believed that
Fred Landry was key in solving this mystery that we
were here. If he was able, we needed him to tell us
what his relationship was to the other victim, the
leprechaun. There was always the possibility that
he was involved in something illegal, as Kennedy
believed. In that case, he likely wouldn't talk, at
least not to us. But those were the chances we were
taking.

Once at the hospital, we learned that Fred had
recently been moved from the ICU and was now
resting peacefully in a private room in a wing on
the third floor. Out of immediate danger, he still
required around-the-clock care.

Landing in the right section of the hospital, we
realized that the floor was a busy one. Machines
were beeping, buzzers were ringing, and there wasn't
a nurse to be found at the desk. There was a jum-
ble of various medical devices and equipment waiting in the hallways, and voices could be heard
coming from some of the rooms, likely from nurses

or other medical staff. I noticed an office behind the nurses' desk and decided to take a chance and poke my head in there. I found a younger woman busily working at a computer.

"We're here to see Fred Landry," I told her. "Can you direct us to his room?"

The woman stood. "Sure. I'm not a nurse but I can get one for you. This is a busy floor, and this hospital is woefully understaffed. That's a common problem today. I'm a hospital social worker," she explained, as she guided me out of the office and around the nurses' desk. "My job is to help patients transition from the hospital setting to their next point of care. Most of the patients on this floor go straight to a rehab center or receive at-home nursing care, some need assisted living. I've been assigned to Mr. Landry but haven't yet had the chance to meet his family. He just arrived on this floor late last night." She checked a page on a clipboard, shrugged her shoulders, and asked after our relationship to the patient.

"I was one of the first to find Fred after he'd been attacked," I told her. "I administered first aid at the scene before the ambulance got there. We are all naturally concerned and just want to check in on him, you know, to sit with him a bit?"

"You're not family?" We watched as she weighed this minor technicality.

"We're *like* family," Kennedy assured her, looking sincere. "And we've brought him flowers." She pointed to the lovely arrangement in the crook of Rory's arm. "Now, be a dear and point us to his room."

Without any further convincing, the girl glanced at the clipboard one last time. "Mr. Landry is in room 307. Doubtful he'll be awake, but you can sit with him for a few minutes. I'll make a note of it on here. I'm also going to ask that you be very quiet when you go in there. This is a quiet hall."

We thanked the social worker, assured her we'd be on our best behavior, and headed for the room. Once at the threshold of room 307, I gave a quiet knock before opening the door. "Mr. Landry?" I whispered. The room was dark and deathly still, a fact that sent the hair on the back of my neck on edge. The moment my eyes adjusted, I saw Mr. Landry's form on the bed, but I instantly knew something wasn't right. Rory, having the same feeling, thrust the flowers at Kennedy. In two strides he was beside the man, lifting the pillow that covered his face.

"Quick, Linds, find a nurse. He's not breathing!"

He wasn't breathing. Somebody had made sure of that. Mr. Landry was now dead. A fact which inspired Kennedy to drop the flowers and start screaming.

CHAPTER 29

"I don't understand what happened," the nurse said. Thanks to Kennedy, every nurse on the floor, and one doctor, were now crammed into room 307. While Kennedy had screamed, I had called the police. Rory had started CPR. But the doctor who'd taken control of the situation had declared that poor Fred Landry had moved far beyond the point of resuscitation. *Moved beyond*, he had said. *Far beyond.* Teddy's macabre remark about hospitals and death now seemed prophetic, curse the talented man! The crying nurse had brought me back to the problem at hand, namely that Fred Landry had been murdered, smothered to death with a pillow. "I had just checked on him," she blubbered, looking both horrified and a little guilty. Apparently, according to the chart at the end of the bed, *just* was more like half an hour ago. The lack of security and staffing on the floor was a cause for concern. In point of fact, we had basically walked right into Fred's room without any pushback. I was the person who had found

someone to help us and make a note of our visit.
Had we known which room was Fred's, we could
have made a visit without anyone knowing. Also, it
was discovered that the electrocardiogram monitoring him had been unplugged. For how long? I
wondered. Obviously, the person responsible for
monitoring the monitor, hadn't noticed. Sheesh!

To be fair, with Fred's attacker found dead on
the open dunes, it was unlikely that anyone thought
he was in danger. We now knew that assumption
had been wrong. Rory, Kennedy, and I had figured
that one out, the moment we saw the pillow over
his face and his lifeless body. Someone who'd been
afraid that Fred Landry might talk had made certain that wouldn't happen. We now knew, beyond
the shadow of a doubt, that there was a murderer
on the loose in Beacon Harbor, and it wasn't a leprechaun or Finnigan O'Connor.

"Tucker!" Kennedy cried, spying her handsome
ex-boyfriend walking through the door. She ran to
him, tears staining her face. Proving that he was
putty in her hands, the young officer held her with
a fierceness that belied all the pain she'd caused
him. The heart is a forgiving organ, I mused.
Sergeant Murdock would not be pleased.

"Tuck," I said, walking over to him. "Glad you're
here." I then took hold of Kennedy so that he
could get to work, and she wouldn't embarrass
herself further. After all, she'd come to Beacon
Harbor with another man. It was going to be a
long day for the young officer.

"We came to talk to Fred," I heard Rory telling
him, as Tuck was trying to come to terms with this
new crime scene. "Clare Hinkle told Lindsey last
night that Fred was recovering. We wanted to see if

he could tell us anything about the leprechaun who attacked him. We came in around eleven this morning and found him here, in his hospital bed, smothered to death with a pillow."

"I don't believe this," Tuck said. "I was planning to make a visit to Mr. Landry as well but got stuck at the station. I was interviewing Mayor Jeffers again. I didn't realize that Fred had been moved from the ICU."

Tuck slowly shook his head as he regarded the lifeless form. The doctor had begun shooing the nurses from the room, every nurse but the one assigned to Fred. "This is bad," Tuck said. Then, addressing the doctor, he added, "Call security. I'm going to need to take a statement from everyone working on this floor. Including you three who found him." This was directed at us. "If you haven't already done so, this floor is to be on lockdown immediately, meaning that no one enters or leaves without being cleared first. How can something like this occur in a hospital?" He looked crestfallen.

"In our defense, Officer," the doctor addressed him, "no one expected this to happen."

Finding Fred Landry murdered in his hospital bed had shaken all of us, particularly Kennedy. After all, she had cut her romantic ties with Tuck and had left Beacon Harbor last fall because of a murder. In some ways she had blamed herself for what happened during last Halloween. The experience had shaken her to the core, and she had needed time away to think about things. I hated to let scary Sergeant Murdock in my head, but I was afraid she was now renting space there. Kennedy was now back in the village and two men had been murdered. Of course, I knew that she had nothing to do with the murders, but I wasn't so convinced where Niall Fitzhugh was concerned.

After giving our statements to the police, and after Fred's family had been contacted, Rory, Kennedy, and I had checked out of the hospital and had driven back to the lighthouse. I prepared a quick lunch for us. Kennedy then went upstairs to take a nap in the guest bedroom I reserved for her. Rory had taken off for the Blarney Stone to break the news to his uncle and Colleen regarding Fred Landry. I was about to return to the bakeshop to do the same when I decided to spend some quality time in the backyard with Wellington first.

There was a reason that dogs were man's best friend. Dogs, I believed, were people pleasers by nature, at least Wellington was. After a romp in the backyard, he trotted right back to the back steps, where I was sitting. He then demanded his usual, an ear scratching, a belly rub, and a Beacon Bite, in that order. Appeased, he then plopped down beside me and listened as I whispered my fears to him, namely my suspicions regarding Niall Fitzhugh. The moment I whispered the name he lifted his head and twitched his ears. Welly was listening.

"Right?" I said. "Hear me out, Welly. Niall knew that we were going to the hospital, and he had a car. We hadn't told anybody else about our plans. It could be merely a coincidence, but Niall also has connections to the Blarney Stone through his textile business. Finn also mentioned seeing a leprechaun in Ireland once, when he was working at his pub. He thought the leprechaun, who we now know to be just a strange little man, was following him. It could be wild speculation, and I hope it is, but what if it's not?"

Welly put one of his saucer-sized paws on my leg in agreement. Maybe he just wanted another treat. But I was on a roll, so I continued. "What if the leprechaun was working for Niall? He was seen at the gas station the night of the leprechaun murder, but he still could have done the deed. Also, he dropped Kennedy off here, then supposedly went to the hotel, but he could have just as easily gone to the hospital instead. Then there's the floor security camera. According to Tuck, a couple of people were seen going into Fred's room after the nurse's last visit. An unidentified doctor, an unidentified aid, another nurse, and a wound-care technician. None of whom bothered to sign in. Tuck and Murdock are checking up on that now, but one of those people did the deed. Do you see what I mean? Niall could be the unidentified doctor . . . or even the nurse or technician." Welly licked my face in agreement. I gave him the Beacon Bite in my hand, and said, "Good. Now all I have to do is warn Kennedy again." I didn't know if I was brave enough for that quite yet. Besides, her fake name, Lillian Finch, was now off the table.

Welly had gone back into the lighthouse, and I had gone to the bakeshop to deliver the news about Fred Landry. As we locked and cleaned up the Beacon for the day, Wendy, Elizabeth, Alaina, and Ryan, my closers, voiced their thoughts and concerns regarding the events that had occurred over St. Patrick's Day. This new turn of events had us all on edge.

At some point while I was working, Kennedy had left with Niall. I didn't have the time nor the will to tell her about my new suspicions regarding him. She hadn't the time nor the will to talk about the incident that had occurred at the hospital, when she had thrown herself into the arms of the man she'd broken up with. I was left with the conclusion that there were just some things we weren't quite ready to talk about yet.

Exhausted, worried, and facing another early morning of baking, I went to bed right after dinner. Rory, after hearing my latest suspicions regarding Niall, agreed to give it some thought. He'd take Welly for a walk, then poke around on the internet before coming to bed. There was no reason to torture him with my early-to-bed, early-to-rise schedule.

As I lay in bed, begging for sleep to come, I couldn't help thinking about poor, defenseless Fred Landry. It was logical to assume that the person who'd killed the man dressed as a leprechaun was the same person who killed Fred Landry in the hospital. The leprechaun had taken a stab at it and had failed. Was that why he was murdered, his failure to kill Fred Landry? And why Fred? What was his involvement in all of this? He had a wife. Maybe she knew. I made a mental note to talk with her in the morning. Then there was Clare Hinkle. Did she know something? She worked with Fred, and so did others. That would have to be investigated as well. The list was growing. Then, just as I was about to drift off to sleep, the thought of gold popped into my mind and robbed me of it. Gold coins in this day and age? Why? Better yet, why bury them in the ground? Also, what were the chances of Finn finding a pot of gold on St. Patrick's Day? Was it irony, or was it some weird plan in a bigger scheme? I wish I knew, but the fact remained that Finn had put the gold somewhere and no one had come forward to claim it. Lucky Finnigan O'Connor.

CHAPTER 30

The fog was thick as I walked along the lake-shore. I could barely make out my hand in front of me, it was so oppressive, and yet I continued walking as if propelled by a force that was not my own. As I walked, I was overcome by a strange, surreal feeling. I felt that I was somewhere between heaven and earth, a quiet place bathed in a luminous blanket of fog. The notion was ridiculous. As I continued walking along the frozen, ice-speckled sand, a gust of wind came out of the west. It blew the fog landward, revealing a thin yellow ribbon in the distance. I didn't know what it was at first, but another gust came, and this time I knew where I was. I was at the crime scene where the leprechaun had been murdered.

The fog thinned, and I realized that I wasn't alone. Another person was standing in the middle of the crime scene, a bearded man, bent in reflection and smoking a pipe. Although I'd never met this person, I instantly knew who he was. The old-fashioned clothing gave him away—from the boxy blue wool coat with the double row of gold buttons and the matching blue pants, to the white starched collar poking above a thick cable-knit sweater. Yet the sight of the regulation wool cap, also of dark blue, with a black visor and the lighthouse insignia embroidered on it (a white lighthouse surrounded by a wreath of gold laurel) left no room for question. I was standing on the foggy shoreline with my lighthouse ghost, Captain Willy Riggs. For some reason, the thought didn't scare me as it should have.

"Captain Willy?" I ventured. At the sound of his name, his head came up and he looked at me with a direct, unnerving gaze.

"A right mess, this is," he stated, referring to the bloodstains on the sand. Dumbfounded, I nodded. He continued. "I've been trying to reach you, send a message, but yours is a busy life."

I acknowledge this with a self-conscious smile. "True, but what are you doing out here?" I was puzzled by the sight of him. The captain's domain was the lightroom. That was where he made his presence known to me. Why was he on the beach?

"Whenever there's trouble afoot, I take notice. It's my job. Yours too. This one is very curious indeed."

"Do you know something about this murder?" I asked, feeling hopeful. Honestly, I'd take all the help I could get, even from the lighthouse ghost.

He shook his head. "To find the who, you must focus on the *what*," he mysteriously offered.

"The *what*?" I repeated. Yet the moment I uttered the words, I knew what he meant. It popped into my mind with the suddenness of a kernel of popcorn. "The gold," I uttered. "I need to focus on the gold."

With his pipe clenched between his teeth, he tapped his forefinger on his cap, indicating that I'd gotten his meaning. For some reason it made me feel proud, special. I then thought to ask, "Are you a ghost?"

The visor on his hat moved from side-to-side, ever so slightly. "Not here."

"But . . . you are a ghost, aren't you? That's why you're still at the lighthouse. I hear your footsteps on the stairs; I smell your pipe. You're the one who turns on the light that's not there anymore—to warn us. How is that possible?"

After another puff on his pipe, he removed it and looked at me. "You ask so many questions. My answers won't make a lick of sense, but I will give you one. Like an anchor the size of a fishhook dangling from the bow of the largest ocean liner, only a wee fragment of my soul remains in the gray space, hooked to my past life and my earthly duty at the lighthouse. I can see that hook now, thanks to you. I could haul her aboard any moment and cast off for good, but I leave it. I chose to leave it. Because you have accepted it, and I may still be of some service here."

"Please don't stay on my account," I told him sincerely. "You should, you know, walk toward the light. Enter into heaven. Enjoy eternity." I didn't want the guilt of having his ghost hanging around the lighthouse because of me.

He smiled kindly. "A soul cannot be trapped here. But sometimes, due to many reasons, a fragment—a wee hook—can remain. Those dunderheads with your dark-haired friend nearly unhooked me." He gave a deprecatory shake of his head. "I like your friend. Keep the dunderheads away. Now focus on the *what*, Lindsey Bakewell." That's when the beeping began.

My eyes flew open with a start and I fought to focus in the darkness. I honestly thought I was awake, but I must have been sleeping. I was in my bedroom, in my bed, with the lingering scent of pipe smoke still in the air. My alarm was going off, and Welly was stirring. A moment later he was beside the bed. In the darkness, his large head resembled that of a grizzly bear waking from a long winter slumber. To Wellington, my early alarm meant a romp in the backyard, or a walk along the shoreline, followed by a dental chew and a string of treats. Mornings were the best part of the day, according to Welly's swishing tail. I turned off my alarm and flopped back on my pillow, fighting to recall the fading dream. I had seen the captain. This was a first, and I didn't know what to make of it. He had come to deliver a message, only I was having a hard time trying to remember what it was. I let out a soft groan in frustration, kissed Rory on the cheek, then slipped out of bed. It wasn't until I was in the shower that I remembered the point of the captain's dreamscape visit. Gold. I needed to focus on the gold!

After another fruitful day at the Beacon, and after yet more discussion over the two murders that had occurred, including Finn's pot of gold, I finally got the time to give my parents a call. After my strange, haunted dream, I couldn't stop thinking about the gold. I really wanted to pick my dad's brain on the subject; for example, what investment strategy would favor hoarding pots of gold over, let's say, blue chip stocks, real estate, annuities, high interest CDs, or even municipal bonds? Although we both had prosperous Wall Street careers, mine arguably shorter than his, gold coins, as an investment, wasn't my forte. Dad would have more knowledge on the subject and would hopefully be able to give me some direction. Since they were in Maui and there was a six-hour time difference between us, I felt it was safe calling after four p.m. Michigan time.

"Lindsey, I'm so glad you called us," Mom said. Since I was Facetiming them, I could tell that Mom had been poolside, sipping fresh pineapple juice while lounging in the sun. She was wearing an adorable Hawaiian-style wrap over her swimsuit. I was envious of her tan. "We've been so worried about you and everyone there! I received a text from Betty yesterday. She told us that Fred Landry was murdered right in the hospital. You, Rory, and Kennedy had gone to visit him! I don't know what's going on, but that charming little village isn't safe anymore. You should close the bakeshop for a couple of weeks and come to Maui with Rory until things blow over."

Dear heavens, I was tempted.

"I'd love to, Mom. Really, I would, but I'm kinda in the middle of things here. Is Dad around?"

After another five minutes of small talk with Mom, Dad finally came to the phone. We chatted for a moment and then I posed my question to him.

"Storing gold coins in a pot buried in the ground is highly risky. We're in the realm of pirates and leprechauns, I'm afraid," he said with a chuckle. "Now, as far as gold is concerned, most people who invest in gold do so to diversify their assets and to protect their wealth from the often-volatile nature of the stock market. In other words, it can be a safe place to park money."

"Thanks, Dad, but I'm well aware of those reasons. Can you think of any other?"

"Well, there is another advantage, and in today's climate it's becoming more important than ever. Simply put, buying physical gold is an off-the-grid investment, meaning that it can't be tracked electronically, like money or other bank-held investments. Of course, there are some rules in place around this, mainly to avoid large-scale money laundering. In this case the gold isn't tracked per se, but the money is. Any cash purchase larger than ten thousand dollars is required by law to be reported to the government. Any gold purchased with cash that is under that amount gets a pass. One thing to note is that there's no way to track multiple cash purchases that fall below that threshold. Regarding gold, Lindsey, there is one more thing to note, which is that investing in gold in the US is also subject to the whims of the government. Take the Gold Reserve Act of 1934, for example, when the government made it illegal for citizens to hoard gold."

I knew Dad could go on all day about gold and investing, but he had already answered my question.

"There are some who believe wide-scale gold

confiscation could still happen," he continued, "but it's doubtful. Now, regarding this pot of gold, my best guess is—"

"Money laundering," I finished for him. "It's hard to believe something like that would happen in a place like Beacon Harbor, but now, with all you've told me, it seems likely. What better way to hide stolen money than by converting it into gold coins and squirreling it away where no one can find it. Either that or leprechauns are real. Thanks, Dad," I told him. "Love you both." I hung up as thoughts of gold swirled in my head.

CHAPTER 31

I was just about to call Rory with my discovery regarding the gold when he came bursting through the back door of the lighthouse. One look at his face and I could tell he was fuming about something.

"What is it?" I asked, jumping up from the kitchen table. "What's happened?"

"My house," he said, his face flushing red with anger. "Someone broke in while I was at the Blarney Stone, and they've turned the place over. It's been ransacked, Linds." The pain of that statement flashed across his face, swiftly replaced by a stoic yet calculating form of resilience. That was the military man in him. Personally, just thinking about his beautiful log home, which we often referred to as "a cabin," being violated in such a way made me both furious and heartbroken. In two strides my arms were around him, offering what moral support I could.

"Why would somebody do . . . ?" The words were barely out of my mouth when I realized that I already knew why. "The gold!" I blurted. Or the *what*, as Captain Willy had called it in my dream. The murderer was out there and now they were looking for the gold. Everyone knew that Finn had it, but nobody knew where he'd hidden it.

"Yes, the gold, damn Finn." Rory took a deep breath to quell his rising anger, making my arms expand with his broad chest. I gave one last squeeze of support and released him. "They broke a window to get in," he explained. "I had just left the Blarney Stone and was on my way to pick you up for dinner when I decided to go back to the cabin first and check on things there. I was running early." He shrugged. "Whoever broke in knew that Finn and Colleen would be at the Blarney Stone. It's the brazenness of the violation," he added, clenching his jaw in frustration. "Also, whoever did this had the audacity to sprinkle glitter all over my hardwood floors. Glitter!" he added again. If the ransacking wasn't enough, the glitter really kicked him over the edge.

"I'm so sorry, Rory. Why the glitter? Do you think there's another leprechaun out there?"

He shook his head. "Leprechauns aren't real, Linds. Like I said earlier, either the glitter is this person's calling card or whoever did this just wanted to tick me off—which they did!"

"Do you know if they found the gold?" I thought to ask.

"Hard to say. I called the police immediately, then Colleen. She's back at the cabin now sorting things out with the police. I didn't want to tell you over the phone. Finn is still at the pub with Bailey, closing it down for the night. Damn the man and his foolish beliefs," he uttered, pressing his eyes shut and causing a vein to appear on his forehead. Rory was an expert at handling stress, but this was a step too far for him, and I didn't blame him. "I told him to give up the gold, but he wouldn't listen to me or even Murdock. He thinks it's his. But it's not his, is it?"

"No," I agreed. "I suppose at this point only Finn can tell us if whoever it was that broke into your house found the gold. As for dinner, we can order some pizza and help clean up the mess. I'll give Kennedy a call. She and Niall can help too."

"Thanks," he said. "But I'm worried about Finn. If he still has the gold, he's going to need to turn it in before something else bad happens. Whoever is behind all this, they've broken into my home, next it'll be the Blarney Stone."

"I agree. Tuck is aware of this as well, correct?" I asked.

"He is. That poor man is having one heck of a day. I've volunteered to help him with a stakeout tonight if one is still needed."

Then, thinking of Tuck, another thought hit me. "Was Niall in the pub by any chance today?"

Rory furrowed his brows. "No. I assumed he was with Kennedy, but we'll have to check to be sure. I know you're still suspicious of him, but there's nothing concrete linking him to the murders or the break-in at my cabin."

"I realize that, but I don't trust him. I suppose it could just be that I don't want to see Kennedy get hurt."

"Regarding Niall, the jury's still out. Regarding Kennedy, she's an adult. She's made choices. Not

great ones, but they're hers. Besides, we have plans
with them for dinner tonight, which you're going
to have to cancel."

"It's pizza at the cabin tonight, with a side of
garbage bags. Not sure if it's their scene, but I'll
ask." For the first time since arriving at the lighthouse, Rory grinned. I was about to phone Kennedy with this new change of plans when Rory's
phone rang.

"What?" he said in a low voice that was filled
with concern. The sound of it sent shivers of fear
down my spine. Rory listened to the voice on the
other end a while longer before asking, "Are you
okay? Did you call the police? Stay right there.
We're on our way."

"What is it?" I asked, filling with dread.

"Uncle Finn. He's at the Blarney Stone with
Bailey waiting for the police. He was just about to
lock up for the night when he realized that his
SUV had been broken into. The passenger-side
window has been smashed and the vehicle has
been turned over. Like my cabin, he was disturbed
to find that glitter had been dumped all over the
front seats and the floormats."

"Not the glitter again," I breathed. "This leprechaun murderer is a real psycho."

He gave a slight nod at this then continued.
"Uncle Finn doesn't believe anything was taken,
but the violation has shaken him. He told me that
he thinks someone is still watching him."

"Good heavens!" I exclaimed, grabbing my coat
off the hook. I took Welly's leash as well. My
nerves were raging and there was no way I was
going to leave him behind with a glitter-sprinkling

killer on the loose. As we left the lighthouse, heading for Rory's truck, I said, "The gold. Finn still has the gold!"

"Indeed, he does, and until he hands it over to the police, he's likely to be the target of more mischief."

CHAPTER 32

Finnigan O'Connor, beguiled by drink and leprechaun lore, had foolishly thought that he'd tricked a real leprechaun into giving up his pot of gold. It made sense to him, a grown man. In fact, he had felt so vindicated by his clever and stealthy actions on St. Pat's Day night, that he had been determined to keep his treasure. But if leprechaun lore had taught Finn anything, it was that leprechauns do not give up their treasure so easily. They are considered roguish tricksters by nature, he'd told us, and they delight in thwarting humans. They would go to any lengths to protect their treasure, including but not limited to break-ins and pesky glitter.

"Thank heavens this person didn't break into the Blarney Stone while you were in there, Da." We were back at Rory's log home, eating pizza while contemplating the mess.

"I had Bailey with me," Finn remarked, fondly petting the dog that slept beside his chair. "And maybe they did too. Bailey was making quite a racket while I was cleaning the pub." He laid a finger beside his right eye. "She saw the wee devil," he informed us.

"If not for dear Bailey you might be dead, Da." Colleen cast him a weary look before taking another bite of her pizza.

"They want their treasure back," he said matter-of-factly. Once the initial anger regarding his SUV had subsided, Finn was back on the leprechaun wagon. "I would too, but they cannot have it."

"Excuse me, Uncle," Rory butted in, looking miffed, and rightly so, "but we're not dealing with leprechauns here and we never have been. We're dealing with a murderer, maybe a few of them. We're in the middle of something bigger and darker than leprechaun gold."

"Can you prove that 'tis not a leprechaun, then? Because I rather think it is." Uncle Finn placed his hands on the table and leaned in, issuing a challenge.

Personally, I found it unbelievable that Finn was still sticking to his story and his gold. I sat at the table next to Rory, silently eating my pizza. Welly was lying next to my chair because I was slipping him slices of pepperoni as I watched the drama unfold.

"*Ahem.*" Niall loudly cleared his throat, breaking the tension. He and Kennedy had come directly to Rory's cabin the moment they had heard the news. To Niall's credit, Kennedy said he'd spent the afternoon with her, shopping in Downtown Traverse City. We had planned to have dinner together at the Moose, but that plan was put on hold for the time being. Niall continued. "I might be able to shed some light on the matter for him."

Niall graced the table with a patronizing grin before continuing. "I've spent a fair amount of time on the Emerald Isle myself, and know a thing or two about leprechaun tales, Finn. The entire point of the leprechaun fable is to warn children against get-rich-quick schemes, and from taking what doesn't belong to them. Not only have you missed the point of the fable, but you took someone's gold and refuse to turn it in to the authorities. Look around you. Look at this mess. How do you not see this?" he asked the older man. "You are not a child, Finn. You are a grown man with a lovely daughter. Your actions have harmed this cabin and your vehicle. What other price will you pay for this stupid gold?"

"Ach," Finn exhaled, as if punched in the gullet. "When ye put it like that, man, I feel shamed. Truly shamed, I do." Finn took a deep breath then hung his head. After a moment of reflection, he decided to confess his secrets.

"On that fateful night, I saw a leprechaun," he told us, pointing to his eyes again. In Finn's defense, there was overwhelming evidence to support his statement. "But in here," he continued, pointing to his head, "I knew that leprechauns did not exist. Sure, I enjoy spinnin' tales for the youngsters. Adults too. Everyone loves a good tale. And there's a possibility, just a wee possibility, that the tales are true. As I've explained, I had a rough go of it in Ireland these past few years. I came to America after me own American dream, like me sister once did long ago, rest her soul." Finn smiled at Rory as he said this, tugging on my own heartstrings a little. "Then, when I found the gold the very night of the Blarney Stone's grand opening, I could barely believe me own eyes. What a grand omen it was! Holding it in me hands affirmed that dream—affirmed why I had come here to begin with. I thought to meself, I am here with me beautiful daughter, in this lovely wee village, running a gift shop and a small pub. Life is good. With this gold it will be glorious. Dear Colleen deserves that much." Finn folded his hands on the table and cast his daughter a loving smile. "You see 'tis not a crime to believe in leprechauns, m'dear. I was so afraid of failure that believing in them was easier than believing in meself."

"Oh, Da," Colleen uttered and gave him a hug.

"Rory, m'boy," Finn said, looking at his nephew, "I'm ready to turn the gold over to the authorities."

The next morning, while I was busy running the Beacon with my crew, Rory took Finn to the police station to deliver the gold. After the harrowing day we'd had, I was very grateful Finn had finally been made to see reason. As Kennedy reminded me, Finn's about-face regarding the gold had been Niall's doing.

"I know he takes a little getting used to," she said, leaning a hip against the bakery counter, "but he means well."

Tom placed her latte and Niall's espresso on the tray I'd set on the counter and cast her one of his charming grins. I had just put two warmed spinach-and-bacon quiches on two bright red plates and was getting the two chocolate chip scones ready that she'd ordered. Being a good friend, I warmed those up as well without her asking. We were nearing the last week of March. The

first day of spring had come and gone. In my opinion everyone in Michigan deserved a chocolate
chip scone for making it through the winter.

"Does he . . . mean well?" I asked. I cast a quick
glance at the man in question. Niall was oblivious,
sitting at a café table near the window while reading a local newspaper. I lowered my voice, adding,
"I'm still not convinced."

"Oh no. We're not going through this again,"
Kennedy seethed. "The last time you cast suspicion on my boyfriend, you had me so scared that I
had to hide behind the brave face of Lillian Finch.
Thanks to you, she's now dead. And no thanks to
Hunts-a-Lot, I'm now referred to as PR. You made
a fool out of me, Lindsey, darling. I won't let it
happen again."

"Here's your scones." I transferred them from
the warming plate to the awaiting ones, threw away
the disposable food prep glove, and hiss-whispered,
"Where was he on Wednesday morning when we
were driving to the hospital?"

"Back at the hotel, doing business," she hissed-
whispered back at me. "When Niall picked me up
after my nap at the lighthouse, I was still so shaken
that I had to go shopping. It was the only thing that
could console me after finding that poor man dead
in his hospital bed after the daylights had been
snuffed out of him by a pillow. The fact that Niall
came with me speaks volumes on his devotion.
Men, as a rule, hate shopping."

"He's the very soul of devotion," I said in a
mocking tone. "He told you that he was at the
hotel, but you don't know that for sure."

"I know what you're thinking," she sneered.
"You think he dropped me off here then drove to

the hospital to murder a man he's never met. That makes so much sense, darling. I'll have to mark it on my calendar and make a note to consider it. But for now, I'd like to eat my breakfast in peace with my older, wealthy, and worldly boyfriend. I can't help that you're attracted to the Paul Bunyan type—a burly man who has a week's worth of flannel shirts hanging in his closet next to his ax collection, and who thinks the height of romance is bringing you dead fish to clean and cook for him." Her face was contorted with anger as she flung the insult at me. I was steaming mad as well. Kennedy and I didn't fight often, but when we did, we knew how to twist the knife, so to speak. Kennedy picked up the tray and was about to walk away when she offered one last parting remark. "It took a lot for me to come back here, Linds. Don't make me regret it."

I turned from the counter and headed for the safety of the kitchen as tears of anger burned behind my eyes. *Stupid*, I thought, wiping the tears away with my fingertips. Wendy was working at the counter. I cast her an apologetic smile. As if reading my mind, she smiled back, dusted off her hands, and headed to the café. I was alone with my thoughts, and they weren't happy ones. It was so stupid of me to confront Kennedy again, I thought. But I couldn't help it. She was my friend, and I was concerned . . . or was I just mourning the death of her relationship with Tuck? Those had been such good days for us in Beacon Harbor, I thought as I plucked two pounds of butter from the walk-in. As I began working on a batch of chocolate chip cookie dough, I realized how much I missed her. Niall lived in London. Ken would go back there with him, where her family lived, where she belonged. We'd call each other from time to time, exchange Christmas cards, and Rory and I would visit once a year, when we could. Growing up was hard.

Kennedy trusted Niall, and it was time for me to shut up on the matter. Besides, I needed to focus my energies on the things that I could control, namely discovering the source of the gold, and bringing a murderer to justice.

CHAPTER 33

It had been a long day, one which made me realize how much I needed a break from the world. After making twelve dozen gooey chocolate chip cookies at the bakeshop, and after eating half a dozen myself in an effort to overcome my self-pity, I felt ready once again to face the world. I then closed the Beacon Bakeshop for the day, took Welly for a long walk along the lakeshore, then went to my personal kitchen to cook a private dinner for Rory and me. Rory, I was sure, was ready to escape as well, having taken his uncle and the pot of gold to the police station, after which he had to be back at his cabin so the window company could replace the window the intruder had broken. He was also cleaning up the last of the mess that had been left there, taking care to look for any clue as to who had done the deed. Colleen and Finn were staying at the lighthouse tonight, but each had their own dinner plans.

I couldn't believe it was Friday already. An entire week had passed since the Leprechaun Parade, and it felt like we were still spinning our wheels regarding the murderers. I looked in the fridge and gave half a thought to making a healthy meal. However, all I really wanted was comfort food. Since I had some thinly sliced corned beef in the fridge, I decided to make Reuben sandwiches for us, with a side of a kosher dill pickle, a bag of thick, crispy kettle-style potato chips, and a plate of freshly made chocolate chip cookies for dessert. Gooey, crunchy, savory, tangy, salty, sweet—all the sensations my tastebuds adored were there, making it the perfect meal to end a stressful week. In my opinion there was no better mood-lifter than a plate of fresh-from-the-oven chocolate chip cookies, followed by a gooey grilled sandwich. Maybe the sandwich should come first, but did it really matter?

After feeding Welly, I took out a loaf of marbled rye, the corned beef, a jar of sauerkraut, four slices of Swiss cheese, a bottle of thousand island dressing, and butter for grilling. As I heated up the pan, I spread the dressing on all four slices of bread. That way one side of the sandwich wouldn't be overloaded with dressing, which was an important part of the sandwich. I then began layering my sandwiches with a slice of cheese, a healthy amount of corned beef, sauerkraut, another slice of cheese, and then topped each with the second slice of bread. Just before I grilled the sandwiches I sent Rory a text, letting him know that dinner would be ready in five minutes.

As expected, Rory was starving and fawned over the simple dinner, grabbing a warm chocolate chip cookie off the tray to tide him over until we climbed the light-tower stairs. Once there, I turned on the heater, put a white tablecloth on the little table between our chairs, then lit some candles. I then set down the plates, put the plate of cookies between us, and poured two glasses of wine.

"Honestly," Rory began, lifting his wineglass, "this place is far better than any restaurant that I've ever been to, and with a view that's hard to beat, even at night."

"I agree," I said, looking out over the dark lake. It was a clear night with patchy, fast-moving clouds. The view from the lightroom was unsurpassed. "However," I added, after clinking his glass, "when eating here one of us has to make the dinner, then we have to haul it up three flights of narrow, circular stairs. But it's worth it." I took a sip of the wine and flashed him a smile.

Over our romantic dinner of Reuben sandwiches and chips, I couldn't help telling him about my suspicion of Niall and my fight with Kennedy. Rory patiently listened as I babbled on. One of the things I loved about him was that he was a good listener and refrained from adding any of his usual snide comments because he knew, deep down, what Kennedy's friendship meant to me.

"She'll come around," he said. "And Niall stays on our suspect board until we can firmly rule him out. Your suspicions of him may be proven yet, in which case Kennedy will thank you profusely. Although it pains me to say it, I don't think a little squabble over a man is going to erase your years of friendship. Now, I have something to tell you, and it's about Finn's gold."

Rory had used military precaution when accompanying Finn as he retrieved the pot of gold, then drove him to the police station where he handed his coveted pot over to Sergeant Murdock.

"Where was the gold hidden?" I asked. Rory shook his head in an expression to suggest idiocy. "In my shed . . . in the wheelbarrow, which he covered with straw. As if to suggest that carting around straw is something I do."

"You've got to be kidding me!" A laugh escaped me as I pictured Finn hiding his gold. "Someone ransacked your house when all they really needed to do was check your shed?" He nodded. "We're obviously not dealing with the top brass here, which is to our advantage."

Rory then told me that once the gold was safely in the hands of the police, the press had been called, and Finn was interviewed. Sergeant Murdock had also given a statement, asking anyone with knowledge of this gold to come forward. It was done in an effort to spread the word that Finn no longer had the gold, and that the matter was now in the hands of the police.

"Finn never told them where he found the gold in the first place. The sly old devil told the sergeant that he didn't want to anger the leprechauns."

"Murdock must have been furious." His nod confirmed my suspicions.

"And here's something else. While heading over to the high school today for a quick meeting with Greg Smith, I saw another rainbow flag, just like the one at the war memorial on the beach." Rory, as a former Navy SEAL and PADI diver, (Professional Association of Diving Instructors) was getting ready to start teaching scuba diving certification classes at the pool facilities in the high school, having teamed up with the athletic director, Greg Smith. Teaching scuba was his passion, and the classes were offered through his aquatic adventure center that would open in the late spring.

Noting the look in his eyes, I sat up a little higher. "Exactly the same?"

"Exactly."

"What are you thinking, Campbell?"

"You know what I'm thinking, Bakewell. I have a shovel in my truck. Grab your coat and a flashlight."

In a matter of moments, and with excitement coursing through my veins, Rory, Welly, and I drove to this new location where another St. Patrick's Day rainbow flag had been hoisted up a flagpole next to the American flag. As Rory pulled into the parking lot of the baseball fields near the elementary school, I cast him a puzzled look.

"I don't see it."

"It's right by the concession stand, in the middle of these fields. Didn't you see it from the road? There's a spotlight on it."

"Guess I missed it. Although I must admit that this is an odd place to hide a pot of gold."

He grinned and slung the shovel over his shoulder with the air of a roguish gravedigger. "So was the memorial at the public beach. It's worth a look." Welly agreed, although his palpable excitement for our nocturnal dealings had more to do with the fact that he had landed in a place with a world of new scents to explore.

With flashlights on, we made our way to the refreshment stand. Once there I was surprised to find another large memorial stone placed at the foot of the flagpoles, this one honoring the man who had bequeathed the land the baseball fields had been built on. Feeling a bit like a gravedigger

myself, I held the flashlight as Rory set about removing the heavy stone. The moment the stone
had been shifted, I inhaled.

"I don't believe it," I uttered as Rory pulled out
another heavy pot covered with a dirty cloth. The
moment he lifted the cloth, the beam from my
flashlight illuminated the gold coins. Rory quickly
covered it again.

"What are the odds?" he asked.

"A billion to one," I answered. "We're definitely
not dealing with a normal criminal." Rory agreed.
I then added, "Remember Finn saying that he saw
the leprechaun he was following adding coins to
the pot—as if he was squirreling the money away,
literally?"

"I do," Rory said. He was in the process of returning the memorial stone. This new pot of gold
was coming with us. "Which means that whoever is
behind this has been hiding these coins for some
time. I wonder how many more pots are hidden in
this town?" He smoothed the dirt around the
stone, gave Welly, who believed he was helping
him, a pat on the head, and stood. "Crazy as this
sounds, Linds, I can't fault Uncle Finn for believing that this is the work of a leprechaun." He ran
his fingers through his hair, and asked, "According
to the fables, leprechauns do this sort of thing."

I shook my head, then reached beneath the
dirty cloth and picked up one of the coins from
the pot. I inspected it closely under the beam of
my flashlight. "This is a one-ounce gold American
Buffalo coin," I said, perplexed. I had never taken
a close look at the gold in Finn's pot. I then reached
for another coin, this time pulling one from deeper
in the pot. "This is a one-ounce gold South African

Krugerrand. Each one of these coins, Rory, is valued at over two-thousand dollars today. Of course, the value of gold fluctuates with the market."

"Investment coins?" he asked, looking intrigued.

"Or, as my dad alluded to, an untraceable way to park money. What we're dealing with here is a very wily, risk-taking, irreverent, money-laundering leprechaun, who's now dead. I say irreverent, because whoever he was working for, or stole this from, obviously didn't know where he'd hidden their money. Since the dates on these two coins are within the past ten years, it's hard to say exactly how long this has been hidden here. Also, due to the very public nature of his hidey-holes, it kind of has the feeling as if Mr. Leprechaun was mocking whoever he was working with. Finn really is quite lucky, you know. Thanks to his ardent belief in leprechauns and his passion for green beer on St. Patrick's Day, he found this gold, which could have sat beneath the ground for another hundred or so years."

Rory ruminated over that a moment. "The poor man died thinking he was taking his secret to the grave with him. Someone must have double-crossed him."

I agreed. "Thanks to Uncle Finn and your sharp eyes, we now have the key to his quirky map. Mr. Leprechaun was hiding his gold under the St. Patrick's Day flags, but why?"

"I have no idea. But we have another pot of gold," he offered, cradling this new pot in his arms as we walked back to the truck. I was carrying the shovel this time. Once in the truck, Rory turned to me. "Babe, we need to take this gold to the police station tomorrow morning, but let's not tell Murdock where we found it."

"She'll be flaming mad, Rory." That was likely an understatement. I wondered if she'd have the power to throw us in jail for that.

"Let her be mad," he said, turning onto the road. "We've unlocked the key to finding the gold, but we don't know how many flags are still out there, or who put them up. Remember, two men died because of this gold. One man was hiding it, and the other, Fred Landry, was attacked by him, then finished off by another. Let Murdock concentrate on the murders. We need to figure out what Fred Landry's role in this was, and who put up those flags."

CHAPTER 34

While Rory took this new pot of gold to the police station, one we hadn't told anyone else about, my job was to figure out who was responsible for hanging the decorative flags around town, particularly the St. Patrick's Day flags under which two pots of gold had been buried. Was there a connection between the flag-hoister and the gold hoarder? I didn't know, but it needed investigating. Lucky for me, the one person who really had her finger on the pulse of Beacon Harbor came to visit the bakeshop nearly every day. If anyone knew who was responsible for hanging decorative flags around town, it would be Betty Vanhoosen. And, lucky for me, the woman was like clockwork. The moment I saw her walking up the sidewalk, I asked Tom to get her latte ready.

"Good morning, Betty," I welcomed her the moment she came through the door. "Are you having the usual?" With Tom working on her latte, I was ready to reach for a large cinnamon roll when she stopped me.

"I'll have a latte," she confirmed, "but I'm going to try the tomato, basil, and caramelized onion quiche this morning. My slacks are getting a little tight and I think the change might be good. Best make that two. I'm going to take one to Bob. He went to his office early today."

As Tom handed Betty her latte, he asked, "Has the doc discovered the identity of the leprechaun yet?" Everyone in town was anxious to learn the truth. Every morning since the murder there'd been a sensational headline in the local paper. The front page of this morning's paper was all about Finn O'Connor, leprechaun hunter, and his pot of gold, which was now safely in the custody of the police. Due to this flurry of gold fever, Rory had been determined to keep this new pot of gold a secret.

Betty thanked Tom, picked up her latte, and took a sip before answering. "He's getting close. He's expecting to get the results of the DNA test back today. Hopefully, that will confirm his suspicion."

"Which is?" Alaina asked, handing Betty a bakery box that contained the two quiches she'd ordered.

"Whether or not he really was a leprechaun, dear. A grizzled little man dressed in green, with no identity, and carrying a shillelagh? To use Bob's own words, *This has been one for the books!*" Betty smiled at Alaina before casting her a cheeky wink. "Anyhow, Bob asked me to invite you and Rory to join us for dinner tonight at the Moose. Although I have great faith in Stacy Murdock, I know that you two seem to have more luck regarding murderers around here."

Betty's invitation was a welcome one. Doc Riggles was required to report his postmortem findings to the authorities, not to us. However, as Betty had hinted at, he would be happy to discuss his work over dinner. I jumped at the offer and thanked her. She was about to leave before I remembered the flags.

"By the way, Betty, do you, by any chance, know who's in charge of hanging those cute St. Patrick's Day flags around town?"

Betty grinned. "Aren't they darling? That would be Molly Butterfield. After all, she *is* the Beacon Harbor Welcoming Committee and the person in charge of the beautification committee."

Molly Butterfield. I honestly didn't know that she oversaw the beautification committee, but that made sense. Molly was a sweetheart. She was a gifted florist and had an eye for making things look pretty, beautiful even. Yet I couldn't quite picture her as the person behind the brutal murders. However, that wasn't saying much. I knew from personal experience that some of the nicest people harbored some of the darkest secrets. I didn't know much about Molly Butterfield other than she had taken a keen interest in Uncle Finn— right from the moment she'd met him. Molly would know about Finn's obsession with leprechauns, as most of us did. Molly had a connection to the decorative flags, but what was her connection to the gold, or the man dressed as a leprechaun? I honestly had no idea. Maybe they were working together? If Molly hung those rainbow flags, and if Mr. Leprechaun was using them

as a marker to hide their possibly ill-gotten gold,
then why didn't she just dig up the gold herself?
And why murder the leprechaun? Also, what was
her connection to Fred Landry? Nothing made
sense. Not much in this strange case did. There
was only one way to figure that out. I needed to
talk with her.

The moment Betty had left the bakeshop, I sent
Rory a text. He was still at the police station, pro-
tecting the secret of where we had found this new
pot of gold. We believed that the gold and the
St. Patrick's Day flags were connected and wanted
more time to investigate this theory. Rory felt that
keeping it a secret was important, no matter how
angry Murdock became. He would come to the
Beacon as soon as he could.

"Sorry, babe," Rory apologized, walking in just
before noon. I'd been anxious to talk with Molly
all morning. I stepped around the bakery counter
and met him at the coffee bar for a discreet welcoming kiss. "We're now officially on the sergeant's
list of disobedient civilians. She wants me to tell
you to cease and desist—to stop sticking our noses
in where they don't belong. The professionals will
handle it from here."

"She doesn't really believe we're going to stop,
does she? I mean, we found a pot of gold."

"She's not happy about that either. Although I
wouldn't tell her where we found it, I did explain
that we were following a hunch. By the way, Tuck is
going to swing by after work and join us for dinner
with Betty and Bob. Did you know he and Colleen
had a date last night?"

"*Really?* I was not aware of that. Thanks for the
update, Hunts-a-Lot."

Both Rory and I turned at the sound of the familiar voice, only to find Kennedy standing right beside us.

"What are you doing here?" I asked her, trying hard not to sound accusatory.

"I was bored, so I thought I'd swing by. It is alright if I swing by, isn't it?"

"Of course," I replied to her questioning look. Kennedy was extending an olive branch, and I was eager to take it. "You're always welcome here, Ken. You know that. Is Niall with you?" I scanned the café as I asked this.

"He's still at the hotel. He's reading a book in the hotel library. It's the middle of the day. Who reads in the middle of the day?"

"Lots of people, I'd imagine," Rory told her. "Especially those on vacation. Aren't you two supposed to be on vacation?"

"We are," she said. "However, reading is rude when you're on vacation with someone else who doesn't want to read. I told him that I wanted to investigate—to find out more about this leprechaun. He told me to let the professionals handle it. He's also told me that I can be exhausting. Can you imagine that? Me, exhausting?"

I shook my head while Rory nodded, sending her a mixed message.

"I just wanted to do something fun, that's why I'm here. After that horror show at the hospital the other day, I want to get to the bottom of this. Also, Lindsey, darling, I'm sorry for blowing up at you yesterday. You were just being you, looking for a possible suspect in these murders. While I admit that I haven't been myself lately."

"Oh, Ken," I said, placing a hand over my heart.

"I'm sorry for voicing my concerns about Niall. I was off base. It's just that I care about you."

"I forgive you, darling. Regarding Niall, I don't think that man has the energy it takes to be a murderer."

Leaving the bakeshop in the capable hands of my employees, Rory, Kennedy, and I headed over to Butterfield's Floral Artistry. It felt like old times once again, and that made me very happy.

We hadn't noticed it before, but hanging next to the door of Butterfield's Floral Artistry was a St. Patrick's Day flag—the very kind that we were interested in. Molly Butterfield was arranging a bouquet on the back counter when we entered her beautiful shop. I had to admit, the place was a feast for the eyes, filled with floral decorations of every size and color. There was no doubt that Molly was an artist. I found it clever how she mixed fresh arrangements with artificial ones. That way they would last longer, I mused. However, she was known for her fresh flowers, which was obvious the moment we walked through the door. The aroma hit like a heavenly smack to the nose, an overwhelmingly beautiful floral scent of roses, lavender, lilies, and possibly the grapefruit-sized hydrangeas as well. I really didn't know which flowers I was smelling, but the scent was lovely.

"Lindsey, Rory, Kennedy." She smiled, turning from her flower arrangement. "What a surprise to see you here. What can I help you with?"

Not wanting to be obvious, we had discussed our plan before entering the flower shop. "We're here to order a flower arrangement for Fred Landry's widow," I told her, watching to see how she'd react to this. If I'd been expecting anything but sorrow, it didn't appear.

"What a terrible tragedy," she said and took out a pen. "I'm happy to help however I can. What did you have in mind?"

After ordering an arrangement to be sent to Fred's house, I then prodded, "We know that you're in charge of the welcome committee, Molly, but we had no idea that you were in charge of village beautification as well."

"True," she said, and raised her arms in the air. "You got me, although I don't like to toot my own horn regarding that. It's just that I believe little touches go a long way in a town like this. You wouldn't think so, but planting gardens in public spaces not only adds a splash of color, and makes the space feel special, but it also helps the local wildlife. Bees are attracted to the blossoms, and those sweet little hummingbirds can't get enough of daylilies, impatiens, hollyhocks, irises, and phlox. Hanging a basket of flowers outside a shop on Main Street does much the same, but also reinforces the image that we're a picturesque village."

"That's very kind of you," Kennedy told her sincerely.

Rory, not much of a flower enthusiast, was anxious to get to the point. "What about flags?"

"Well, Mr. Campbell, most establishments are responsible for hanging their own American flags."

"Right. True. But what about those bright-colored St. Patrick's Day flags that I've seen around town? You have one here. Who hangs those?"

Molly grinned, then thrust her hands into the air again. "Guilty as charged. Aren't they adorable? If you'd like to be part of our decorative flag program—for instance, to have one placed outside your new aquatic adventure center, or the bakery, Lindsey—I'll be happy to add you to the list. We send out a flyer every January. I guess you didn't read it?" Here she cast Rory a pointed look. Undoubtedly such a flyer had ended up in the trash. Mine as well. I had a guilty smile on my lips as she continued. "We order new ones nearly every month. They run from ten to fifteen dollars each, and we bill your account, depending on which one we choose. We supply the monthly flag. It's your responsibility to hang them on a flagpole."

"Interesting." Judging from the look of disinterest on his face, Rory wasn't about to put himself on that list. "However, what about the flags that aren't on private property?"

"Are you referring to the flags that fall under the jurisdiction of the village?" she asked, casting him a look of suspicion. "I don't know why you're concerned about those, but we order those as well. In fact, those were the first flags we ordered. It was only after getting so many comments on those holiday flags that we opened it up to the community."

"Do you hang those flags?" I asked.

"Actually, you should probably talk with Lisa. As my assistant, I've put her in charge of our flag beautification program. She orders them and delivers them. Hanging them was never part of our program. Lisa," she called into the back before I could stop her. I believe we got the gist of the decorative flag program, or whatever it was called. "Do you have time to explain how the community decorative flag program works?"

A moment later, Lisa popped out of the back room with a lily tucked behind one ear, allowing the rest of her light brown hair to fall like curled ribbons to her shoulders. "Oh, hey," she said upon seeing us. "You have questions?" She looked puzzled. "It's pretty basic. If you want in, you just have to sign up on our website, or I can add you to the list. The Easter flags have already been ordered, but I can get you in the rotation for the Memorial Day flag." She looked hopeful.

"I'm good," Rory said, dashing her hopes. "Not much of a fan regarding decorative flags. That's Lindsey's department. She's the one who's been eyeing them."

"Sure have," I said, forcing a smile. "Sign me up." Kennedy, I noted, was biting her lip in an effort not to giggle.

"That's great, Lindsey." Lisa looked genuinely delighted. "Take my word for it, your customers are going to love it. It's what makes this job so much fun. Adding a touch of beauty to this place we call home."

I was officially on the list and had prepaid for a flag I didn't want, although I didn't have the heart to tell Lisa. I then asked her who hung the flags on village property.

Lisa smiled. "All I do is deliver them to the office manager of each building. Honestly, I'm not sure who hangs them, but I always smile when I see one of our decorative flags around the village."

I thanked Molly and Lisa for their time. We were about to head out the door when Molly addressed Rory.

"Rory, do be a dear and tell Finn that I'll be by

the cabin this evening. That handsome uncle of yours is a gem, and I never suspected him of any wrongdoing. If I did, we wouldn't have a dinner date tonight, would we?"

Tightly clenching his jaw, Rory pretended not to hear her and walked out the door.

Men, I mused. He was the one acting as if he'd just been roped into the flag-of-the-month-club, and not me. Sheesh!

CHAPTER 35

"I don't know what just happened back there, but I'm going to say that it looks like our leprechaun had a sense of humor regarding those decorative St. Patrick's Day flags. I believe he thought that he was being ironic. It must be that. I guess I don't pay much attention to decorative flags in general, but judging from the lack of them around town, it appears that not many shop owners are enrolled in the program. However, I can't believe that either Molly or Lisa is involved in this."

"I agree with Lindsey," Kennedy piped up from the back seat. "The only thing those two can be accused of is sabotaging their good works with unsightly flags. The only real piece of intel we discovered is that Rory's uncle is going on a date tonight with a middle-aged hottie—and that date is being held at his newly righted cabin. That's got to rankle, Hunts-a-Lot."

"I don't care about the date," Rory grumbled. "I don't much care that it's taking place in my cabin either. What rankles, if you must know, is the fact that Molly wanted me to deliver the message to him. That's a hard pass. Not going to happen on my watch. Finn's his own man and can handle his own affairs, regardless of how irresponsible he's being." I noticed that Rory's knuckles had turned white as he gripped the steering wheel.

"I doubt she meant anything by it," Kennedy offered. "She was just being cheeky. Finn's hook with the ladies is undoubtedly that sexy Irish accent of his. Remove the accent, and your uncle's merely a middle-aged drunk with a poetic soul and a passion for tweed."

"Not helping," Rory growled, keeping his focus on the road ahead. "But you're right. He's a novelty and he's taking advantage of it. He's also being highly irresponsible by dating while his life is in danger. The murderer is still out there. Just because he's turned in the gold doesn't mean he's off the hook. He found it in the first place. He knows where it was hidden. We know too, and we now believe there's more out there."

"What?" Kennedy breathed. "What do you mean by more out there?"

Rory, realizing his mistake, uttered an expletive. "Nothing. It's nothing."

"Don't tell me that you two found more gold under one of those stupid flags?"

There was no use lying. "We did," I confessed. "Last night. But we've turned it in to the police."

"I don't believe this. If there are two pots of gold, there's bound to be more out there," she reasoned.

"We know," Rory and I said in unison.

"Well, what are we doing here? We should be out trying to find more flags."

"This is exactly why we didn't want to tell you, Kennedy." Rory cast her a stern look in the rearview mirror. "And you need to promise to keep this a secret as well, until we've discovered who's behind this."

"Agreed. I understand," she said. "I only wish I had been there with you."

"Ken." I hooked my arm around the back of my seat to look at her. "You'll get the chance. I promise. We'll search together for more. But for now, we'd like to concentrate on figuring out who's behind the murders. Do you have to run back to the hotel, or would you be interested in talking to Fred's widow with me?"

"The widow. Definitely the widow."

Rory, who was going directly to the Blarney Stone to lay down some ground rules for his uncle regarding dating while the murderer was still at large, dropped Kennedy and me off at the Beacon first. Once there, I picked out a selection of our most delicious baked goods—including giant cinnamon rolls, pecan rolls, cherry and cheese Danish, chocolate chip scones, and six grasshopper brownies—and filled a bakery box for Mrs. Landry. I didn't think the shamrock sugar cookies were appropriate under the circumstances. Regarding the death of a loved one, words often failed, but a thoughtful bakery box was always appreciated. I was sorry to think that I didn't even know her first name.

After letting Welly out to do his business, and after a quick call to Betty for an address and a name, Kennedy and I drove three miles out to the immaculate, cottage-style home of Lottie Landry.

"Mrs. Landry?" I said the moment a woman opened the green front door. The woman nodded, allowing Kennedy and me to introduce ourselves.

"I know who you are, Lindsey," the woman said, struggling to produce a welcome smile. Lottie was a petite woman in her late forties, with sad brown eyes and thick hair of the same color that was halfway to gray. "Won't you come in? Please excuse the mess. As you can imagine, it's been a difficult week."

As far as I could tell, the mess Lottie was referring to extended to a stack of newspapers on the stairs, a forgotten laundry basket, and a man's coat that had been draped over a wingback chair in the living room. Other than that, the house was as neat and tidy on the inside as it was on the outside. We followed Lottie to the kitchen, where she set the bakery box on the counter. She then motioned for us to take a seat.

"I've been thinking of you two and Mr. Campbell," she said. "After the incident, the hospital called me and told me that you three were the ones who . . . discovered Fred." Here she paused to regain her swiftly crumbling demeanor before continuing. "In the hospital bed." She hiccoughed. "With a pillow over his head. The poor dear. Who . . . who could do something like that to that dear man?" The pain of loss was still so raw that the mention of her husband unleashed a flood of tears. It broke my heart. Kennedy's too. She reached across the table and took the older women's hand.

"Oh, luv," she cooed, dropping her gentrified accent for a more colloquial one. Ken seldom did that, but when she did, one felt like they were being wrapped in a big cozy hug. Lottie needed that hug. "There now, Lottie, dear. Never ye mind the tears. Let them fall. Lindsey will make us some tea." The look in Kennedy's large, dark eyes caused me to excuse myself from the table and get to work.

"Good idea," I said, then began rummaging around the kitchen for a kettle and some tea. While I worked, Kennedy continued to soothe the grieving woman. By the time I brought three mugs to the table, Lottie Landry had gained her composure.

"I'm not sure what you think you can do," she told us plainly. "The police have already been here, asking the same questions. As far as I know, there was no reason for either the attack on Fred by that leprechaun fellow on Friday afternoon, or what occurred in the hospital Wednesday morning. That leprechaun fellow is off the hook for that one, I'm afraid, being dead already. I honestly can't understand why anyone went after Fred?"

"Your husband was the village treasurer," I stated. "Could he have been involved in illegal dealings either willingly or against his will? If you know something, Mrs. Landry, there's no harm in saying so now. It won't leave this table, but what you tell us might lead us to the person responsible for Fred's death." I could tell that the mere notion of her husband being involved in illicit dealings greatly upset her.

"Not my Fred. He was honest to a fault, especially when it came to money. He'd been working for the village for nearly twenty years without incident!"

"Was he acting strange lately?" Kennedy asked. Lottie shook her head. However, a moment later another thought had come to her.

"There wasn't anything out of the usual, mind you," she began. "Fred was always complaining about headaches at work. But now that you mention it, about a week before the attack from that leprechaun fellow, Fred was particularly upset with the accounting software the village was using. I doubt they're related. Accounting software, according to Fred, was riddled with issues. Yet I could tell that this particular problem he was having seemed to really get under his skin."

"Do you have any idea why?" I asked.

"Not really. He wouldn't say much about it, other than it was giving him headaches. Fred was very type A. He liked things neat, tidy, and predictable. One of his rules was that work issues had no business at home, and I agreed. However, he did remark over dinner one night that he was going to be purchasing an entirely new software program for the village. He was looking into it. The mere thought of learning new software and getting others on board with it was also giving him headaches."

While switching software programs could really throw a wrench into the works, it wasn't what I'd consider means for murder. Lottie was a sweet woman, and from everything she'd told us it was evident that she and Fred had enjoyed a happy marriage of twenty-five years. I was sad for her, thinking that it had ended far too soon. By all accounts, Fred Landry didn't deserve to die, so why was he killed? The only answer I could think of was that Fred, having a type A personality, had stumbled onto something that he shouldn't have. Whether it was an anomaly in a software program alerting him to wrongdoing or catching someone at work in the act of gaming the system, I needed to figure out just what Fred Landry had stumbled upon.

CHAPTER 36

"Good evening, Doc, Betty," Rory said by way of greeting as we took a seat at their table. "Tuck will be here shortly," he added, noting the extra chair. "He was just pulling in the parking lot when we came in."

Thank heaven for that. I, for one, was starving and was happy that Betty had invited us to join them. Dinner at the Moose was always a pleasant experience, once one got over the "up north" décor and the owner's penchant for decorating the walls with the heads of local forest animals. Rory, unbothered by the atmosphere, loved the place. Betty and Doc did too. As for me, animal heads aside, I was growing addicted to their fried perch dinner, but I had learned that the local whitefish, the pan-fried nutty trout, and the fish and chips were winners as well. Sure, there was a full menu of other tasty offerings. Lamb chops, steaks, duck, and chicken were favorites, and there were those who took a chance on the imported crab, shrimp, and lobster dinners as well. However, when living near the Great Lakes, I had learned that the local fish, including the catch of the day, was unsurpassed. In the offseason the Moose offered a more limited menu.

"I'm so glad that you could join us. Bob has some interesting news to share, isn't that right, dear?" Betty looked like a child who was bursting to tell a great secret. "Oh, here comes Tuck. Tuck, dear. Over here!" If Tuck had any misgivings about where he was supposed to sit, thanks to Betty the entire dining room could direct him to our table.

The doc offered a kind smile as the young police officer, now in his favorite blue jeans and sweater, took a seat. "It is interesting," Doc said, but didn't offer more on the subject. In fact, Doc's eyes had narrowed suspiciously behind his wire-rimmed glasses. Shocked, I turned my head toward the door, and realized his cause for alarm. Kennedy, dressed to the nines, had appeared on the arm of a decidedly suave looking Niall Fitzhugh.

Karen, that wonderful, if not sassy, middle-aged waitress, was trying her best to direct the couple to the other side of the room where a table for two awaited. Karen adored Rory, tolerated me, and had a visible ax to grind with Kennedy, largely due to my friend's penchant for wine, and her snarky remarks.

"Whoa, Ms. Kapoor." Karen had my friend by the arm. "As they told our dear Lord, there's no room at the inn, especially not for you. But there's a nice, romantic table for two beneath Bullwinkle."

"You're sitting us under that unlucky moose head?" Kennedy glared at me before feigning outrage. "Our friends are just there. Lindsey, don't turn away, darling." Was I turning away? I didn't mean to.

"Your reservation said table for two," Karen reminded her. "Not with the party of five."

"Well, can't you just pull up a couple of chairs for us here?" Niall said, trying to be helpful. He waved in greeting, looking as if he'd rather join our table than be alone with Kennedy.

"Let me ask them." Karen huffed and headed for Betty.

Rory leaned in and whispered to me, "How did she figure it out?"

"Don't look at me. I didn't say a word."

Tuck leaned over, and offered, "She sent me a text earlier, asking what I was doing for dinner. She thought I was having dinner with Colleen. I told her that Colleen was at the cabin, third-wheelin' it with her dad and Molly, on account that Finn's life is still in danger. Anyhow, I told Kennedy that I was having dinner with you two instead. Dang it!" He cringed, listening to himself. "This is my fault." His eyes lifted and homed in on his ex with something akin to hero worship. "I have to admit, she not only looks great in that dress, but she also possesses excellent sleuthing skills. I swear I never told her where we were eating." Without waiting for the word from Betty and Doc, Tuck began scooting his chair over, making room for Kennedy. I wondered if he even realized Niall was holding her hand.

"You bonehead," Rory averred, just before offering a smile to the approaching couple.

"Of course, Kennedy and Niall can join us," Betty told Karen. "The more the merrier!"

"Betty, dear. Do you think that's wise?" Doc had the good sense to look skeptical.

"Kennedy is looking into this case as well," Betty reminded him. "With these four heads working together on this leprechaun issue, we can rest assured it'll be solved. Kennedy should know, Bob."

"Leprechaun issue?" I asked and shot Doc Riggles a pointed look.

"I have a party of eight that's just about ready to leave," Karen told us in a manner that demanded everyone's attention. "You all just hang on a minute. Stuffing seven at a five-top isn't happening on my shift. I'm preparing a bigger table for you."

"Excellent idea, Karen. And don't forget to bring the wine, darling," Kennedy reminded the waitress's swiftly retreating backside. "Three bottles to start with."

Karen, a professional, had made a good call. The larger table was greatly appreciated as we ate our meals and discussed the murders using the information we'd gathered so far. Tuck added to the discussion, stating that the police were looking closely at every employee working for the village. Even Mrs. Hinkle had been questioned several times.

"Village Hall must be at the center of this," he stated. "The attack on Fred wasn't random. He was targeted—"

"By the leprechaun," Kennedy added with a cheeky wink. "We know. He was hoarding the gold, only nobody's reported any missing. How sensational. Isn't that right, Doc?"

"It's highly unusual, just like the person at the center of this mystery. Let's order dessert, shall we?"

Dessert? I cringed. The doctor had been stalling all evening, due, no doubt, to Kennedy and Niall's presence at the table. I knew that Doc trusted Kennedy. It was Niall he'd been leery of. As the medical examiner, he'd been hinting at something truly extraordinary, but had yet to reveal his findings. It was a nerve-straining game. Everyone had been tap-dancing around the elephant at the table, which was the fact that the doc had examined a person thought to be a leprechaun. My heart was pounding in my chest, just thinking about it. What would the tabloids say? *Murderous member of the fairy folk found in Beacon Harbor? Leprechauns are real, and why you should be scared?* I had the terrible feeling that my worldview was about to shift, and not in a good way.

Everyone had placed their dessert order while Doc was wasting yet more time by deliberating over the chocolate cake or the key lime pie.

"Get the pie," I snapped, "and tell us what you found! I'm dying to know!"

The doc, true to form, made us wait until dessert and coffee had been served. I'd never taken Doc Riggles for a diva, but I had to admire his skill for building medical drama. He had an audience, and he wanted to keep us on the edge of our seats. The fact that he kept referring to the victim as "the leprechaun" caused me to prepare for the worst.

"Well, I must admit that this one had me stumped," he told us, then paused to take a sip of coffee. "He did a good job convincing us all, and maybe even himself as well, for I suspect that any person of that stature struggling with a rare genetic disorder, must wonder about the cards they'd been dealt at birth, and what it might mean."

"Disease?" Rory asked, his face pinched with scrutiny.

"Of course, Rory. Despite what your uncle would have us believe, leprechauns don't exist." This he stated matter-of-factly, as if he hadn't been fooled himself!

"What disease did he have?" I asked.

"I wasn't sure at first. There are so many, as you know. The other puzzling fact was that there was no record of this person in any of the usual databases. That had us all stumped. I took some DNA samples and sent them off to that lab. I then hit the medical books. By the time the tests came back, I was nearly certain that I had guessed correctly. You see, apparently the man we took to be a leprechaun in actuality suffered from a rare, incurable genetic disorder known as Werner syndrome. Very few people have it, but those that do share certain characteristics. Werner syndrome is defined by a lack of a pubescent growth spurt, leaving its victims short in stature. They also tend to be thin, with a pinched look to their face, and bulging eyes. People who suffer from the disease also age prematurely. In short, the man who was seen parading around Beacon Harbor dressed as a leprechaun, and might I add convincingly so, was in fact suffering from a rare genetic disorder."

"How awful!" I exclaimed, suddenly feeling very sorry for the little man we'd mistaken for a leprechaun.

The doctor leaned in, adding, "Now here's where it gets interesting. Because this is such a rare disease, I was able to search through medical databases, looking through records hoping to find a match. And I believe that I found one."

"That's huge, Doc," Rory said, looking both relieved and impressed. "Good work."

"Although the findings have gone to Sergeant Murdock," he told Tuck, "I've written it all down for Rory and Lindsey as well. If this village wants to put an end to this sad, strange case, I believe it's best that we all work together." As the doc handed a folded piece of paper to Rory, he explained, "I believe the victim's name was Shephard Mulvaney. Although he looked sixty, he was just thirty-five years old. His last known place of work was for a company in Grand Rapids called Business Solutions."

Kennedy, with her phone in her hand and working her thumbs like the professional she was, suddenly looked up. "Business Solutions is a software company that specializes in personalized business software."

"Oh my gosh," I blurted as warning bells began going off in my head. "Fred Landry. His wife just told Kennedy and me that he was having issues with the software they were using at Village Hall. What if he was using software from Business Solutions? That could be the connection we're looking for!"

"I say it sounds plausible," Niall offered prosaically, right before taking the last bite of his cheesecake. Up until this point, the Englishman had been quiet, soaking it all in. "I have some experience with bespoke business software, but I've not heard of that company."

"Of course not," Kennedy reprimanded. "It's an American company, and they cater to smaller businesses."

"Got an address for this company, PR?" Rory asked.

"Sure do. Here you go." Kennedy texted him the company website.

"Up for a road trip, babe?" Rory tossed me a grin. I matched his grin and nodded. "Looks like we're going to Grand Rapids tomorrow to talk with Shephard Mulvaney's former boss. Don't worry, Tuck. We'll report our findings as soon as we get back."

"I'm counting on it," Tuck replied, looking a bit glum that he wouldn't be joining us. Tuck had been tasked with keeping Finnigan O'Connor out of trouble.

"And since I grew up there, I'm going to take you to lunch at my favorite deli, Lindsey. I hope you love it as much as I do."

"I can't wait. What's it called?" I asked.

"Founders Brewing Company."

"A brewery? A brewery is not a deli, Rory," I pointed out.

"Technically you're correct, Bakewell, but they also serve sandwiches. That makes them a deli in my book."

CHAPTER 37

"So, he wasn't a leprechaun? That's disappointing." Teddy, attempting to wrap his head around what I was telling him, looked skeptical. While we baked, I'd been filling him in on all the latest developments, including what I had learned last night from Doc Riggles. "Don't get me wrong, Linds. A genetic disorder like that must be terrible, but I was kinda hoping . . ." Teddy let the thought drop as he shook his head. "I've never heard of this Werner syndrome thing, but it still doesn't explain why he was dressed as a leprechaun and was seen hoarding gold."

Using a hefty amount of sarcasm, I said, "Well, that is the mystery, now, isn't it, Teddy?"

"I chalk it up to embracing the spirit of the holiday—you know, if you've got the features of a leprechaun, go for it. As your super-hot, supermodel mother once remarked to me, one must learn to use their assets." With two donuts in each hand, Teddy plunged them into the maple glaze as he talked, pulled them out, set them on the tray, and sprinkled them with succulent chunks of cooked, thick-cut bacon. Hog Heaven donuts were a perennial favorite at the Beacon.

"Eww." I made a face and threw a raw blob of sweet roll dough at him from across the counter just as he had placed the finished donuts on the bakery tray. "You just called my mom super-hot. Honestly, Teddy. She's in her mid-sixties!" Of course, this made him grin. "But you just might have a point there. He fit the part, didn't he? Do you suppose somebody made him dress up like that? You know, the person he was working for?"

"You assume that he was working for somebody, but maybe he was a criminal mastermind, like Babyface Finster, a cartoon character in the old Looney Tunes show. Did you ever watch Looney Tunes reruns when you were a kid?" I shook my head, having no idea what he was talking about. "Babyface Finster was a bank robber who had the physique of a baby. Because he looked like a baby, he pretended he was one to evade capture after he'd rob a bank. Finster was very devious—"

"Listen to yourself," I mock-chided. "You're talking about a cartoon character! Shephard Mulvaney was a real man."

"As they say, life imitates art. Also, I heard you and Rory found another pot of gold the other night. How do you explain that? See, my Babyface Finster theory has merit. Man steals gold, buries gold, and dresses like a leprechaun to evade capture, only he didn't, did he?"

As Teddy worked and talked, my jaw dangled. No one was supposed to know about that second pot of gold. I was just about to ask him how he knew when he offered, "Oh, sorry. Kennedy sent me a text yesterday. I wasn't supposed to mention that . . . to you." He had the decency to look guilty.

"I can't believe she told you! We were trying to keep it a secret from her as well."

"I know. She said Hunts-a-Lot let it slip. He'll never live that one down, I bet."

"Teddy, we don't want anyone else to know about that gold, got it? There might be more of it out there, which means that Rory's uncle might still be in danger, having discovered the lepre-chaun's secret hiding place to begin with. Tuck is keeping a close eye on him. After all, someone, namely the murderer, is after him."

Genuine concern crossed Teddy's face. "Got it." He then mimed zipping his lips shut, adding, "Mum's the word." Why didn't I believe him? Probably because Teddy Pratt, when being fed in-formation by Kennedy Kapoor, was as bad as Betty Vanhoosen when it came to scintillating gossip. Sheesh!

"Look, I'm going to need you to run the bake-shop this morning while I go to Grand Rapids with Rory. We're trying to leave by nine. Although it's Sunday, we've arranged to meet Mr. Mulvaney's for-mer boss and hopefully get some answers. Alaina and Ryan are closing today. They know what to do."

"Lindsey, don't worry about it. I'll take care of things here. Just go. Solve this mystery. We all know that you will. All I ask is a Dirty Bastard for my efforts."

"What?"

Teddy grinned. "It's the name of my favorite beer at Founders. Heard you were going there today as well. Lucky you! Dirty Bastard's a Scotch-style ale for manly men, like Rory and me." He gave his chest a little fist-bump as he said this. It made me giggle. "Bet he'll be ordering a pint or two to go with those deli sandwiches he told you about." He was just teasing me now.

I sliced my cinnamon roll dough and was fitting each large slice into the baking pan for the last rise, when I told him, "My first mistake was introducing you to Kennedy. Honestly, you two are like naughty children."

Welly was sprawled across the back seat of Rory's truck as we drove the two and a half hours down to Grand Rapids to talk with Shephard Mulvaney's former boss. Welly loved road trips. He loved pressing his wet nose against the window while staring out at the passing landscape. Yet after an hour of watching the trees go by, he settled down and decided to take a nap. Lucky Welly. After a quick visit to Rory's favorite brewery for a sandwich (yes, they had some, and they were delicious!) and after stocking up on specialty craft beer, including a case of Teddy's favorite, we then took Welly for a long walk before heading to Business Solutions.

"Brad Tinkerman," the man said, shaking our hands. Brad, a tall, trimly built man with a dimpled chin and a mop of thick brown hair, was the manager of software development at the company. "We're normally not open on Sunday, but I thought this would be the best place to meet under the circumstances. I was sorry to hear about Shep's untimely death. I understand you have some questions regarding him?"

"Thank you for agreeing to meet with us," I said.

"We recently learned that he used to work here. We'd appreciate it if you could shed some light on Mr. Mulvaney for us. Any information you give us might help solve his murder."

Brad shook his head. "Can't believe anyone would want to murder poor Shep. Do you work for the police?"

"We're private investigators," Rory told him, which wasn't exactly a lie. We were investigating the murder, privately, but were by no means professionals. Rory, however, had a certain unspoken military air about him that inspired confidence. Mr. Brad Tinkerman seemed satisfied with his answer.

"The truth is, Shep hasn't worked here for at least five years," Brad told us. "He left us because he told us that he was moving to Florida to be with his parents. Due to his illness, he told us that he was retiring. Although he wasn't anywhere close to retirement age, the disease he suffered from was taking a toll on him. Can't remember what it was called, but it prevented him from growing beyond the size of a fifth grader."

"What did he do here?" I asked.

"Shep was a senior software developer, and quite good at it too. He was an interesting fellow. Very smart but a bit of a loner. Although he got along with his coworkers, he didn't go out of his way to make friends here. Never talked of family, but he knew his business. No complaints in that department. He did talk of his hobbies, though. He was a ham radio enthusiast. He also collected model trains. I'm sorry, but that's about all I know about the man."

While I pondered the sad and unusual life of Shephard "Shep" Mulvaney, Rory thought to ask, "What kind of software do you specialize in?" Brad gave us his pitch, stating that Business Solutions designed business software to fit a company's growing needs, mainly inventory tracking, payroll, accounting, detailed quoting systems, billing, and whatever else a company desired. We then asked Brad if he could look at their client list for us, to see if the Village of Beacon Harbor was a client of theirs. After a few quick strokes on his keyboard, Brad brought up the client list.

"Sure is," he answered with his eyes still glued to his computer screen. "In fact, it looks like we have quite a few clients up that way."

"Is there any way you can tell if Mr. Mulvaney designed those products?"

"There's a good chance that he did. The Village of Beacon Harbor has been with our company for over ten years."

CHAPTER 38

"There's our connection," I said as we headed back to Beacon Harbor. We had been in Grand Rapids longer than we'd expected. It was a beautiful city, and the sun had popped out, making it nearly impossible to leave. Rory had enjoyed giving Welly and me a tour of the town, including a trip to East Grand Rapids to visit the lovely home he'd grown up in. We'd also taken Welly to a dog park, then grabbed takeout from Rory's favorite burger chain, Burger Guys, before hitting the road. During the tour, I'd made a quick call to the Beacon Bakeshop to make sure all was well. The bakeshop was now closed for the day. "There must have been something wrong with the software Fred was using," I continued. "What had he discovered that had gotten him killed? From what Brad Tinkerman told us, Shep Mulvaney seemed like an okay person. I also found it interesting that Shep hadn't worked there for the past five years, which is odd."

"Remember," Rory began, then paused to take a sip of his soda. "Most of the leprechaun sightings we marked on that map had been in the vicinity of Village Hall. Shep was casing the place and might have been stalking Fred as well. If Fred was using the software Shep developed, he might have called Shep directly with his complaint. Maybe that's why Shep attacked him?" Rory, like me, was airing his theories.

"Pride? That Shep didn't create a good enough program? That doesn't seem like cause for a beating. Also, why was Shep dressed like a leprechaun? He would have blended in better if he'd just walked in there and had it out with Fred in person. But he didn't."

"This is driving me nuts," Rory admitted. "Nothing makes sense. We need to go straight to Village Hall and take a look at that computer."

It was Sunday night, and Village Hall was closed on Sundays, which we both knew. Rory assured me that he could break in, that he had tools, but I didn't think that was a good idea, not since I had Clare Hinkle's phone number. I made a call to the older woman and explained the situation.

"Wait right there," she said. "I'm already in my nighty, but I'm not in bed yet. I'll just throw on some comfy clothes and meet you at the back door in fifteen minutes."

Still in the truck with Welly, I rolled down the window and held up my phone so that Rory could see it. He was pacing along the backside of the building, looking for the easiest place to enter. "Clare Hinkle is on the way. Also, I should probably call Tuck and let him know about this."

Rory stepped out from behind a large bush. "Good idea. But for the love of God, Lindsey, don't mention a word of this to Kennedy."

Mrs. Hinkle arrived on time, armed with a set of keys. "This is highly unusual, you know," she said, thrusting a key into the door. "However, on account of dear Fred, I'm happy to help. What else do you need me to do?"

Just then Tuck arrived in the parking lot, and with him was Kennedy. Welly, who was waiting patiently before the back door of the building with us, saw his friends and gave a welcoming bark.

"I don't believe this," Rory uttered disparagingly. "What is she doing with him? He's not only a bonehead, he's a glutton for punishment as well. Where is Niall?"

Good question. Niall wasn't with them. "Look," I said, pointing at the beverage carrier in Ken's hands. "They've brought drinks."

"Thought you might need some coffee, seeing as you two might be facing a long night of computer sleuthing," Tuck said, gesturing to the four tall coffees in the carrier Ken was holding.

"Thank you," I said, appreciatively. "A hot cup of coffee certainly won't hurt." We all walked into the dark building and waited for Mrs. Hinkle to turn on the lights. A moment later she met us in the hallway and escorted us to Fred's office. As we followed her, I asked Kennedy what she was doing with Tuck.

"I waited all night while Niall was on an important business call. Then, once the call had ended, he declared that he was heading for the sauna. Can you believe it? I took one sauna with him already, and that was enough. All that sweating is for the birds. I told him to go ahead and that I was going to pop out for a breath of fresh air. I drove to Hoots Diner and found Tuck just sitting there, staring at his phone."

"Did you know he was going to be there?"

"What? Me? Of course not, darling. It was pure chance."

It was hardly chance. Tuck's favorite evening hangout while on duty was that diner, and Ken knew it. In a sleepy little village like Beacon Harbor the police often needed someplace to while away their shift, or pop in for a quick cup of coffee and a bite. During the morning hours the Beacon Bakeshop was the place to be, but once noon rolled around, Hoot's Diner fit the bill. They were open until midnight every night.

"I overheard your call and ordered the coffee," she explained. "Don't forget, I know how you work. I also don't enjoy being out of the loop, which I know that I am."

"Well, you're here now, and I'm glad of it. You should probably send Niall a text. We might be here a while. Also, please be kind to Tuck. Okay?"

Once in Fred's office, I immediately went to his computer. "Do you, by chance, know his password?" I asked Mrs. Hinkle.

"I do. We all use a similar login with minor variations to access our interoffice system, which isn't connected to the internet. I believe that's what you're here to look at. If Fred was using a personal account as well, I'm afraid I can't help you with that."

In a few minutes I was logged onto Fred's computer. Armed with a cup of hot coffee, and with Welly sleeping at my feet, I went to work. I wasn't a forensic accountant, far from it, but I did have a knack for spotting anomalies, especially in strings of numbers. The moment I began I realized that it was going to take hours looking through pages and pages of complicated billing codes, tax assessments, disbursements, expenditures, and payroll. Accounting, I mused, was boring as heck. I found so many random numbers and spreadsheets, that I was struggling to make sense of them. While I worked, and it was a one-person job at best, the others talked quietly and took walks around the building in an effort to entertain themselves. After the first hour, Mrs. Hinkle had gone home, making us promise that we'd lock the building when we left. At one point Kennedy must have left too, only to return with Niall. I was too busy to notice just what Tuck thought about that.

After three hours of scanning through pages and pages of spreadsheets, I was just about to call it a night when I decided to go through the billing codes once again and track them against the most recent round of water bills that had been sent to residents of the village. That's when I saw it. The anomaly I was looking for. It was so subtle that I almost missed it. Everything looked good, passable, and lined up nearly perfectly. Nearly. And that was the problem.

"Dear heavens!" I exclaimed, sitting back in Fred's office chair for the first time all night. I could hardly believe my eyes.

"What is it?" At the sound of my voice, Rory and Welly came bursting through the office door. Tuck, Kennedy, and Niall followed him.

"I think I've found it," I told them, still reeling from my discovery. "If Shephard Mulvaney designed this software program, then he was an evil genius!"

CHAPTER 39

It was unimaginable, it was so slyly deceptive. As the gang pulled chairs around Fred's desk, and after giving Welly a much-needed hug (I needed Welly hugs as much as he did!), I told them about my discovery.

"This software program that the village has been using for the past ten years, and possibly longer, has been overcharging every bill sent, and other random transactions by only a few pennies. No one pays attention to pennies—especially on a monthly bill." I shook my head, just thinking about it. I then explained, "The bills are randomly altered by a few cents, from three cents up to twenty-seven, to always create an uneven number. Odd numbers are important here because it's been proven that brains take longer to process odd numbers than even numbers. Odd numbers are harder to remember. Shep must have known that. Then, the moment the bill is paid, the altered system, which keeps track of the overcharge by using individual account numbers, instantly siphons these pennies off every transaction without visible notice so that the billing matches up with accounts received at the end of each month, making this robbery nearly undetectable. A few pennies here and there seem innocuous, but they can add up quickly over time, especially when taken from every transaction. That's genius! Once I realized what was going on, I was able to track these pennies. They appear to be sent to a holding account called VWC, but at the end of every day the account returns to a balance of two-thousand dollars. So even if someone was checking this account, which it doesn't look like they had any reason to, it would appear normal."

"Damn," Rory uttered, holding me in a look of glowing pride. "Excellent work, babe!"

"This is incredible," Tuck remarked. "Fred must have found out about this." Tuck then removed his cap to run his fingers through his smartly cut blond hair. It was a nervous habit of his. "That's why he was attacked by Shephard Mulvaney, I'll bet."

"I agree." Kennedy smiled at him, then added, "Though his choice of murder weapons seemed a bit wanting. Remember, Fred Landry was attacked with a shillelagh. Who uses a shillelagh?"

"Leprechauns and Irishmen," Niall added, as if that were obvious. "What I'm curious about is how you—a baker—figured all this out when the professionals couldn't?" He held me in a scrutinizing gaze.

"I did work on Wall Street, Niall," I told him, not liking the implication he was making. Just because I chose to spend my days kneading dough instead of making large quantities of it and investing large quantities of it for other people, didn't mean I couldn't add.

"Also," I continued, "and the obvious answer to your question, Niall, is that no one working here had a reason to look for it. The system works seamlessly. I'm an outsider looking for something, and only realized it when I started checking the water bills. I'm sure every bill sent out is affected by this. While I was looking at the water bills, I calculated the actual amount a resident used, added the billing code to that number, then found the total amount billed to that resident. The program then bills the resident the overcharged amount, which is just pennies. A resident wouldn't have any way of knowing they've been overcharged, and the village wouldn't be aware of it either. This is because once the overcharged bill is paid, it matches the correct amount in the system. Most people pay online these days anyhow, which also worked to Shep's advantage."

"It's that dummy account I'm curious about," Rory remarked. "Do we know what VWC stands for?"

I shook my head.

"I haven't a clue," Tuck admitted. "However, it's a good bet to assume that Shep had control of that account."

"Too obvious," Niall said. "This VWC account is obviously a holding account for this money laundering scheme. Usually, a money laundering scheme's first order of business is to take a large sum of money and scale it down to little bits that can be deposited in various accounts to make it hard to detect by the authorities. The cunning of this wee fellow was that he seemed to be flipping that on its head. He was taking little amounts, putting them in a holding account, then transferring a daily balance to either one or possibly many accounts where these ill-gotten gains were swiftly adding up. The second phase of this process is known as layering."

"Layering is where the ill-gotten money is then blended with legitimate money such as being placed in the stock market, or even used to purchase other financial products like gold coins," Rory added for him, looking suspiciously at the Englishman. "How is it that you seem to know so much about money laundering, Niall?"

All eyes were on Niall as he bristled. "How is it that *you* know so much about money laundering, Campbell?"

"My former rank and military background required it," Rory told him, narrowing his eyes at the Englishman.

"Answer Rory's question, Niall." Tuck's interest had now been piqued, making him flip into cop mode again. "What are you not telling us?"

"This is ridiculous," Niall snapped. "You all are acting crazy again."

"Are we?" Kennedy rounded on him. "You are no stranger to imports and exports, darling. That's basically the bread and butter of money laundering, according to the movies. Also, more importantly, all the Irish imported goods that have made their way to this town have your hands all over them. What are the odds that you'd be connected to both establishments? In point of fact, you promised me that Ellie and Company would have an exclusive line of Irish walking capes, only to find out that you made the same deal with Colleen O'Connor at the Blarney Stone, which is just down the street from our clothing boutique! I was promised an exclusive line by you, my boyfriend. If you can't be trusted on something as simple as that, how am I supposed to trust you regarding a brutal leprechaun murder, money laundering, and hidden pots of gold?"

"We're back to that again, are we, PR?" Niall's handsome face turned red behind his perpetually haughty expression. "It's called conducting business. My company has the best products in the industry. I thought I explained that to you."

Tuck McAllister's normally cheerful expression hardened remarkably as he asked, "Was Shephard Mulvaney working for you, Niall? I'd appreciate an honest answer."

"What? No, you numpty!" Niall was visibly riled by us. "I see what's going on here. It's the classic small-town mentality of turning on the outsider. You all reason that I must be guilty because my arrival here happened to coincide with a puzzling murder, and you have no one else to blame. How very small-minded and unprofessional of you all. But I won't be your scapegoat. And you're just mad," he added, jabbing a finger at Tuck, "because I'm dating your ex-girlfriend, whom I'm beginning to realize is just as mental as you all are! Might I remind you once again that I have no connection to the unfortunate Mr. Landry, or Mr. Mulvaney, and that I don't need to squirrel my money away in pots of gold in a village that I'm visiting for the first time? Also, I shall have you know that my net worth is the equivalent of a million pots of gold. Like every reasonable person on the planet, I prefer to keep my wealth in bloody banks! Bugger the lot of you!"

"I guess . . . I guess that does make sense," I offered. "Sorry, Niall."

"Good point," Rory added, flashing the man in question a look of apology. "You're correct, Niall. I know it's not a good excuse, but it's been a long week. We're tired, and we're just grasping at straws at this point. My apologies."

"I'm sorry too," Kennedy apologized. "There's a murderer still on the loose, and it makes me suspicious of everyone, including you. The truth is, I don't really know you, Niall. You're always on the phone. You're always preoccupied with something. And when we do go out, it doesn't seem like you're enjoying yourself. I wanted you to come here to meet my friends, but I now believe that was a mistake."

"I agree," Niall told her. "Americans," he scoffed, adding an eye roll for good measure. "It's time to go home. I've had quite enough of this place. I'm going to see if we can get a flight out tomorrow; that is, if the officer will let me leave."

Just then Tuck's phone rang. "McAllister," he answered. His eyes were still glued to Niall. "Okay. On my way."

"What is it?" I asked, the moment Tuck ended the call. He was grabbing his coat.

"Colleen called 911. Someone's trying to break into the cabin."

"I'm coming with you," Rory said, grabbing his coat as well. He handed me his keys just before he dashed out the door. I had to hold Welly by the collar. "Stay here and lock up. I'll meet you back at the lighthouse."

"Be careful," I said, and gave him a kiss on the cheek.

As Tuck was leaving, he said to Niall, "You're not cleared to leave town just yet, but I'm working on it."

CHAPTER 40

After locking up Village Hall for the night, Niall, having had quite enough of us, had taken the rental car keys from Kennedy, and declared that he was driving back to the hotel. Kennedy, still a ball of raging nerves, and very conflicted regarding her feelings for the man, told him that she was spending the night at the lighthouse with me. She had some thinking to do. She also wanted to make sure the O'Connors were okay, but I interpreted that to mean Tuck. I imagined that Welly was also anxious to get home. It was past our bedtime, and he had only eaten a hamburger patty in the car to tide him over. Judging from the amount of drool dripping on the back seat of Rory's truck, I could tell that my pup was hankering for a bowl of kibble.

"I'm sorry about Niall," I ventured as I drove toward the lighthouse. I was worried about Rory as well and gave a thought to driving straight to the cabin to make sure everyone was okay but decided against it. The cops were on the case, and Rory could hold his own. They didn't need Kennedy, Welly, and me to interfere.

"Oh, Linds." Kennedy gasped and let out a little sob. "I really know how to muck things up, don't I? He seemed so perfect when I'd met him in London. He was a lot of fun there too, but bringing him here was a mistake. The moment he lied to me about those walking capes, I knew it was over. I was just lying to myself, hoping I could make it work."

"Oh, Ken." I wasn't a fan of Niall Fitzhugh, but my heart broke for her. She had a history with men, which included her penchant for sabotaging her relationships before they had a chance to either blossom or naturally draw to an end. For instance, she could have defended Niall tonight. I believed deep down that she didn't really think Niall was involved in any wrongdoing in Beacon Harbor. I was the person who had thrown suspicion on him first, convincing her to believe me. That largely had to do with my own suspicions regarding the man. Yes, I'd been jaded. Tuck McAllister was my friend, and Niall was an outsider who had captured Kennedy's affections. Regarding Tuck, it was evident the minute she arrived, that she wasn't over him. She'd expected him to still be pining over her, but he had moved on, and rightly so. I loved them both, but I wasn't convinced that Kennedy and Tuck should be together.

As the lighthouse came into view and Welly began whining softly, she said, "I miss it here. I miss working at Ellie and Co. I miss my friends. I even miss Welly's drool, and you know how much it disgusts me." She reached into the back seat and gave Welly a rub on the head.

"Wow, you really do miss us."

"I also miss this." She wiggled her hand between the two of us. "I don't like murder, mind you, but I have to admit that there's a real satisfaction that comes from bringing the baddie to justice."

"I agree."

"So, who do you think is behind all of this?"

I parked Rory's truck in the space alongside the garage side of the boathouse and turned off the engine. "That's a good question. I'd say the person trying to recover the lost gold is responsible. We'll find out soon enough from Rory if the police were able to apprehend the guy behind all of this. Hopefully they catch him tonight. However, if tonight's a bust, why don't you come with me to Village Hall tomorrow. The bakery's closed, and I really want to ask Mrs. Hinkle about that mysterious account."

It had been a struggle to fall asleep, but eventually I had. It felt like I'd been out for only a moment when Rory came in and woke me with the news that whoever had tried to break into his house after Finn and Colleen had gone to bed, must have been scared away by Bailey. There was damage to the side door, indicating that someone had tried to pry it open. They didn't get very far before they realized their mistake. Bailey was inside. Finn's faithful dog wasn't about to let anyone harm her people. I thanked him for the news, told him that Kennedy was spending the night, and fell back to sleep.

Having the day off, I slept until nine. After a shower and taking care of Welly, I then went to the kitchen to brew a pot of tea for Kennedy. Rory had already made coffee. Smelling the tea and the warming scones, Kennedy arrived in the kitchen dressed and nearly ready to go. After our quick breakfast we decided to walk to Village Hall, taking Welly with us.

"I hope you don't mind that we brought Welly?" I asked, meeting Clare Hinkle in the lobby of the building. "After being cooped up so much yesterday, I felt he could use a good walk."

"Welly is welcome here anytime. After all that's happened in this building, I find his mere presence comforting."

I thanked Mrs. Hinkle as we followed her to her office.

"You hinted on the phone this morning that you found something important. I'm just dying to know what that was."

Kennedy and I were seated on the other side of her desk. Welly had found a comfy spot along the wall. I nodded and told her about the diabolical software program I had discovered. The news of the program the village had been using made her go white in the face, which for an elderly woman, wasn't a flattering look.

"Lindsey, I can't believe this. This is just terrible!" The way she was clutching her sweater at the level of her heart made me nervous that she was going to suffer a heart attack or a stroke. Clearly the older woman hadn't been expecting to hear that the village had been unknowingly cheating taxpayers and citizens out of their hard-earned money.

I then had to ask her the hard question. "Do you think that Fred could have been involved in this?"

Clare thought about that for a moment, then shook her head. "Fred Landry wasn't the sharpest tool in the shed, if you get my drift." She gave her old noggin a tap with her finger as she said this. "But if Fred was anything, he was honest. He was also diligent. I can't believe that he didn't spot the problem right away."

"I don't think you should be too hard on him. The program was designed to appear as if it was working just as it should have. We believe that Fred might have stumbled on an anomaly that caused him to dig deeper into the program."

"Oh!" she gasped, recalling something. "I think he did. He must have. Poor Fred. It was a few days before St. Patrick's Day. I nearly forgot. Fred was very troubled by something but wouldn't say what it was. He was grumbling about faulty software. Since he's also the person in charge of purchasing the accounting software the village uses, he told us at our staff meeting that we were going to be scrubbing our current software and switching to another system immediately. That's always a nightmare. I was half suspecting a mutiny over that one."

"He must have contacted Shep Mulvaney," I said. "He was the man who'd developed the software to begin with."

"I don't know anyone by that name," Mrs. Hinkle told us. "But it wouldn't surprise me if Fred called somebody." Her hand flew over her heart again. "He must have called somebody to complain! That's why that little leprechaun fellow came here and attacked him." Her eyes flew to me then as she asked, "That terrible little man wasn't behind this—this faulty software that's been stealing from people, was he?"

"You can never judge a book by its cover," Kennedy remarked. "That terrible little man was a genius . . . according to Lindsey."

I nodded, then addressed Mrs. Hinkle once again. "The fact that Shep Mulvaney was murdered suggests that he wasn't working alone. Others might be involved in this scheme as well. I have another question for you that I hope you can answer. Last night while investigating this software program we found a suspicious account. All the stolen money seems to pass through this account before it disappears. We need to know who this account belongs to. The account is called VWC. Does that mean anything to you?"

"VWC? Are you certain?" Mrs. Hinkle looked highly skeptical. Kennedy and I nodded in unison. "Are you sure the stolen money is deposited there? That doesn't make sense. The village makes a yearly deposit into that account of two thousand dollars. Members of the Garden Club have also been known to donate to that committee. Yet whenever I've been asked to check into that account there's never very much in there."

"Who does that account belong to?" I prodded.

"VWC is the acronym we use for the village welcoming committee."

My heart sank. The village welcoming committee? It couldn't be. I looked at Kennedy, then explained. "Molly Butterfield *is* the village welcoming committee!"

Ken's lips were poised somewhere between a grin and a frown as she uttered, "Oh my. Molly Butterfield! A woman with a flower shop and secrets. Utterly diabolical. This explains the unexplainable, darling, namely the reason for her fawning attraction to Finn O'Connor."

CHAPTER 41

"Thank you!" I cried to Mrs. Hinkle as Kennedy, Welly, and I made for the door. It was nearly unimaginable that sweet Molly Butterfield could be behind the stolen money and the murders, but as I've learned during my short stint with crime-solving, the culprit is usually the one you least expect. Molly traded in kind works, bringing flowers to new residents and businesses as well as taking it upon herself to beautify the town with small, artistic gestures. Her kindness had certainly overshadowed her darker nature. After all, with the help of the man named Shep Mulvaney, it appeared that she was also stealing money from the village. It now didn't seem like a coincidence that she was also behind the decorative flags. As Welly pulled me to the front door of the village hall building, I couldn't quite work it all out in my head—it was a puzzling case to be sure—but we had a name. And that name had just sent the fear of God in me.

"I'm calling Tucker," Ken declared, pressing a

button on her phone. Apparently, she still had her former lover at the top of her "favorites" list.

"I'm calling Rory," I announced as we hit the sidewalk. Wellington, sensing our urgency, was trotting like a pacer at the end of his leash, propelling me along with him as I attempted to talk into the phone.

"Rory," I said the moment he answered. My voice was not only breathless, but it was shaking from the quick pace we'd set. Why had we decided to walk? "We figured out . . . who that VWC . . . account belonged to." I paused to take a breath, much to Welly's dismay. "Welly, heel!" I snapped. Welly stopped trying to pull me to the lighthouse and sat instead. "Molly Butterfield!" I cried into the phone.

"What?" Rory sounded confused. "What about Molly Butterfield?"

"We believe that she's the person behind all of this, including the attempts on Uncle Finn's life!"

"No way. Are you certain?" Like me, it appeared that Rory was having a hard time wrapping his head around this concept.

"We learned that VWC stands for Village Welcoming Committee. That's Molly's account! Where are you?" Kennedy had caught up with me, and we started jogging again.

"At the cabin. I left you a message this morning. Due to recent events, I'm installing security cameras. I'm also trying to catch up on some paperwork."

"Is Finn with you?" I asked.

"No. He's at the Blarney Stone."

"Hold on a sec." I pulled the phone from my ear and addressed Kennedy. "What did Tuck say?"

"He's on his way to Butterfield's Floral Artistry as we speak. He also commended us on our good work!"

"Good news," I told her. I then relayed the information to Rory.

"Linds," he began, cautiously, "Molly spent a lot of time in the pub during the grand opening of the Blarney Stone. She could have easily taken Finn's shillelagh while he was working, and he never would have realized it."

"Good point. She could have hidden it in one of the bins she had used to transport all those flowers!" It was all becoming so clear to me. "Why hadn't we thought of that before?"

"Because we had no reason to suspect Molly until now. If she is behind all of this, Linds, she's dangerous. She's already killed two men. I'm calling Tuck now to make sure the police search that flower shop."

"The police are already on it, Rory," I remarked as the lighthouse came into view. "We're almost home. See you in a few."

Kennedy, Welly, and I had just walked through the lighthouse door when Tuck called Kennedy again. I was in the process of removing Welly's leash when the look in Ken's eyes stopped me.

"What is it?"

"Molly's not at the flower shop, Linds," she informed me with a look of concern. "Lisa told Tuck that Molly left earlier to prepare a private lunch for her and Finn. They're having a lunch date! At the Blarney Stone! What if she means to poison him with her beautiful, delectable lunch?"

"Poison?" The thought was terrifying. "But why would she do that?"

"Maybe because she's a nutter and has already murdered two men?" There was a hefty amount of snark as she offered this. "Think about it. Molly poisons Finn, then tells him he's been poisoned, and makes him tell her where he found the gold if he wants to live."

I stared at her for a moment processing this. She did have a point. Finn was putty in Molly's hands. The man was smitten with her and loved the attention she showered on him. If she'd been the one searching for the pot of gold, what was to stop her from drugging him or poisoning him to make him talk? Finn was a stubborn man on a good day, but if his life was threatened, I believed he'd talk. My heart pounded at the thought.

"Quick, Ken! We need to get to the Blarney Stone. We've got to stop Finn from eating that lunch!" Kennedy agreed. With Welly leading the way, we ran to get my Jeep.

By the grace of God and some fast driving, we pulled into the Blarney Stone's parking lot just as Molly Butterfield was making her way to the entrance of the shop. She had dressed for her murderous date in a darling, flare-skirted coat of spring green over a pair of wide-leg jeans and was carrying an innocent-looking wicker picnic basket in one arm. In the other arm she held a lovely bouquet of white roses and green carnations interspersed with other eye-pleasing greenery. The woman might be a psychotic killer, I darkly mused, but she certainly had a flair for the finer touches.

"Stop here!" Kennedy demanded, her hand poised on the door handle. I pulled to a stop at the head of the walkway. "The flower-peddling strumpet! Finn won't be able to resist that romantic picnic hamper, and we'll never reach her before she reaches him!" With that, Kennedy jumped out, yet instead of racing up the walkway as I had anticipated, she let Welly out instead.

"Get Bailey!" she sang in a high voice that excited my pup. Welly didn't need to be told twice. He leapt out of the Jeep and ran to the door, grazing Molly's picnic basket in his haste.

"Whoa!" Molly cried, as the picnic basket launched skyward. Unfortunately, she still had a tight grip on the handle. Bless her, she didn't let go, but the impact was too much, causing her to spin around and lose her balance. She teetered a few paces on unsteady heels, then stepped off the walkway where one of those heels got stuck in the icy mud. "Oh nooo!" she cried, just before crashing to the unforgiving ground in an explosion of flower petals and potato chips.

The moment Molly went down, Finn flew out of the door to help her. Bailey was right on his heels. The two giant dogs, acting as if they hadn't seen each other for weeks, began romping around the front lawn of the gift shop.

"Don't eat anything in that picnic basket!" I called to Finn as Kennedy and I ran to Molly.

"We think it might be poisoned!" Kennedy added.

Finn looked both outraged and confused. Then he saw the flashing lights from Tuck's police cruiser as it pulled into the parking lot. Rory's truck was right behind it. Finn's bright blue eyes narrowed as they settled on Molly again, this time with all the suspicion the mud-splattered woman deserved. "Oh, Molly," he sighed in dismay. "What mischief have ye done, m'dear?"

"Theft and murder," Tuck answered as he pulled out a pair of handcuffs from his utility belt. "Molly Butterfield," he began, standing over the stunned woman, "I'm arresting you under suspicion of embezzlement and the murders of Shep Mulvaney and Fred Landry. You have the right to remain silent."

CHAPTER 42

Molly Butterfield, proclaiming her innocence, had gone kicking and screaming into custody. It wasn't a pretty sight. I'd nearly felt sorry for her until we were told that a shillelagh had been found in her flower shop, hidden in the back of a closet. The shillelagh, believed to be Uncle Finn's, had dried blood on it and glitter. Finn, deflated and saddened that the woman he'd been seeing had been playing him all along, had gone to the police station to identify the shillelagh. A short while later he had called his daughter at the Blarney Stone. Rory, Kennedy, and I had been there with her, waiting for the news.

The moment Colleen ended the call she informed us, "Da found his shillelagh. Molly's denying that she'd taken it, but she must have gotten ahold of it during the grand opening and smuggled it out of here without us knowing. Sergeant Murdock believes it's the murder weapon, but they won't know for certain until they get the report from the lab. Poor Da." Colleen shook her head with palpable sadness. "Seeing his beautiful shillelagh like that—all caked with blood and sparklin' with glitter—has broken his heart. He told me that even if it turns out that 'tis not the murder weapon, he wants nothing to do with it. We have plenty here. He'll just have to choose a new one."

"Poor Finn," Kennedy remarked. "But I applaud his sentiments. That stick obviously is carrying a lot of bad juju after being used to murder a man."

"You're still clinging to juju?" Rory flashed her a deprecatory sideways glance. Kennedy and I had learned all about juju when we'd gone to visit a psychic medium last Halloween. Rory obviously didn't give a thought to such things. "Good or bad, Kennedy, it's just a walking stick."

She rolled her eyes at him as she mumbled, "Simpleton."

That was my cue to take control of the discussion. "Regarding Molly's duplicity, I imagine that wound is going to take a little longer to heal."

"I agree," Colleen said with a nod. Then a grin came to her lips as she added, "However, what me father will truly be mourning is the pot of leprechaun gold he found and had been made to give over to the police. Women come and go in his life like the changing of the seasons. But gold? Doubtful he'll ever get over that one."

"Just think of the stories he'll be able to tell now," Rory reminded her.

"Ah, the stories." The thought made Colleen smile again. "They're bound to be grander, for sure. Folks will flock to his wee pub to hear them. After all, Finnigan O'Connor really did bait a leprechaun and found the unlucky man's gold."

* * *

We were all relieved that this puzzling case had
been solved. Well, mostly solved. There were still
questions, and those we pondered over dinner at
the lighthouse. I invited our small group of friends
to a simple supper of chili, cornbread, and a healthy slice of Baileys cheesecake. St. Patrick's Day
was over, and I was very glad about that. But the
Baileys cheesecake had been a hit with our customers, prompting Teddy and Wendy to keep baking them.

"I can't believe that woman stole me shillelagh
only to debauch it with the blood of a leprechaun."
Finn shook his head, still holding to the fantasy
that Shep Mulvaney had been a leprechaun.

"Not a leprechaun, Da," Colleen corrected. "He
was a man, same as you, God rest his soul. Although,
according to Tuck here, the wee man was a criminal mastermind."

"He wrote a very clever software program," I
told them. "But we still don't know how he managed to implement it, or what his connection to
Molly Butterfield was."

"That's easy." Kennedy set down the napkin she
had used to blot her lips. "They were obviously ro-
mantically involved. Molly likely told him that she
was breaking it off, which caused him to double-
cross her. He'd obviously taken all the money and
hidden it from her in a ploy to get her back,
which, as we know, backfired."

"You're making this up," Niall accused, although
he was clearly entertained by her theory. He then
addressed the table at large, adding, "Kennedy has
a very active imagination. Too active for my taste.
In point of fact, I realized that this whole time

she's somehow convinced herself that I'm involved in all this malarky. Have you told them yet, PR?"

With a swooping hand gesture, she deferred to him. "Go ahead, Niall. Spill the beans."

"Now that the murderer has been caught, I'm leaving town tomorrow morning. For good. It's been a pleasure, but one I do not wish to ever repeat. I'm depositing Kennedy into your care."

"In other words, darlings, this"—she wiggled her finger between herself and Niall—"is over."

"Sorry to hear it," Tuck said in a manner that was utterly unconvincing. That remark drew a sharp, almost pained look from Colleen. Kennedy merely smiled.

"It was mutual," Kennedy informed the table.

"May I leave, Officer?" Niall asked, although we all knew that regardless of what Tuck said, Niall Fitzhugh was leaving town in the morning, come hell or highwater.

Tuck was quick to nod his approval, after which Colleen asked, "And when are you leaving us, Kennedy?" With the announcement of Kennedy's single status once again, the undercurrent at the table seemed to shift, this time causing Colleen to be on her guard. Kennedy shrugged, indicating that she didn't have any plans. Rory, growing uncomfortable in the silence, stood from the table and took his empty bowl to the kitchen for a second helping of chili. Finn followed him, as did the dogs. I decided it was time put a pot of coffee on and slice the cheesecake.

While everyone was enjoying dessert, including Niall, who seemed to be enjoying his visit immensely now that the pressure of his tenuous relationship with my friend was over, Tuck admitted, "Molly's not talking. She is denying everything, including the fact that she knew Shep Mulvaney."

"What about her computers?" Rory asked. "Have the police been able to track her activities on the VWC account?"

Tuck took a sip of coffee before replying, "Her computers have been confiscated and while it's clear that she has full access to the VWC account, there haven't been any false transactions detected yet. In other words, we don't know where the stolen money is going. The village deposits two thousand dollars a year in the VWC account. There's also evidence that Molly, on occasion, uses her own funds to cover some of the costs she incurs while performing her welcoming committee duties. So far, everything is checking out on that end. Regarding the food in the picnic basket, that's been sent to the lab. If any of the food or the wine in that basket has been tampered with, we'll know. However, these things take time."

"According to everything Lindsey and I learned at Shep's former employer in Grand Rapids, this embezzlement scheme they were running was going on for some time, upwards of ten years." The mere thought of the clever theft made Rory shake his head in wonder. "Molly is obviously trying to protect herself by denying everything. Once they can link her to the stolen money, and the two murder scenes, it won't matter. Good work, Tuck."

"Good work, everyone," Tuck added, raising his coffee mug in the air. "I, for one, am looking forward to things returning to normal around here. Although, admittedly, it was pretty cool when Finn recovered that pot of gold."

"Indeed, it was, m' boy! Do you think you can

talk the good sergeant into giving me one wee coin of it? Just to give credence to me story, you understand?"

Tuck assured him that he'd check into it.

"By the way," Niall broke in, "do we know why that little man was dressed as a leprechaun in the first place? I was halfway to believing that this town was infested with leprechauns."

Everyone shook their heads while Kennedy offered, "Flair? Irony? Take your pick. The man was struck down with a shillelagh on St. Patrick's Day night, which leaves one to believe that he was mocking his business partner."

"I agree," Colleen said, casting a hooded glance at my friend. "Anyone who converts stolen money into gold coins, then puts those coins into a little black pot, and hides that black pot under a rainbow—"

"No!" Finn cried. "Ye'll not be givin' that secret away, m'dear."

"Why not, Da? Everyone here already knows where the gold was hidden."

"What?" Tuck and Finn expostulated at the same time. The two men looked at each other, one confused, and one quite angry.

"You all knew where the gold was hidden?" Tuck's handsome face had turned an unhealthy shade of red. "You knew and you didn't tell me? I'm offended."

"We couldn't tell you. It was Da's secret. Also, if the police knew where the gold was hidden, they'd dig it all up, making it harder to draw out the murderer. Think about it. If all the hidden gold had been confiscated by the police, the murderer would hardly go to the police and claim it. The murderer could leave town and the mystery would never be solved. We were only thinking of you, dear," Colleen told him while gently laying a hand over his.

"There's no harm in telling me now. Where was the gold hidden?" Tuck's beseeching eyes held to Colleen's. The dear young woman crumbled under that look like a cupcake in the rain.

"Beneath the flags with the shamrock, the pot of gold, and the rainbow on them," she declared.

"Molly Butterfield orders those holiday flags for the town," Kennedy added, casting Colleen a smug look. Tuck seemed oblivious.

"Molly clearly didn't know where the gold had been hidden." Tuck looked puzzled by this revelation. "Are you telling me that you found that pot of gold buried under some ridiculous flag Molly ordered for the town as a holiday decoration, and yet she didn't know about it? What in the name of St. Patrick has been going on in this town?" He looked as confused as we felt.

Niall brandished his empty fork at the young officer. "I'm going to take a stab in the dark here. Shenanigans," he declared just before bursting out in laughter. It was the deep belly laughter of a man enjoying himself. It was so infectious that I almost joined him. "Plenty of good old Irish shenanigans! You're obviously dealing with some real psychopaths here. Best of luck to you all."

CHAPTER 43

It felt good to be back at the Beacon Bakeshop again, working beside my staff while chatting with our customers. I had relayed the entire incident to them during our morning meeting. Everyone had been relieved it was over, and Teddy, regarding Rory and me as heroes, was beaming with pride as he told our customers what had happened.

It was a busy morning. Word of Molly Butterfield's misdeeds had traveled fast, filling the morning bakery hours with wild speculations, congratulations, and quite a few customers mumbling, *I knew she was too good to be true, giving those beautiful flower arrangements away like that!*

Last night, after Kennedy's announcement of her breakup with Niall, she had officially moved back to the lighthouse for the time being. Once our guests had left, Kennedy and I went up to the lightroom with a steaming mug of herbal tea in our hands to have our much-needed girl chat. It was apparent that Kennedy had enjoyed her time

with Niall, but she admitted that they weren't a
good match. Beacon Harbor had been the cru-
cible for their relationship, and it hadn't survived.
Kennedy had also admitted that her time away
from Beacon Harbor had been good for her. I
knew from personal experience that it could be
truly confusing at times trying to figure out what
one wanted out of life. However, I also believed
that every time you figured out what you didn't
want brought you that much closer to where you
needed to be. Kennedy was still on that journey.
She had missed Beacon Harbor and her work at
Ellie & Company. I could tell she was getting excited for May, when Mom would be back, and
they'd open the boutique once again with a whole
new line of fashionable yet comfortable clothing
in time for the tourist season.

There'd been one more thing that I had wanted
to express to Kennedy. Rory and I were genuinely
glad that she was back, but I had made it clear that
I didn't think it was a good idea for her to rush
into another relationship so soon after her
breakup with Niall. It was no secret that she was
still attracted to Tuck McAllister, Beacon Harbor's
hottest man in uniform. Tuck had finally moved
on and Colleen had been very good for him. I felt
that they deserved a chance at happiness. I had
urged Ken to let it be. However, even I knew that
talking sense to Kennedy was at times like asking
Welly to ignore a pound of bacon that had fallen
on the floor. Welly understood my words. He even
tried to heed them. But in the end, he'd snap up
the bacon . . . even at the risk of upsetting me.
That was because, like Kennedy, some of Welly's

baser urges superseded reason. The heart wants what the heart wants, even if it's only a pound of bacon.

It was almost noon, and I was just about ready to remove my apron and pop into the lighthouse for a bite of lunch and to take Welly out for a walk, when Rory came into the Beacon. He looked flustered.

"What is it?" I asked.

"I just got off the phone with Tuck. Molly's not cracking. She's maintaining her innocence and is claiming that she has no idea who Shep Mulvaney is, or what Finn's shillelagh was doing at her flower shop."

"Is that unusual?" I asked him. "By denying everything, she's making it harder for the police to prove her case. Maybe that's her strategy?"

"It's getting harder, alright," he said. "They still can't connect Molly to Shep Mulvaney, and they still have no idea where the money is going that's floating though her account."

I thought about that for a minute, then went to fetch Welly and my coat. "Meet me out back," I told Rory. "We need to go to Village Hall again. Something's not adding up here."

After alerting my staff that I had one more errand to run (my poor staff, they were getting tired of my errands!), we left Welly in the car as we went to talk with Mrs. Hinkle again. As we passed Fred's office at the top of the stairs, I noticed that the forensic accountants were hard at work in there, trying to sort out the details of Shep Mulvaney's deviously clever embezzlement software.

"Good afternoon, Mrs. Hinkle," I said as Rory and I walked into her office. Mrs. Hinkle's office was across from Fred's on the other side of the staircase. Although she had a decent view of Fred's office, it was partially blocked by a half-wall that protected the stairwell. "I was wondering if you might answer some more questions for us regarding Fred Landry's murder?"

"Of course," the older woman said with a kindly smile. "Come in, won't you? The police were here earlier asking all kinds of questions. They've brought in a team to go over Fred's computer." She made a gesture to the office across the hallway. "I hear congratulations are in order. I never would have thought it, but it appears that Molly Butterfield was behind this whole terrible thing."

"Actually, Mrs. Hinkle, that's part of the reason why we're here," Rory told her. "I was talking with Officer McAllister this morning. Although Molly Butterfield is the owner of the VWC account, it doesn't appear that she's benefiting from the embezzled money. They can't locate the account the money is flowing into from that account, nor does it appear that Molly has access to it."

"Is that so?" A look of pure curiosity crossed the older woman's face. "Then where is it going?"

"That's the question," I said. "Also, we know that Shep Mulvaney developed the business software the village is using, but we can't find a connection between him and Molly Butterfield. Did Molly ever work here?"

"That is a good question. Let me look through the records." Mrs. Hinkle then excused herself and left the office, heading down the stairs. Fifteen minutes later, she returned with a very peculiar look on her face and a slip of paper in her hand.

"Forgive me, but I don't have access to employee records here. However, when I made a visit to Phyllis Helman's office in the human resource department, I was able to peruse past employees. Molly Butterfield has never worked here. However, I did come across something I think you'll find interesting." Clare Hinkle handed Rory the slip of paper she was holding.

"Good grief!" Rory exclaimed, reading the paper.

"What does it say?" I was dying to know.

"Linds, I think we've just made a terrible mistake," Rory admitted, looking dumbfounded.

"What? How?" The longer Rory stared at the paper in his hands, the more unease I felt.

"It appears that ten years ago, around the time the software was implemented, Lisa Baxter used to work for Fred Landry."

"She was his office manager," Clare interjected, helpfully. "That was before her divorce."

"Lisa Baxter is Molly's assistant," I said as every nerve in my body began tingling uncomfortably. "She was with Molly at the grand opening of the Blarney Stone! She has access to the flower shop and Molly's account!"

Rory pulled out his phone. "I'm calling Uncle Finn now. If Lisa Baxter is behind all of this, he's still in danger." Rory let the phone ring until it went to voice mail, then hung up and dialed another number. "Finn's not answering. I'm calling

Colleen." However, when Colleen's phone went to voicemail, Rory grew nervous. "She's not answering either."

"Let's go," I told him, heading for the door. "They might still be at the Blarney Stone."

CHAPTER 44

We drove across town to the Blarney Stone, only to find it locked when we got there. It was Tuesday afternoon. The shop should have been open. This alarmed me as well as Rory. Welly was highly agitated by something as well. It wasn't until he started barking loudly before the door that we heard a bark in reply.

"Bailey's still inside," I remarked. "She must be locked in the office. That's not normal, Rory."

"I agree," he said, digging a hand in his pocket. "This entire situation is not normal. A locked shop, Bailey left inside, and they're not answering their phones?" Rory looked troubled as he held up a key. "Thankfully, I have a backup. Uncle Finn insisted."

The moment the door was unlocked, Welly ran inside and led us straight to the office. Just as I had thought, the door was closed. The moment I opened it, Bailey ran out, greeting us with nervous kisses and her tail tucked under her hind legs.

"Poor Bailey," Rory said, giving the anxious dog

an affirming hug. "It appears that they left in a hurry."

"Where do you suppose they went?" This I asked as Bailey and Welly made a beeline to the front door. Bailey started to whine. I'd been around my dog long enough to know that he could smell things that I couldn't. For instance, if I left the lighthouse alone to take a walk on the beach and someone happened to let Welly out, he'd follow my scent until he caught up with me. I knew Bailey had the same instincts and drive. The O'Connors were her people, and I believed that she could sense they were in trouble.

"I don't know where they went, but I'm calling Tuck." Rory pulled out his phone to make the call.

"I'm calling Ken to let her know," I told him as I went back to the office to get Bailey's leash. For some odd reason Kennedy wasn't answering her phone either. All I got was her voice mail. *"Can't get to the phone right now, darling. Please leave a message."* I walked back into the gift shop to see if Rory was having better luck.

"I told Tuck what we have learned regarding Lisa Baxter. He's heading over to the flower shop as we speak to question her."

"Doubtful she'll be there," I said, feeling the hollow ache of doom in the pit of my stomach. Just then my phone dinged, indicating that I'd gotten a text. I looked at my phone and realized that Kennedy had sent it. However, it wasn't one of her usual texts. Ken was fond of emojis, but this one was entirely made up of them. As I stared at the pictures, my phone dinged again. Ken had sent the same text twice. However, this second text wasn't quite the same. When I saw the emoji of a gun in the string of pictures, the hair on the back of my neck prickled. "Oh no!" I cried, looking at Rory. "I think that Kennedy might be with them. I don't know for sure, but . . . I think she's in trouble. Look at this."

"Why would she be with them?" He looked perturbed as he took my proffered phone. "That makes no sense." It might, I thought, if one were to imagine that Kennedy had gone to confront her rival for Tuck's attention at her rival's place of work. Either that or she'd just happened to be at the Blarney Stone purchasing Irish imports when the baddie came waltzing in. I hoped I was wrong, but the text indicated otherwise. I watched as Rory examined the honeypot emoji, the letters Au, and a toy gun emoji. There was also an American flag and a goat.

"You might be correct," Rory conceded. "The pot, Au for gold, and the gun would indicate that someone, presumably Lisa Baxter, is making them reveal where the pot of gold was hidden."

"Or she's making them dig up another pot of gold for her. Whoever is behind this, they obviously believe there's more gold out there. Poor Ken!" I cried, thinking of my friend. The last time we had confronted a baddie we had almost gotten ourselves killed. The incident had destroyed Ken's confidence. I couldn't imagine how she felt now with another gun, if I was reading the text correctly, pointed at her.

"Sorry, Linds," Rory offered sincerely. "I don't know how she got messed up in this, but she did. However, if she's with Finn and Colleen, Kennedy is the only one who was able to send a text."

"It's one of her gifts," I admitted. "She could

text blindfolded if she had to. Oh, no! You don't think they're blindfolded?"

"Lord, I hope not. Back to this text, Linds, what do you suppose the meaning of the American flag and the goat are?"

I shrugged as I thought about that. And then it hit me. "She wouldn't, would she?" I looked at Rory as I uttered this.

"Don't tell me this has something to do with Clara?" The mere thought caused a troubled frown to appear on his face.

"No. Not Clara," I said, thinking. Clara was a lovely little white nanny goat that had spent some time at the lighthouse with us. Clara now belonged to the Jorgenson family, who regarded her much like a family dog. I looked at Rory. "If Kennedy was in trouble, she wouldn't endanger the Jorgenson family. The only person I can think of who brings to mind a goat is Daphne Rivers. Remember? The crazy goat lady? She owns the Happy Goat Lucky Goat Farm a few miles outside of town."

"I know Daphne."

"Kennedy does too. She also knows that Daphne is very protective of her herd. I think Kennedy is trying to trick whoever is behind this into believing that the gold is hidden beneath an American flag on a goat farm."

"I would say that's utterly ridiculous, Bakewell, but I'm considering the source."

"Good man. Let's go!"

With both dogs loaded into the back seat of the Jeep, Rory and I drove out of town heading for the Happy Goat Lucky Goat Farm. As we drove, Tuck had reported back that Lisa Baxter wasn't at the flower shop or at her house. Another point of interest that he delivered was that Lisa Baxter lived in the same neighborhood as Mayor Jeffers. Bingo! That would explain the leprechaun sightings in that neighborhood. But if Lisa was behind this, what was her connection to Shep Mulvaney? As I thought on this, Rory delivered one more message from Tuck.

"I think we're right about that goat farm," he said, looking at me as I drove. "There was a 911 call from Daphne Rivers complaining about a green SUV that drove into her goat pen."

"Finn owns a green SUV!" I declared. "This confirms Ken's cryptic message!"

As we raced to the Happy Goat Lucky Goat Farm, Rory relayed our suspicions to Tuck.

The moment we pulled into the farm's driveway, I spotted them in the field. The sight of Lisa Baxter aiming a gun at Kennedy's head as Finn, Colleen, and Daphne Rivers stood behind her, gave me a fright. Bailey must have been frightened too, due to the sound of her anxious whining that had reached critical levels in the back seat. Her whining was partially drowned out by the pounding of my heart in my ears. I was so frightened at the scene unfolding in the field, that I feared I was going to collapse. The reason I didn't was because I was focused on Kennedy. My fashion-forward friend, who abhorred manual labor in general, clearly didn't know how to use a shovel. She was stabbing the head of it into the snowy ground beneath a flag depicting the silhouette of a goat. As for the goats, not one was to be seen.

"Lisa's pointing a gun at Kennedy," Rory remarked, as I parked the Jeep. However, the moment he left his seat to get out, Welly and Bailey

leapt over the back seat and jumped out after him.
I got out as well. Before I knew what was happening, the two dogs began racing through the snow-covered field towards Lisa and her gun.

Welly, with a bark to rival thunder, made his presence known as he galloped at speed beside Bailey. It was the sound of his bark that caused Lisa to turn. It was just the opening Kennedy needed. Gripping the shovel like a baseball bat, she swung it at Lisa's head, knocking the woman to the ground. Finn jumped on top of her. Daphne jumped on top of Finn, obviously unwilling to take any chances. Colleen went for the gun while Kennedy stood beneath the goat flag leaning on her shovel. As Rory and I ran to them, the first goat appeared at the top of the hill, heralded by the tinkling of a bell. It was the handsome bellwether, Bode-Goaty. This I knew because I had met Bode-Goaty once before. Sensing mischief, Bode-Goaty emitted a loud bleat, calling the others to him. Then the goats descended on the humans like a horned, bouncing swarm of locusts.

CHAPTER 45

Thanks to the arrival of the Beacon Harbor Police, and to the quick actions of Kennedy Kapoor, Lisa Baxter had been arrested, and the goats had once again been brought under control. Uncle Finn and Daphne were also integral in subduing the fuming mad Lisa Baxter.

As we made our way back to the Jeep, I commended Kennedy for her quick thinking.

"The crazy loon believes there's still pots of gold hidden somewhere," she told us, taking a seat in the back with Welly. "When we heard that, I, for one, wasn't about to give up Finn's secret. Also, for the record, I thought Molly was behind everything. I never suspected her sweet-tempered little helper to be involved. Anyhow, when she came into the Blarney Stone and began brandishing that hefty pistol, I realized my mistake. Lisa demanded that Finn tell her where the gold was hidden. The look on his face made me realize that the daft Irishman would take the secret to the grave with him. That's when I jumped to his rescue. My only conscious thought was to stay as far away from the truth as possible. That's when the goat farm popped into my head. Due to our previous encounter last August with that mama bear goat-lover, Daphne Rivers, I had a feeling that if she saw anyone drive into her goat pen, she'd grab a gun and hunt them down. Well, I'm sorry to say that Daphne's mellowed a bit since then. She didn't bring a gun. She brought her loud, sassy mouth instead, breaking one of Sir Hunts-a-Lot's golden rules. Never bring a sassy mouth to a gunfight."

"I'm honored you listened," Rory teased as he pulled out of the driveway.

"I'm glad you thought of it," I told her. "When I saw that goat emoji, I had a feeling you'd taken the hunt to the goat farm. I'm just glad we got to you in time."

"I was stalling," Kennedy admitted. "I pity the fool who ever puts a shovel in my hand again and demands me to dig a hole. The audacity is galling! She had it coming to her." That made me laugh.

"I, um, have another question." I turned to look at her. "What were you doing at the Blarney Stone today? I thought we agreed that you'd leave Colleen and Tuck alone."

"I never agreed to anything, darling," she informed me with her signature hauteur.

"You weren't trying to convince her to remove her grip from Tuck?"

"You think I went there to bully that Irish siren? Why is it that you always think the worst of me? If you must know, Linds, I was simply making her an offer on a shipment of Irish walking capes. After much reflection, I just don't think they fit the Ellie and Company brand. They belong in an Irish gift shop, and not in one of the nation's hottest fashion boutiques."

Rory looked at my friend in the rearview mirror with something akin to respect in his eyes. "Know what, PR? You surprise me, but in a good way. That's very kind of you."

"Thank you, Hunts-a-Lot. I'm touched you think so. I'd also like to thank you both for welcoming me back into the fold, so to speak. It feels good to be back together again—just the three of us, living under the same roof. There's no telling what mischief we'll get up to next."

"I like your optimism," I said, grinning at her.

"That lighthouse isn't big enough for the three of us," Rory uttered, gripping the steering wheel tightly. "It really isn't."

"It'll work for now," I assured him with a kiss on the cheek. "Let's go home and celebrate the fact that this time we got the real culprit."

After feeding the dogs and making sure they were set for the time being, Tuck, Colleen, Finn, Kennedy, Rory, and I headed up the light-tower stairs with our dinner trays, ready for a quiet, celebratory dinner. I had ordered pizza and salad. Kennedy had brought the wine, and Finn supplied the imported Irish beer. It was the perfect, portable, lightroom meal. With the Edison lights glowing softly above us, and with a few candles lit as well, we all took a seat, anxious to hear what Tuck had to tell us about Lisa Baxter.

"It's hard to believe that Lisa Baxter was the mastermind behind the money-laundering scheme," he told us, right before taking a huge bite of Chicago deep-dish, loaded with sausage, mushrooms, and green peppers. The pizza was a favorite take-out of mine. Having grown up on New York–style slices, I embraced the thick, cheese-stuffed Midwestern pie. It was out of this world, and a real treat. It was obvious that Tuck loved it too. We had to wait for him to swallow before he could continue. "The blow to her head was nasty." Tuck raised a brow at Kennedy before continuing. "However, once she recovered enough, she was able to tell us her story. Shep Mulvaney was her younger brother," he explained. "Both were small in stature, Shep noticeably more so, and both needed the money. Lisa was going through a bad divorce at the time, and Shep was drowning in medical bills from his condition. Knowing that her brother was a senior software developer for Business Solutions, Lisa had convinced Shep to write a software program that would be modest and nearly undetectable, especially not by busy government employees. She even bragged that with the overinflated property taxes, gouging water bills, dog licenses, and whatnot, that no one would notice if a few pennies went missing. She knew from working at Village Hall that prices went up all the time, and nobody asked questions. Most people just accepted it."

"That's a brilliant plan," Colleen said, holding Tuck in a loving gaze. The look caused Kennedy to roll her eyes, while Colleen added, "Most people won't think twice about an extra ten cents when they're paying a three-hundred-dollar water bill."

"That was her point," he assured her. "She was bragging about it. She also talked about how clever she was when she decided to involve the VWC account. When Lisa had learned that village tax dollars went to a flower shop so that new residents would receive a bouquet of flowers, she nearly fell off her seat. Remember, Lisa and Shep were going through hard times. She saw the frivolous spending of money as an opportunity. She also realized that the VWC account was the perfect foil. Shep agreed, and he set up a backdoor dummy account behind the real account. Lisa told her then boss, Fred Landry, that a technician from the software company was coming in to upload a new software program that would make their jobs easier and save money in the long run. Everyone wants to save money! It was an easy sell, and Shep came to Village Hall to install this new, deceptive, software program right under everybody's nose. Lisa, spearheading the project, had taught everyone how to use it. Once she saw that the software program was working like a charm, she resigned from her job at Village Hall to take a job with Molly. That way, Lisa could monitor their progress from the VWC account at Molly's shop, without Fred Landry or others at Village Hall growing suspicious. Their scheme worked seamlessly for over ten years. The trick was handling the syphoned money. Shep had been in charge of that. Every week he'd withdraw the ill-gotten money from their dummy account, purchase gold with it, then deposit the gold into a bank lockbox for safekeeping."

"That's brilliant!" Finn declared. "So that's where the coins came from." He rubbed his chin as he thought on this. "However, ye say it was in the bank, and yet I found it buried in the ground. How did that come about?"

"That's the odd part," Tuck agreed. "And that is what eventually led to their undoing."

"That and the fact that Fred Landry had finally figured it out," Rory offered.

Tuck nodded. "Six months ago, Lisa realized that the gold was missing from the lockbox. At that time both Lisa and Shep had a key to the lockbox so that they could make minor withdrawals as needed. When Lisa found the lockbox empty, she grew extremely nervous. It was also around this time that her brother had started acting strangely."

"How so?" I questioned.

"She told us that he was acting shifty and was more aggressive than usual. She explained that because of his rare genetic disorder, people have always teased him about looking like a leprechaun. Their parents had babied him, and Shep had lived at home all his life. When their parents died, the old farmhouse twenty miles north of Grand Rapids was left to him. She also said that her brother was heavily into ham radio and had made lots of connections around the world. Lisa had always encouraged him that way. She thought that the anonymity of the format and the wide range of the radio signals really let his true personality shine through. What she hadn't realized until six months ago was that he'd met a woman over the radio waves."

"I knew this had something to do with a woman," Finn remarked.

"Well, Lisa was unaware of it until recently. Shep had become shifty, and he had started dressing strangely, wearing a lot of green. He had even dyed his hair bright orange and had grown a beard. When she questioned him, Shep told her that he didn't have Werner syndrome. Doctors had diagnosed him with it because they had no answer for what he was. He told her that he was, in fact, the deformed child of the fairy folk, otherwise known as a leprechaun. He denied being her brother, and told her that he'd been switched at birth, the healthy child going to the fairies, while he was left with their parents. The joke was on them."

"Dear heavens," I said, placing a hand over my heart. I honestly felt very sorry for the poor man. "Life can be difficult for any of us, but I cannot imagine what it must have been like for Shep Mulvaney. He was denying who he really was."

"This has the mark of a woman written all over it," Finn remarked again, throwing a sage wink out there for good measure.

"The man had gone mental, Finn," Kennedy offered, narrowing her eyes at him. "Pity for you, but there are no such things as leprechauns."

"Not so fast, Kennedy." Finn, with a jaunty grin on his face, pointed his finger at her. "He might just be speakin' the truth. According to legend, leprechauns are indeed part of the fairy folk. They are small, tricky, love hoarding gold, and are always male."

"He was mental, Da!" Colleen upbraided him. "Mental! There are no such things as leprechauns."

Tuck cast a wary eye at them both before he continued. "Either way, Lisa knew that her brother had become delusional, and very greedy as well. He wouldn't tell her where he'd put it, only that it was safe from the feds. Then, when he sold the farmhouse and banked the money, she finally confronted him. Shep was living in an abandoned cabin in the woods a mile from Lisa's house. She told him that he could stay with her if he didn't dress like a leprechaun. Shep refused the offer on

the grounds that he was a leprechaun and had
found a woman in Ireland who loved him because
he was one. He was planning to take his share of
the money and leave the country. Lisa was good
with that plan."

"I honestly can't blame her," I offered.

Tuck continued. "Lisa was biding her time until
she could get her brother to release her share of
the money. Then, as fate would have it, a week before St. Patrick's Day Lisa got a call from Fred
Landry. He had finally found the discrepancy in
the software program, and had put two and two together. Fred had been beside himself once he realized what had been going on right under his nose.
He was able to trace the issue all the way back to
Lisa and the strange man who had installed the
software to begin with. Lisa, knowing that they'd
been caught, told her brother that she would help
him get to Ireland if he'd handle Fred. It was
nearly St. Patrick's Day when Lisa saw her brother
peeking through the flower shop window dressed
as a leprechaun. She realized then that Shep was
going to murder Fred and place the blame on a
St. Patrick's Day icon. For a moment she thought
it was a flash of brilliance on her brother's part, especially since there was a leprechaun parade in
town the day of the attack. She also knew that he
was particularly interested in the new Irish shop in
town, and that her involvement there on opening
day might help her. When she learned that Shep
had botched Fred Landry's murder, she knew that
she had to confront her deranged brother and
make him tell her where he'd hidden the gold.
During the party at the Blarney Stone, Lisa formed
her plan. That's when she stole Finn's shillelagh.

She knew her brother was dangerous and knew he carried a shillelagh. If things went wrong when she confronted him, she thought it best to place the blame on Finnigan O'Connor, a man who believed in leprechauns."

"The wee witch!" Finn exclaimed. "So that's why she took me shillelagh! It breaks me heart to think that beautiful stick was misused in such a way."

"Lisa admitted that Shep had been very drunk when he met her on the open dunes," Tuck continued. "Shep was mocking her. Lisa knew that he had hidden all their gold and demanded that he tell her where it was. However, after dancing around in circles, pulling handfuls of glitter from his pocket and throwing it at her, and mocking her, Lisa realized that he meant to keep all the gold for himself. She couldn't make him talk, so she attacked him with the shillelagh instead. Since Shep had one too, it was quite a battle, but in the end, Shep was a weak man. Lisa admitted that it had been dark, and at one point she'd dropped the stolen shillelagh. She picked one up, thinking it was her brother's, but it was the one she'd stolen from Finn instead. After she had killed Shep, Lisa grew scared. Shep was dead, Fred had found her out, and she still didn't have an ounce of the gold they had worked so hard to get. Then, however, Lisa heard about Finn finding a pot of leprechaun gold. She knew that was her gold and told us that she had tried to do everything she could to get it back. She was doing her best to remain under the radar while all this was going on. However, when she realized that Fred was recovering from his attack and that the police would be questioning him, she disguised herself, walked into the hospital, snuck into Fred's room, and finished the job her brother had started. Poor Fred. His murder had been a desperate act perpetrated by a pair of desperate criminals."

"What about the glitter?" Rory asked. "Lisa sprinkled glitter all over my house when she broke in. What was the point of that?"

"'Twas in me SUV too," Finn added. "I think she was trying to make us believe there were more leprechauns about."

Tuck nodded. "You're correct there. Lisa told us that for some crazy reason, Shep thought that by sprinkling glitter around at the crime scene it would give more credence to his new identity . . . as a leprechaun. Lisa used it to confuse us and to perpetuate the myth. However, she also admitted that she never imagined that an Englishwoman with a shovel would be her undoing." As Tuck spoke, he graced the Englishwoman in question with one of his heart-melting smiles.

"Thanks to Kennedy and her quick thinking, we can now finally put this case to rest," I said. I then raised my wineglass to Kennedy. "Congratulations, my friend. It's good to see you back in form."

Kennedy blushed. "It feels good to be back," she admitted, before hoisting her glass and taking a sip. As she did so, the Edison lights flickered. Unsettled, Ken's eyes shot to the lights in question. "I forgot about the lights," she uttered.

Rory grinned at her. "I think the captain might be happy that you're back as well."

We toasted the captain, and our success, after which Finn leaned forward, and asked Tuck, "You said the wee leprechaun split up the gold and hid it? Did Lisa happen to say how many pots there were?"

Tuck shook his head. "Not exactly. No. The truth is we have no idea and neither does she."

Finn's spirits were brightened by that news.

Kennedy cast a flirtatious wink at the older man, knowing that Tuck was watching. "Well, Finnigan O'Connor, what are your plans regarding your hunt for wife number four?"

That made the older man grin. "I'm still on the hunt, but I have me eyes set on Molly Butterfield. She really is as sweet as she appears. And I owe her a grand apology. I plan on taking her on a wee picnic of my own. We might even bring a shovel."

CHAPTER 46

"Bakewell." I turned around at the familiar voice and was pleased to see a smiling Sergeant Murdock making her way to the bakery counter. It had been three weeks since the St. Patrick's Day murders, and the sergeant had been busy ever since.

"It's good to see you, Sergeant. Are you having the usual?"

"Just a latte for me, thanks, and two dozen donuts to go. Everyone at the station has been working hard lately, so I thought I'd bring breakfast. Village Hall has been set to rights once again, as have several other municipalities in the area. It appears that the late Shep Mulvaney and his sister had sold that devious software program to other communities."

"I had heard about that. Do you know how much they got away with?" I asked, preparing two bakery boxes for the donuts she ordered.

"It's been estimated at upwards of five million. As you well know, not all of it has been recovered."

Here she cast me a wink and took the latte Tom handed to her. "Also, it comes to mind that I haven't properly thanked you and Campbell for helping us on this one. I specifically remember asking you and Campbell not to meddle in this, but you did, as you always do. It's highly annoying. However, you seem to have a knack for these things. It's almost a shame you're a baker. You would have made a good cop."

I was blushing at the compliment. "Thank you, but I'll stick to baking. However, I'm here if you need me." I flashed her a smile, then began filling her order.

"There is one thing that you might be able to help with, Bakewell. Campbell's uncle, Finnigan O'Connor."

At the mention of the name, my hand stilled on a chocolate donut. I took a deep breath and plucked it from the tray, hoping the sergeant hadn't caught it.

"Took Brian and the kids to the Blarney Stone Saturday morning." Brian was the sergeant's significant other. "Apparently, Finn is now hosting a Celtic story time, where he spins tales of Irish folklore, particularly about leprechauns. There's green punch and a snack he offers that he calls leprechaun bait. Then he tells the kids of the time he caught a real leprechaun who came to visit the Blarney Stone on St. Patrick's Day evening. He's good at spinning tales and tells the kids how he left some bait out for the little trickster, and how the leprechaun took it, and led him straight to a pot of gold."

"Well, he's not wrong, is he?" I said, handing over one dozen of the two she ordered. "What's the harm in telling stories?"

"None. It's quite cute. He hands out recipes for leprechaun bait at the end of story time. It's a mixture of Rice Chex, pretzels, peanuts, Lucky Charms, mini chocolate-coated candies, all mixed with melted white chocolate. You can even add green sprinkles to make it more festive. It's delicious."

"I've had some," I told her, wondering where she was going with this. "It's yummy."

"It is," she agreed. "Now, to my point. We don't believe that all the gold has been recovered. Finn never told us where he uncovered that first pot of gold. You and Rory never revealed where you found that second pot of gold. And we have reason to believe that more might have been found but never turned over to the proper authorities."

I swallowed, placed the second bakery box on the counter, and smiled at her. "What makes you think that?"

"It's something Finn tells the children that come to his story time. He says that the leprechaun who came to Beacon Harbor left behind a trail of gold, and if they're lucky they just might find a coin. I thought he was just winding them up until yesterday. I got a call from the grade school. Apparently, a little boy named Jimmy Wexford found a gold Krugerrand on his way to school. He told his teacher that he found it on the sidewalk in front of the Blarney Stone. Finn, of course, is denying everything. Also, Little Jimmy Wexford isn't alone. Two other children claim to have found similar gold coins on their way to school. You wouldn't know anything about that, would you?"

"I have no idea," I told the sergeant, and thanked her for coming in. It wasn't entirely a lie.

Rory and I had suspected that his uncle Finn had found another pot of gold, but never dared to ask the question. We had agreed that there were just some questions we didn't care to know the answer to. Truthfully, I was thrilled that the Blarney Stone was in Beacon Harbor. Even Kennedy had come to terms with the fact that her ex-boyfriend was happily dating the lovely Colleen O'Connor, although I suspected she was hatching a plan of her own to get him back.

Rory, after Lisa Baxter had been caught, had surprised me with a gift of a beautiful Irish walking cape all my own. I couldn't believe my eyes. He knew that I had wanted one, and had asked his cousin to help him pick one out for me. It was perfect! I was ecstatic to finally own an authentic Irish walking cape and wore it whenever the weather allowed. On chilly spring mornings Kennedy and I could be seen walking down Main Street towards the Blarney Stone, wearing our walking capes, as Welly trotted excitedly before us. Welly was excited because he knew we'd pick up Bailey and take her with us as we walked around town. And if Rory and I were in any doubt about the lost gold, we had only to look at the Blarney Stone itself. If one looked closely, they could see the signs. Every morning Uncle Finn proudly hoisted the American flag. That wasn't odd at all. It was the other flag that Rory and I had noticed. It appeared quite suddenly beside the front door one day. This new flag was a decorative one and was distinctly Irish. It depicted a shamrock with a rainbow leading to a pot of gold. It was familiar. It was fitting, I thought. It also invoked memories of a strange St. Patrick's

Day, where one wily Irishman had baited a leprechaun and had brought home not only a pot of gold but an unbelievable story to tell. I was growing very fond of that wily Irishman. His daughter too. Most importantly, every time I see that jaunty little flag flying beside the gift shop door, it never fails to make me smile.

RECIPES FROM THE BEACON BAKESHOP

Are you in the mood to try some delicious St. Patrick's Day treats? I hope so. Here at the Beacon Bakeshop, we believe that there's no better way to celebrate a holiday than with tasty treats your family and friends will enjoy. Below are some favorite recipes inspired by the Emerald Isle. They're so delicious they just might have you dancing a jig!

Traditional Irish Scones

Prep time: 15 minutes. Cook time: 12–15 minutes. Makes 6 scones.

Ingredients:
2 cups all-purpose flour
1 teaspoon salt
3 tablespoons sugar
1 teaspoon baking powder
1 teaspoon baking soda
½ cup (one stick) cold butter (Irish butter is best), diced small
½ cup buttermilk, plus 1 tablespoon extra for brushing on scones
1 large egg, beaten
½ cup raisins (optional)

Instructions:
Preheat oven to 425°. Line a baking sheet with parchment paper.

In a large bowl add the flour, salt, sugar, baking powder, and baking soda. Stir until mixed.

Next, add the cold butter cubes. Using your fingertips, rub the butter cubes into the flour mixture until all the butter is incorporated and the mixture resembles fine breadcrumbs. You may also use a pastry cutter, but Irish bakers prefer to use the fingertip method. It's actually quite satisfying!

Next, make a well in the middle of the flour mixture. Add the buttermilk and the beaten egg. Using a fork, gently stir until a soft dough forms.

Add the raisins at this point and knead into the dough until they're evenly distributed.

Transfer dough onto a lightly floured surface and gently pat, forming a 1-inch-thick circle. Using a 2-inch biscuit cutter, cut the dough. Transfer the scones onto the prepared baking sheet, repeating until all the dough has been used.

Brush the top of each scone with additional buttermilk.

Bake in oven for 12 to 15 minutes, or until the scones are a beautiful golden-brown color. Let cool for 10 minutes. These scones are so good with clotted cream, crème fraîche, or butter, and strawberry jam!

Colleen's Famous Irish Soda Bread

Prep time: 15 minutes. Bake time: 50–60 minutes. Makes 1 large round loaf.

Ingredients:
4 cups all-purpose flour
1 cup sugar
1 teaspoon baking soda
1 teaspoon baking powder
¼ teaspoon salt
⅓ cup melted butter
1⅓ cup buttermilk
1 egg
1 cup raisins

Instructions:
Preheat oven to 350°. This recipe works great in a cast-iron skillet. If you don't have one, line a baking sheet with parchment paper.

In a large bowl, or the bowl of an electric mixer, combine the flour, sugar, baking soda, baking powder, and salt. On low speed, stir in the melted butter, the buttermilk, the egg, and the raisins. Mix just until a soft dough forms. Don't overmix the dough. It's going to be a little sticky. Using your hands, form the dough into a large ball. Place the shaped dough into the cast-iron skillet or on the prepared baking sheet. Using a sharp knife, cut an X into the top of the dough. Bake for 50–60 minutes or until the bread has a nice golden-brown crust. Enjoy!

Lindsey's Delicious Irish Beef and Guinness Stew

Prep time: 20 minutes. Bake time: 2 hours 30 minutes. Serves 6.

Ingredients:
2 pounds of beef chuck, cut into 1-inch cubes
6 slices of bacon, cut into 1-inch chunks
3 tablespoons all-purpose flour
1 large yellow onion, chopped
4 garlic cloves, minced
5 medium potatoes (waxy potatoes like red or Yukon gold work best), peeled and cut into 1-inch pieces
4 large carrots, peeled and cut into ½-inch pieces
2 ribs of celery, cleaned and cut into ½-inch pieces
2 large parsnips, peeled and cut into ½-inch pieces
1 8-oz. package of baby portobello mushrooms, washed and sliced (optional)
1 bottle (16 ounces) Guinness Extra Stout
1 cup good beef broth
3 tablespoons Worcestershire sauce
¼ cup tomato paste
1 teaspoon dried thyme
1 teaspoon dried rosemary
2 bay leaves
salt and pepper to taste

Instructions:
Sprinkle beef cubes with some salt, pepper, and the 3 tablespoons of flour. Toss to coat and set aside.

Using a Dutch oven or heavy pot, fry the bacon

pieces over medium heat until tender. Remove with a slotted spoon and set aside, leaving the bacon drippings in the bottom of the pan.

Using small batches, brown the beef pieces on all sides in the bacon fat and set aside until all the beef is browned. Add more cooking oil if necessary, then cook the onion until lightly browned, about 10 minutes. Next, add the garlic and cook one more minute. Add the vegetables (including mushrooms, if using them) and cook for another 5 minutes. Pour in the bottle of Guinness and bring to a boil, scraping the bottom of the pot to incorporate all the bits. Boil for 2 minutes.

Next, return the beef and bacon to the pot along with all the remaining ingredients. Give the pot a good stir and bring it back to a boil. Reduce the heat to low, cover the pot, and simmer for another 2 hours. You can also transfer the Dutch oven to the oven. To do this, preheat oven to 325°, then put the entire pot, covered, into the oven, making sure to stir it every 15 minutes or so.

Once the stew is tender and delicious, salt and pepper to taste. Serve it with a warm slice of Irish soda bread. Enjoy!

Baileys Irish Cream Cheesecake

Prep time: 30 minutes. Cook time: 1 hour 15 minutes. Inactive time: 6 hours.

Ingredients:

For the crust:
1 regular full-size package of Oreo cookies (36 sandwich cookies)
6 tablespoons unsalted butter, melted

For the filling:
3 8-ounce packages full-fat cream cheese, softened
1 cup full-fat sour cream
1 cup sugar
3 large eggs plus 2 egg yolks at room temperature
1 teaspoon instant espresso powder or strong instant coffee
1 tablespoon of hot water (to dissolve espresso powder)
½ cup Baileys Irish Cream liqueur

For the chocolate ganache:
6 ounces (1 cup) semisweet chocolate chips
½ cup heavy cream
¼ cup Baileys Irish Cream

Instructions:
Preheat oven to 350°. Prepare a 9-inch springform pan for the water bath by covering the outside of the pan with heavy-duty aluminum foil on the bottom and halfway up the sides. You want to make the pan as watertight as you can. Lightly spray the inside of the pan with non-stick cooking spray. Put Oreo cookies in a

food processor and reduce to fine crumbs. You may have to do this in smaller batches. In a large mixing bowl, combine the cookie crumbs with the melted butter and mix well. Press the mixture into the bottom of the springform pan and halfway up the sides. Bake crust for 10 minutes. Remove and set aside to cool. Reduce oven temperature to 325°.

Add the softened cream cheese and the sour cream in the bowl of an electric mixer. Beat until completely smooth. Add in the sugar and continue to beat until smooth, scraping sides and bottom of the bowl as needed. Next add the eggs and the egg yolks and continue to beat until smooth and velvety.

In a small bowl mix the instant espresso powder with the hot water and stir until completely dissolved. Next, stir in the Baileys Irish Cream until combined. Gently fold this mixture into the cream cheese mixture until combined. Pour the filling on top of the partially baked crust.

To make the water bath, place the springform pan in the middle of a large roasting pan. Fill the roasting pan with an inch of hot water and place in the oven. Bake the cheesecake for 1 hour and 15 minutes.

Once the cheesecake has been baked, turn off the heat and leave the cheesecake in the oven, allowing it to sit undisturbed for an additional 40 minutes. Remove the cheesecake from the oven and gently run a sharp knife around the edge of the cake. Cover loosely with plastic wrap and place in the refrigerator for at least 6 hours.

One hour before serving the cheesecake, make the ganache. Place the chocolate chips in a medium bowl. In a small saucepan over medium heat, gently heat the cream until it begins to bubble along the edges. Pour the cream on top of the chocolate chips and let sit for 1 minute. Using a whisk, incorporate the chocolate into the cream and whisk until smooth and glossy. Whisk in the Baileys Irish Cream. Let the mixture cool completely before pouring over the cheesecake. Return the cheesecake to the refrigerator for one more hour. Once the ganache has set the cheesecake is ready to serve. Enjoy!

Heavenly Chocolate Guinness Cake with Baileys Buttercream Frosting

Prep time: 20 minutes. Cook time: 45 minutes. Serves 12

Ingredients:

For the cake:
1 cup Guinness Stout beer
½ cup (1 stick) butter, cubed
2 cups sugar
¾ cup baking cocoa powder (I use Hershey's)
2 large eggs, room temperature
⅔ cup sour cream
3 teaspoons vanilla extract
2 cups all-purpose flour
1½ teaspoons baking soda

For the frosting:
4 tablespoons butter, softened
2 tablespoons heavy cream
2½ cups powdered sugar
2 tablespoons Baileys Irish Cream

Instructions:
Preheat oven to 350°. Cover the bottom of a 9-inch springform pan with parchment paper. Spray the sides with nonstick cooking spray and set aside.

In a small saucepan combine the Guinness with the butter cubes and heat over medium heat until all the butter has melted. Remove from heat. Next, whisk in the cocoa powder until smooth and blended.

Place the sugar in a large mixing bowl. Pour the warm chocolate mixture over the sugar and whisk together until smooth.

In a small mixing bowl, place the eggs, the sour cream, and the vanilla. Whisk together until smooth. Whisk this mixture into the chocolate mixture. Combine the flour and baking soda. Whisk the flour into the chocolate mixture until smooth. Pour the batter into the prepared pan and bake in the oven for 45 minutes or until a toothpick placed into the center of the cake comes out clean. Remove cake from oven and cool completely.

To make the frosting, place the softened butter and one cup of the powdered sugar in the bowl of an electric mixer and beat until combined. Add the cream and mix well. Add the rest of the powdered sugar and the Baileys Irish Cream and whip 3 minutes, until frosting is smooth and fluffy. Frost the top of the cake. Enjoy!

Visit our website at
KensingtonBooks.com
to sign up for our newsletters, read
more from your favorite authors, see
books by series, view reading group
guides, and more!

BOOK **CLUB**

BETWEEN THE CHAPTERS

Become a Part of Our
Between the Chapters Book Club
Community and Join the Conversation

Betweenthechapters.net